THE WHITBY WAILERS

JOHN REGAN

ISBN-13:9798568776130

Published in association with JV Publishing
jvpublishing@yahoo.com
Tel: 07860213358

DEDICATION

For Harry Regan (Dad) 05/08/1932 – 25/10/2020.

ACKNOWLEDGEMENTS

It goes without saying that to produce anything worthwhile, requires help from others. The process of writing a book such as this is aided and abetted by numerous people – some, who only subtly assist, and others, profoundly. A huge thanks to Vicky for providing invaluable help on structure, editing and proofreading. A great deal of the words contained within, are hers. My appreciation, also, to the people who purchased and read my first six books: The Hanging Tree, Persistence of Vision, The Romanov Relic, The Space Between Our Tears, The Fallen Leaves and The Lindisfarne Liturgy. Your support is greatly valued. Finally, to anyone who is reading this book. I hope you find it enjoyable, and any feedback is always appreciated.

December 2020.

DISCLAIMER

Many of the places mentioned in this book exist. However, the author has used poetic license throughout, to maintain an engaging narrative. Therefore, no guarantee of accuracy in some respects should be expected. The characters depicted, however, are wholly fictional. Any similarity to persons living or dead is accidental.

CHAPTER ONE

November 2019 …
Marion plucked the dog lead from the back of the cottage door and clipped it on to the unenthusiastic pug's collar. 'Come on, Pip, it's only raining a little bit. The vet says you need more exercise.'

As she opened the door, she looked back over her shoulder. 'We won't be long, Belle.'

Isobelle appeared at the top of the stairs. 'I thought you'd already taken Pip out?'

'I have,' Marion said. 'But I just fancied another stretch of the legs.'

Isobelle shrugged as her friend pulled the red wooden door firmly shut. Marion smiled to herself as she caught sight of the brass plaque above the letterbox. Pausing, she listened. In the distance, the faint, but insistent barking of another dog could be heard. 'Come on, Pip,' she said. 'Let's see who's making all that noise, shall we?' Pulling her collar up high against the biting cold wind and drizzle, she strode off. Her breath beading into moisture, as the heavy mist of the early November evening hampered her visibility, making seeing more than a few feet impossible. She carried on regardless, knowing the paths and walkways well enough to navigate them in the dark and disagreeable weather. Continuing in the direction of her neighbour, Geoff, who lived a few doors away from her cottage, Marion quickened her stride towards his property, hurried down a cinder track, and stopped.

She tugged off her thick glove and lifted the latch on the gate as another dog raced towards her barking furiously. 'Shush, Freddie,' she said, and patted the animal on the head. 'What are you doing out here at this time on your own? Come on, let's see where your dad is.' The three of them made their way down the track with Geoff's dog, Freddie, still barking frantically. She bent lower. 'What is the matter with you?' she said to the dog, soothingly, trying to placate the excited canine. She screwed her eyes up and looked towards Geoff's cottage. The back door swung wide open, banging against the wall of his kitchen. She took a few steps forward and grabbed the handle.

'Geoff! Are you ok?' Freddie ran into the house and then back out again. He jumped and barked at Marion's feet before taking off down the path and around the front of the house. 'Freddie!' She pulled the door closed and ran after him, afraid that he wouldn't stop in time and would plunge through the thin wire fencing that offered little protection from the drop ahead. 'Freddie, stop!' She managed to grab the dog's collar and pull him back from the edge, sliding to her knees with the effort. 'What is the matter with you?' Her words faltered as she noticed a gap in the fence. The wire and wood bent forwards over the drop, hanging loosely. Marion crawled closer and looked down to the beach below. The tide in this part rarely fully covered the sand and rocks, the opaque moonlight shone onto the slime and seaweed beneath her. As the wind dropped briefly, a flash from the lighthouse illuminated an outline on the ground below. Marion squinted trying to decipher the shape as another flash from the lighthouse traced the same journey. She realised what it was. Marion put a hand to her mouth and stifled a scream.

Whitby, February 2019 ...

Isobelle sat on her own in the front room of the home she now shared with Marion. A small, cosy cottage set in the middle of a terraced street, each dwelling identical inside and out but with the owner's personalities marking their territory. Only Geoff's house differed from the rest. Set back slightly from the others in Haggerlythe Street, marginally bigger, and boasting a back garden instead of a yard. The views across to the lighthouse spectacular at any time of year and in all weathers. The pulsating light, the heartbeat of the town, like a great sentry keeping guardian over the harbour. Isobelle loved it here. Relishing the peace and tranquillity of the space she shared with her closest friend. The gentle sound of the waves and the stunning sunsets over the bay visible from the cottage window.

She sipped her drink as sad memories elbowed their way into her head. Her mind unwillingly drifted back to the events which had brought her here nine months ago.

Middlesbrough 2018 ...

Isobelle sat at the kitchen table and stared into the garden. A robin hopped about on the verdant lawn as the sun glistened off the dew-covered grass. She picked up her teacup and drained the contents. *'Tea and sympathy,'* she said to herself.

A woman entered and smiled thinly at Isobelle. 'The hearse is here,' she said.

Isobelle stood and sucked in a lungful of air. 'Come on then,' she said. 'I'm getting quite good at this.'

Isobelle gazed out of the car window as it turned into the crematorium. The huge number of black-clad mourners snaked along the path from the chapel, stretching out to meet her. The car glided to a halt behind the hearse, and Isobelle stepped out. People, their faces etched with sadness, stared towards her from all directions. Cast adrift in this vast ocean of grief, she resisted the urge to flee. The memories of making the same journey less than a year ago still blazed starkly.

'Belle,' a voice said. She turned around to face Marion, her oldest friend. 'I'm sorry I wasn't there at the house. There was a crash on the moor road. I thought I'd be late.'

Isobelle took hold of her friend's hands and squeezed them. 'You're here now,' she said.

Marion moved aside and placed a hand on a man stood nearby. 'This is Geoff,' she said. 'My neighbour. He brought me here today. I hope you don't mind, but I couldn't face the drive.'

'Geoff.' Isobelle held out a hand.

'I'm sorry for your loss, Isobelle.'

She smiled meekly. 'Thank you.'

Isobelle shook herself free from the unwelcome intrusion of memories, picked up her cup and trudged into the front room. She slumped into the armchair and sighed. Looking to her left, she caught sight of the photo on the sideboard. The picture of two young girls smiling back at the camera, her and Marion blissfully unaware of what adult life had in store for them. Isobelle picked up the picture and studied the face of her younger self and gently brushed away the dust that had gathered on the glass.

She had known Marion since senior school and remembered the shy, young redhead who had moved to Middlesbrough from Whitby. Isobelle, beautiful and confident, had felt sorry for Marion and took her under her wing. Something which Marion was grateful for then, and still now. Their friendship enduring the turmoil of adolescence and the boys that had come and gone throughout Isobelle's life. Marion, always there to pick up the pieces of a broken teenage heart, chose to stay single, insisting that boys were too much trouble. Things changed for them when Bill came into Isobelle's life. She was twenty, and at three years her senior, this mature, handsome, fun to be with man, had swept her off her feet in no time at all.

Now, aged sixty-two and with two dead husbands in her wake, she cupped the steaming tea and wondered, a little dramatically, what would become of her.

Marion walked into the room, bringing the cling of cold air from outside with her. 'Freezing out there.' She shivered.

Isobelle continued to gaze ahead, not hearing Marion's words. 'Belle, I said it's ... What's up with you?' Marion touched her friend on the shoulder to shake her to the present time.

'I was thinking about Bill,' Isobelle said softly.

'One or two?' Marion said.

Isobelle looked at her friend and raised her brows. 'What?'

'Were you thinking about Bill one or Bill two?' Marion repeated. 'I know it's not funny having two dead husbands with the same name, but it still makes me chuckle. We should call you Uma.' Marion laughed at her own joke but stopped when she spotted Isobelle's glare. 'Sorry, Belle. I can see you're not in the mood for fun.'

'Fun is fine, Marion, but lose the wisecracks.' Isobelle stood and moved to leave the room, but Marion blocked her way and placed her hands on her friend's cheeks.

'Belle, I wish you'd tell me what's going on in your head.' Marion touched a finger to Isobelle's temple. 'Just talk to me, like the old days.'

'I'm sorry, Marion. I'm just so tired, I think I'll turn in. We'll talk in the morning.'

Marion slumped into the vacated chair, as the dog curled up in front of the fire, and mused over her and Isobelle's relationship. She had never had a man in her life, always waiting to repair the cracks in Isobelle's. Her darling Isobelle. These men that she chose were never good enough. If only she knew how much she was loved by the person right in front of her. Marion stood and walked over to the bureau, pulled down the front, and reached for the key to the cupboard below. She paused, noticing the hook that housed Geoff's front door key.

She stooped and opened the larger cupboard below. Lifting different discarded papers and receipts, she found the photo album and took it out. Marion sat back in her chair and turned the first page of the thumb-worn book. Pictures of school days. Isobelle, dark and beautiful, faded Marion into the background. Not that she had minded being in the shadow of Isobelle. Her friendship the envy of many of the girls in their year. And now, they had the perfect home together. But Geoff asked her to bring Isobelle along to the pub quiz on the pretence of joining their team. Why couldn't he have just left them to get on with their lives? She had noticed the attraction between the pair on their first meeting, at Bill's funeral the previous year, but what crushed her was that Isobelle had mentioned nothing. Marion admonished herself. 'Poor Geoff,' she found herself whispering. It wasn't his fault. He was just one of a string of men that had fallen under the spell of Isobelle over the years. Although Marion believed that her friend had been faithful to both her husbands, she knew that Isobelle revelled in her own attractiveness, delighting in the effect she had over the opposite sex. Marion felt guilt course through her for harbouring any animosity towards Geoff. The poor man was clearly smitten and obviously helpless in resisting Isobelle. She sighed heavily, put down the photo album and reached into the cupboard for a bottle. 'Brandy will do nicely,' she said softly to herself. Placing a large balloon glass on the table by her side, she pulled out the stopper and filled it a third full. She put the drink to her lips and drank greedily, savouring the warm effect the liquid had as it slid down her throat.

CHAPTER TWO

Islington, London, 1978 ...

Vincent sat on the brown velour sofa and carefully spread the tobacco along the length of the paper, before rolling it into shape. Satisfied with his effort, he placed it to his lips and lit the cigarette. 'Come on, Mick,' he shouted. 'It's about to kick off.'

His friend hurried into the room carrying six cans of lager and plonked them down on the small coffee table. He cracked open a can, spraying foam onto his Arsenal shirt. 'Shit.' He wiped his hand down the now soaked cloth. 'All over my top.'

'Don't worry, it'll wash out.'

Mick's eyes widened. 'Are you mad? I can't wash this shirt, that would be unlucky.'

Vincent rolled his eyes. 'We don't need luck today, my friend. Ipswich Town have no chance.' He rubbed his hands together. 'Come on The Gunners.'

Two hours later they sat in quiet reflection, holding a can of lager each. 'Glad your shirt brought us good luck,' Vincent said.

'One bloody nil. How the hell did that happen? I'll chuck this shirt in the bin.' Mick gulped at his can. 'Glad we didn't have tickets now. Who wants to see your own team lose at Wembley?' He stood, walked over to the fridge in the corner of the bedsit, and took out two more cans. 'Might as well drown our sorrows.'

Vincent nodded his agreement and put his feet on the coffee table. 'No amount of alcohol will wash away that.' He pointed towards the television.

Mick stood next to Vincent and held out the can. 'We have more pressing things to discuss. I know you're avoiding talking about it, Vin.'

Vincent took the drink from Mick, pulled it open, and took a large gulp before speaking. 'You know I'm not happy about going on this job.'

'We need a driver, and you're the best I know. You could do with the money. Get yourself out of this bedsit.'

''I don't like the idea that you're doing this job with Barry Hunt,' Vincent said. 'He's a nutter. Just like his dad.'

'I need the cash, mate. It'll set Yvonne and me up.'

Vincent shook his head. 'He worries me. He'll do something stupid. He's going to get you into real bother.'

Mick patted his friend on the shoulder. 'I've told you, it's all sorted. Every detail has been checked and then checked again. Barry is a pro where security vans are concerned.'

Vincent took another drink from his can. 'What about Yvonne? Is she happy with you going on this job?'

'Vincent, I never mix business with pleasure. What Yvonne doesn't know Yvonne can't worry about.' Mick nudged him. 'Come on, Vin. You're like a brother to me. You know I wouldn't let anything happen to you.'

'If you say so.' Vincent shrugged and nodded. 'I'm doing this for you, Mick. Just make sure that Barry doesn't do anything stupid.'

Mick put an arm around his friend. 'He won't. It'll be a piece of cake.'

Vincent smiled. 'I've got to admit it would be nice to get out of this dump and away from Islington. I'm going to take the money and get far away from here.'

Mick slapped Vincent on the back. 'That's more like it. Where are you thinking of going?'

'I've always fancied living by the sea.'

'Be a bit quiet for a young bloke like you.' Mick slumped onto the chair. He sipped at his can and ran a hand through his hair. 'Even with my more mature outlook. You can't retire to the seaside at twenty-four.'

'Well, you're twenty-nine, old man. I just want a quiet life. No more waiting for the police to knock at the door.'

'Vincent, you worry too much. But if that's what you want, that's what we'll do. You, me and Yvonne. Retirement, here we come!' He chuckled as he lifted his can.

Vincent glanced at Mick and felt a flush of guilt. He knew that after this job, he wouldn't see him again. Mick, and his family, had been good to him, but he knew deep down that Mick would eventually get himself into deep trouble. He didn't want to be around when he did. This security van robbery was a step up from his usual burglary. Robbing a shop or business premises was one thing, but this … The thought hung in his head with a heaviness that threatened the weight of tears. And Mick's girlfriend, Yvonne. She was trouble too. Vincent still admonished himself for their one-night stand. He allowed her, and the beer, to get the better of him. Hopefully, Mick would never find out about it and all the other men she'd seen over the years behind his back.

'Vin,' Mick said. 'You were miles away.'

'Sorry, mate.' Vincent fixed his friend with a stare. 'You promise me this is the last job you'll go on with Barry?'

'I've told you we're retiring to the seaside. Just think of all the fish and chips.' Mick said.

Vincent gazed across at the photo frame on top of the television. His younger self and his father stood in front of Whitby Abbey. 'I hate fish. I just need to know this is this last one you'll do.'

'Definitely,' Mick said. 'Right, I'm off to see Barry to sort out the final details. I'll see you later. If Yvonne comes looking for me, tell her I'll be back soon. And remember, what she doesn't know can't hurt her.'

Minutes later, someone knocked softly. Vincent stood behind the door anticipating the arrival of the visitor. 'Yvonne, come in. Mick's not here.'

Yvonne reached her arms around Vincent's neck and kissed him. He pulled her hands away and stepped back.

'Vincent, come on, let me cheer you up after the football,' she said.

'I told you,' he said. 'Last time was a mistake.'

She laughed and pushed a strand of hair behind her ear. 'I won't say anything if you don't.'

'Don't you say that to everyone?'

Yvonne glared at him. 'What do you mean by that?'

'Barry. I know you two are seeing each other. I saw you outside The Lion last week with your tongue down his throat.'

Yvonne ground her teeth. 'Mick doesn't know, does he?'

He shrugged. 'I haven't told him, but you're not exactly discreet.'

'If Mick found out, Vin ...'

'Not my problem.'

'Please, Vin. Don't tell him, he'll be devastated.'

Vincent's shoulders drooped. 'I won't tell him if you end it.'

'I will, I promise.'

1978 - Two Days Before the Robbery ...

Yvonne lay awake but kept still. Her breathing soft and shallow. She lifted the sheet carefully, swung her legs over the side of the bed, and planted her feet gently on the threadbare carpet below. She stood and stared over at Mick as he snored gently, mouth opening and closing with each breath. The smell of alcohol pervading the cramped room. Turning, she padded her way out of the bedroom and into the kitchen. As she waited for the kettle to boil, she placed a hand on her stomach. Mick will go mental, she thought. How could she have been so stupid to get pregnant? It had to be Barry's, but she couldn't be certain. If only she and Mick had continued to have sex more often. His constant drinking and lack of enthusiasm had put paid to that. She would have to tell Barry. She couldn't pass it off as Mick's. She racked her brains and tried to calculate approximately when she had conceived. Maybe she could lie to him about the dates? Convince Mick that the child is his. Yvonne poured the water into the mug and sat on a chair cradling the tea.

1978, The Day Before the Robbery …

'Rustle up some drinks,' Mick shouted to Yvonne. 'The boys are here and parched.'

Vincent entered and slumped onto a chair. 'Barry's on his way up, I saw him getting out of his car.'

'Good. We'll need to run over the plan again.'

Vincent stood and took hold of Mick's arm. 'Are you sure about this, Mick?'

'Vin.' Mick put an arm around his friend. 'You worry too much.'

'But Barry … I don't like him. He's a loose cannon.'

Mick laughed. 'We've been through this. When we've done the job, we'll be set up for life. You … we … won't have to worry about Barry.'

Barry swaggered in. 'All right, Mick.' He glanced at Vincent. 'Vinny boy?'

'Yeah.' Mick glanced at Vincent. 'We're good, aren't we, Vin?'

Vincent forced a smile. 'Yeah. We're good.'

'Yvonne's making the tea,' Mick said. 'I'll just go and get the map.'

'I'll give Yvonne a hand with the drinks,' Barry said.

Vincent eyed him and folded his arms.

Barry entered the kitchen and put his arms around Yvonne. 'All right, darling?'

Yvonne wrestled free from his grip. 'Barry,' she whispered. 'Mick might come in.'

Barry smirked. 'I thought you liked the danger?'

'Not here.' She handed him a tray with tea and biscuits on it. 'I need a word later,' she said.

'Yeah. Come around to my flat this afternoon, and we can have as many words as you like, gorgeous.' He winked and left the room.

Barry pointed to a street on the map. 'This is where we hit the van.'

'Are you sure?' Vincent said. 'It looks a bit—'

'I've had a look at the area,' Barry said. 'It's the best place.'

'There you are, Vin,' Mick said. 'Barry's checked it out.'

Barry looked at Vincent. 'You wait here,' Barry said, and pointed at another street. 'Me and Mick will meet you there. Then you drive to the other car and drop us off. Dump the car, and we'll all meet up later. It's the easiest two-grand you'll ever make.'

'Good,' Mick said. He looked at the clock. 'I think we should have a beer to celebrate.'

'It's a bit early,' Vincent said.

Barry laughed. 'It's never too early.'

Mick stood and disappeared into the kitchen.

Vincent looked at Barry and narrowed his eyes. 'Don't go doing anything stupid,' he said.

Barry sneered and glared at Vincent. 'You just do your job, Vinny boy. You're only on it because Mick wanted you. Do your job, and there won't be a problem.'

Yvonne tapped on the door of Barry's flat and waited. She glanced about nervously as Barry opened the door and ushered her inside.

He took hold of her as Yvonne pulled herself free from her coat and hung it on a chair. 'Hello, darling,' he said, and kissed her.

Yvonne wrestled from his grip. 'Can we talk first,' she said.

'Talk? I thought—'

'I have something to tell you.'

He glanced upwards and wandered into the lounge, closely followed by Yvonne. He held out tumbler with whiskey in it.

She shook her head. 'No thanks.'

He placed the glass down, lit a cigarette, and dropped onto an armchair. 'Talk you said?'

She sat opposite him and fidgeted with her fingers. 'It's just …' She stared directly at Barry. 'I'm pregnant.'

He smirked and took a drink from the glass. 'What's that got to do with me?'

'You're the father.'

He laughed. 'Really?'

Yvonne rubbed her face. 'I didn't mean to get pregnant, Barry. It was an accident. I—'

'I'm afraid it's Mick's problem, not mine.'

'We haven't had sex for ages,' she said. 'It can't possibly be his.'

'And you're trying to pin this on me?'

'I'm not trying to pin anything on you. You're the—'

Barry laughed. 'I can't have kids. Mumps.' He allowed his words to permeate.

'Mumps?'

'Yeah, mumps. A pretty severe case. The doctors told me I wouldn't be able to have kids. Whoever fathered your nipper …' He pointed at Yvonne's belly. '… wasn't me.'

'But I don't understand.'

'Of course you do, Yvonne. If Mick's not the dad, it must be one of the other fellas you've been with.'

'There's no one else.'

Barry stood. 'Come on, Yvonne. Do you think I'm stupid? You're a slapper and always have been. A bit of fun, I grant you. But a slapper nonetheless.'

She stood. 'You bastard.'

'That makes two of us.' He pointed at her stomach. 'Get out.'

Yvonne raced towards the door, but Barry caught up with her and grabbed her arm. 'Don't go doing anything silly like telling Mick.' He clamped a hand around her throat. 'That would be a stupid thing to do.'

'You're hurting me,' she said.

He released his grip and grinned at her as he slid his hand down and underneath her short dress. 'How about one for old time's sake?'

Yvonne struggled against him. 'Get off me,' she said. 'I'll scream.' He smirked at her and backed away. She smoothed down the front of her dress.

He pulled her coat from the chair and tossed it at her. 'Piss off,' he said. 'And don't bother coming around here again.'

Yvonne raced outside, coat in hand, and quickly descended the stairs. She stopped at the bottom and gathered her breath. If Mick and Barry weren't the father of her baby, it had to be Vincent. She closed her eyes, placed her hands over her face, and began to sob.

1978, The Day of The Robbery …

Vincent jumped from the car and ran as fast as he could with no idea where he was heading. In the distance, he could hear the whine of a police siren. His mind whirred with images of what had just happened. Suddenly, a hand on his shoulder brought him to a halt.

'Vincent! Slow down, I can't keep up with you.' Mick's voice came in gasps as he struggled for breath.

Vincent shrugged Mick's hand away but stumbled as he tried to keep running. Losing his balance on the wet towpath, he lurched forwards.

Mick grabbed at his jacket to stop him from hitting the ground. 'Stop! Vin, just stop a second.'

Vincent dropped to his knees and looked up at his friend. 'Mick. Why did you lie to me? No guns you said. I can't believe you've done this.' Fear and exhaustion cloaked his voice.

'You're like a brother to me. I would never lie to you, Vin. I had no idea Barry brought a gun. I didn't know until the police arrived and all hell broke loose.'

'How bad is Barry injured?'

Mick rubbed at his face. 'I don't know. He was shot in the leg.'

'Jesus, Mick. He'll grass you up. He'll tell them about me.' Vincent stifled a sob as his future came to a standstill. His plans to get away. No more crime, no more waiting to be caught. A future by the sea.

Mick fished inside his pocket and pulled out some keys. 'You make your way to the second car. Take the money with you.' He thrust the bag towards him. 'We'll meet up later. Near the lock-up.'

Vincent looked at the keys in his hand, and then at his friend. 'But what if …? And how did the police get there so quick? Someone must have tipped them off.'

'I don't know. Just go. Hide the money somewhere.'

He continued to stare at Mick.

'Just go, Vin.' Mick glanced behind him as the sound of a siren neared. 'Just go.'

Vincent had no idea where he was running to. Tears stung his eyes as he battled with the emotions raging inside him. He had to get home and grab what he could. The sudden pain of a stitch in his side forced him to a halt. He looked up and spotted the car about fifty yards ahead. He glanced about the deserted street and headed for the vehicle.

Racing from his bedsit, he threw the holdall onto the back seat of his escort and jumped inside. *Think, Vincent. What would Mick do?* He spoke the words to himself. He wished Mick was here to help him. He had always looked up to him, they had been like brothers after Vincent's dad died, and his family had taken him in. But now, Mick was God knows where. His head darted to his right as someone tapped on the door of the car.

Yvonne stood outside. 'Vin,' she said.

He waved her around to the passenger seat, and she climbed in beside him. 'I've got to get away from here,' he said. She nodded, and he roared off.

The car shuddered to a halt on the gravel path. 'What did you say?' Vincent said.

'The police have Mick. They were waiting for him at the flat.'

He covered his eyes with his hands. 'Why the hell did he go back?'

'I told him the coast was clear.'

'And it wasn't?'

Yvonne turned her head and stared outside. 'I tipped the police off.'

He grabbed hold of her arm. 'Why would you do that?'

'Because he should never have listened to Barry. He should never have involved you.'

'He'll go down for years. Barry shot a guard.'

She sighed. 'They would have caught him. Mick had nowhere to run.'

Vincent fiercely gripped the steering wheel. 'What am I going to do? I'm lost without Mick.'

She placed a hand on his arm. 'It said on the news that he's still alive.' Vincent frowned, and Yvonne continued. 'The guard,' she said.

He glanced over his shoulder at the bag of money. 'All this for …' His words dried up to nothing.

'We could still have a future. Me and you, Vin.'

He frowned. 'What are you on about? Your husband's been arrested, and you're talking as if nothing's happened. There is no us.'

'I'm sorry. I'm sorry. I just thought …'

He reached and grabbed the door handle. 'You need to go.'

'Please don't.'

He opened the holdall. 'There's money here.'

'I don't want money. I want you.'

Vincent turned to face her. 'I can't do this, Yvonne. Mick will go down for years because of you. I can't forgive that. I'm not about to steal his wife from him as well.'

'Please, Vin.' She put a hand to his cheek. 'It was always you I wanted. I've always—'

Vincent swatted it away. 'I'm sorry, I'm going. You'll never see me again. Just get out.'

She grabbed hold of his arm. 'But I'm pregnant. I did this for our baby.'

He shrugged her off. 'I can't believe anything you say to me now. Just go, Yvonne.'

She climbed from the car. 'Vinnie, it's our baby.'

Vincent pulled the passenger door shut and sped off.

CHAPTER THREE

1978, Two days after the robbery ...
Vincent climbed from the Ford escort and stretched his back. He had been driving for over five hours – not daring to stop, and needed to rest. Taking out his tobacco pouch, he rolled a cigarette and leant back against the vehicle as he drew deeply from it. He gazed across the estuary of Spurn Point and studied the dark and brooding sea, perfectly matching his mood. He needed to lose his car, just in case Mick or Barry had told the police about his involvement in the robbery. Vincent opened the boot and removed a small can of petrol, a sleeping bag, and a large holdall, containing a few items of clothing, and most importantly, lying at the bottom, £25,000 pounds in crisp new notes.

Although it would take him two days to walk to Whitby, he considered it a better option than using public transport. Tonight, he would rest at a deserted warehouse and set off on foot the following morning after disposing of the car. Should he set it on fire and risk it being seen from miles around? Or roll it into the crashing waves? *'What would Mick do?'* he asked himself, as he had done so many times throughout his life. Memories from two days ago pulled at his conscience, and he slumped onto the dry, sandy grass. *'Mick wouldn't have slept with your girlfriend.'* Vincent answered his own question. Lying back on the turf, he fought to keep his emotions from breaking through. A pulse pumped at his temple as tight muscles constricted his throat. He clutched the holdall to him like he was comforting a friend, buried his head into the stiff fabric, and wept.

Vincent, exhausted from the drive and his emotional dam finally breaking down, settled himself inside the warehouse and ate some of the food he had hurriedly packed for the journey. Finishing his meagre rations, he walked outside into the evening darkness, reasoning that night was the best time to move the car. The early May air was starting to chill as Vincent fired up the engine. He whispered his thanks as it started first time and sat in the Ford, allowing the warmth to creep through his body, before driving it into the furthest corner of the warehouse. He reluctantly pulled himself free of the comfort of the vehicle and into the cooler evening, performed a final check of the car, and wiped down any surfaces he may have touched. He locked the door and trudged outside.

The walk ahead was a long one, but he knew it would be too risky to take the car any further. He bundled up his sleeping bag, flung the holdall over his shoulder, and set off towards Withernsea. This first part of the journey would take no more than four hours, then he would find somewhere to sleep for the rest of the night and set out again in the early hours of the morning.

Vincent sat and rubbed the sleep from his eyes. He glanced down to his right and viewed the tattered old photographs he had been looking at before he fell asleep. Scooping them back up, he smiled at his younger self, stood with his dad at the top of the 199 steps in Whitby. He allowed his mind to drift back through the years as he continued to study the pictures.

Whitby, 1963 …

Vincent stood with his father as the cold wind slapped at their cheeks and threatened to lift the woollen hats from their heads. 'Not far now!' his dad shouted through captured breaths. 'Come on, we're nearly there.'

At nine years old, Vincent found the excitement of the seaside exhilarating. Even the whipping cold and salty, wet air couldn't dampen his spirits. To spend this rare alone-time with his father, his hero, he would endure anything.

'197,198, 199! We've done it, Vincent,' his dad said. 'Look down at the steps we've climbed.' He laughed and smiled at his son. 'Let's see what I've got for you.' He removed his glove and reached into his jacket pocket. 'Tooty-Frooties, whatever will they think of next?' he said, allowing Vincent to see the packet of sweets. He led Vincent towards a high stone wall to shelter from the still algid wind. 'There you go. I think we've earned a little treat. Aunty Dot is getting fish and chips for us when we get back. How does that sound?'

Vincent grinned at his father and gratefully took the sweets from him. 'Chips, no fish, Dad.'

'Ha, ok, no fish,' he said. 'Let's head back now. Aunty Dot will be waiting.'

'Why wouldn't she do the steps, Dad?'

'Well, she's lived here ages and climbed them many times I bet.'

'I'd never get tired of climbing them,' Vincent said. 'This is where I'll live when I'm a grown up.'

Vincent's dad looked down at him and laughed. 'What will you do here? Be a fisherman? One that doesn't like fish?' He chuckled at his own joke. They made their way back down the steps. The wind now settled, allowing the mist to carpet the harbour and creep its way toward them, bringing with it a damp chill. Looking out to the left, the lighthouse stood guarding the town. The evening just dark enough for the light to be needed. The pair descended the stone steps and continued along the cobbles towards the cottage at the very end of Haggerlythe Street.

'Come on, you two,' a female voice shouted from the doorway. 'The fish and chips are getting cold.' Dot beckoned them inside, the warmth of the room embracing the pair and turning their cheeks pink. 'Right, young Vincent,' Dot said. 'Wash your hands, please.'

Vincent left the heat of the room into the chill hallway and bounded up the stairs. Quickly washing his hands, he made his way back down but stopped at the foot and listened.

'He seems happy, Rob,' Dot said. 'Just what he needed some good Yorkshire air and away from all that trouble in London with his mother.'

'I know, but it's not forever. I have to take him back next week. He still thinks his mother will come back for him, but it's getting less and less likely. Last I heard she's in Spain. I can't snatch him away from his gran. She has looked after him while I was … away.'

Dot frowned as she piled the chips onto warmed plates. 'Just make sure you don't have to go away anytime soon then.' She looked at her brother. 'Please stay out of prison.'

Vincent came running back into the room, and they sat at the table to eat. He looked at the pair of them, his face etched in a deep frown.

'What are you looking so worried about?' Dot asked him.

Vincent shoved greasy chips into his mouth. 'Nothing, Auntie Dot.' He smiled. 'It's just been the best day. But I'm still not eating fish.' He looked from his dad to Dot, and the three of them laughed together.

Vincent's dad pulled the blanket over his son. 'Make sure you get a good night's sleep. We have a big day tomorrow. Lots more adventures.'

Vincent yawned. 'Dad,' he said, 'have you been to prison?'

His dad stopped at the door. 'What put that daft idea in your head?'

'I overhead you and Auntie Dot.'

His dad wandered back across to him and sat on the bed. 'I've done some stupid things in my life, son. But that is going to change.'

'What's it like in prison?'

'Vincent …'

'Is it like that film we watched?'

His dad rubbed his head. 'Not good. Don't worry about it.' He looked sternly at his son. 'Just make sure you stay out of there. Get yourself a good trade.'

'I will, Dad,' he said, and sleepily closed his eyes.

1978 …

Vincent collected the photos together and sighed. The times he had visited his aunt were so special. Before he was born, his dad had been in and out of jail for one petty crime or another. Vincent had learnt later, off family members, that the last stretch inside for eighteen months, cost him his marriage to Vincent's mother. Tempted by a better life, she had left him in the care of his grandmother, promising to send for him when she got settled. She hadn't, though, and Vincent's dad, who had found a job on a construction site, fell to his death when Vincent was only eleven. He had continued to live with his grandmother until she died. At sixteen, he was taken in by Mick's relatives, and the bond between the two men had grown. He mentally shook his head and pushed away any thoughts of Mick, tucked the pictures inside his jacket pocket, gathered his belongings, and set off.

Whitby, 1978 …

'All right, I'm coming as fast as I can!' Dot wiped her hands on the front of her apron and placed the tray of biscuits into the hot oven. She could see a tall figure silhouetted through the glass of her front door with the sunlight behind them. Unbolting the door, she opened it and stood looking at the young man before her.

'Aunty Dot. It's me, Vincent.' He grinned.

'Good Lord, Vincent. What on earth are you doing here? Look at you, you're filthy. Come in.'

'It's a long story, Aunty Dot.' He stepped into the small hallway. 'Something smells good.'

She closed the door behind him, and Vincent lunged forward to hug her. 'It's wonderful to see you.'

'I'm not being funny, Vincent, but you smell awful.' She wriggled free from his grasp and held him at arms' length. 'Right, bath first, then food. Then you can tell me why you're here. Something tells me I'm not going to like it very much.'

Vincent settled into the steaming water and closed his eyes. It felt so good to be here. He could almost forget the terrible events of the last couple of days. Almost. But as he glanced across at the holdall, lying on Dot's bathroom floor, the images flooded back into his mind. What had happened to Mick and Barry? And why had Yvonne told him the baby was his? Was she even pregnant? He couldn't be sure about that.

'Vincent! Have you fallen asleep in that bath?' Dot's words brought him around from his thoughts.

'Five minutes, Aunty Dot.' Forcing his mind back to the here and now, he looked at the pink, floral dressing gown on the back of the door and decided that would have to do. The few clothes he had brought were all filthy and damp. Easing out of the warm water, he dried himself and pulled on the gown.

Dot stifled a laugh at the sight of Vincent in her pink dressing gown. 'Eat this, Vincent.' She placed a plate in front of him. 'Homemade steak and kidney pie, that'll put the colour back in your cheeks. Finish that, and you can have some of my freshly-baked biscuits. I think you need food and then bed. We can talk in the morning.' She ruffled his wet hair. 'I'm guessing if anyone comes asking, I'm to say I haven't seen you?'

'Thanks,' he said. 'Not just for the food. Thanks for everything.' He forced a smile, and she kissed the top of his head. Vincent picked up his knife and fork and concentrated on the meal in front of him. He felt bone-weary and glad of the reprieve until the next day. He would tell Dot the whole story, she would know what to do.

Dot rose early the next morning after a restless night. She walked down the stairs into the kitchen and put the kettle on to boil. Having made the tea, she sat at the large wooden table cradling a steaming hot cup in her hands and tried not to think about what Vincent would tell her. Too many times she had sat at this table waiting for Vincent's dad, to come downstairs and tell her of some crime he was on the run from. Dot heard movement upstairs, filled another cup with tea, and waited for her nephew.

'Morning, Vincent. Did you sleep well?' Dot waved her hand at the wooden chair opposite her.

He sat down and took a drink of tea. 'I was exhausted. I fell asleep straight away, but I've been awake for a while. I need to tell you what's happened. I really don't know where to start.'

Dot sighed and touched his hand across the table. 'Just start from the beginning. I can help you, but I need to know everything.'

Vincent told Dot how he had been involved in the security van robbery in Islington. How his job was to be the getaway driver, and take Mick and Barry to a second car. But within minutes of arriving on the scene, all hell broke loose. The vehicle Mick and Barry had been in had skidded in front of the security van, causing it to stop. The pair were only supposed to threaten the guards with pickaxe handles, Vincent had no idea that Barry had a gun. The police had turned up because Yvonne tipped them off.

'Mick definitely didn't know Barry had a gun?' Dot said. 'Can you be certain?'

Vincent rubbed his face. 'That's what he told me.'

'Do you believe him?'

'I think so,' he said. 'Mick wouldn't have lied to me. I'm sure.'

'Mick always looked out for you.' Dot stood up and filled the kettle once more. She picked up a newspaper and showed it to Vincent. 'The guard is in hospital, he's not dead. But Mick and Barry will be going down for a long time.'

'What about Barry's injury?'

'It says he's being treated in hospital.'

Vincent looked at the paper, and a picture of the security guard stared back at him. 'Thank God they didn't kill him.'

'What I don't understand …' Dot said, carrying a fresh pot of tea to the table. '… is why Yvonne set him up? I thought she's his wife?'

Vincent looked down at his hands. 'Yeah, she is.'

'So why would she …?' Pouring the tea into cups, she stopped suddenly and looked at Vincent. 'Oh, I see. You and Yvonne. You've been carrying on behind Mick's back, have you?'

'It wasn't like that. I didn't mean it to happen. It was just a one-night stand. Yvonne's flighty. I'm certain there were others. Her and Barry … Well, I can't be sure, but …'

'Well,' Dot said. 'You're away from her now.'

'She told me she's pregnant.'

Dot took a sip of her tea. 'And?'

'She claimed it's mine,' he said.

'And is it?'

Vincent shook his head. 'She's lying. Yvonne was furious I was leaving. I'm not even sure she's pregnant. I don't know. She could have just been making it up.'

Dot clasped her hands together. 'Does she know where you are?'

Vincent shook his head. 'No. I talked about coming north, but I didn't say where I would go.'

'These girls, always trying to trap a bloke into staying. Well, she'll not find you here.' Dot moved over to the cupboard and took out a frying pan. 'How does eggs and bacon sound?'

After breakfast, Dot told Vincent she had some errands to run and that he must stay in the house until she had thought through what they should do. Vincent, still tired from his journey, settled down on the settee to watch the television and within minutes fell asleep.

Dot walked into town and to the small corner shop run by her good friends, Elliott and Babs.

Babs smiled warmly at Dot as she entered the shop. Although over twenty years younger than Dot, they had struck up a friendship when

Babs moved to the area, bringing with her a husband and a baby. It was through Dot's acceptance of their situation, and the fact that the locals valued Dot's opinion, that they had been welcomed into the town.

Babs had worked in London as a product demonstrator in a big department store and met Elliott there. She fell in love instantly with the darkly handsome, mountain of a man from Jamaica. He worked as a security guard in the store, and after some months of skirting around each other, he plucked up the courage to ask Babs to accompany him to see a film. Their romance blossomed, but both their families were opposed to them being together. When Babs told her mother and father she was carrying Elliott's child, they asked her to leave and vowed never to speak to her again. Elliott's family felt the same. So, they got married and headed north, finally landing in Whitby.

Dot had felt maternal towards the young, frightened Babs with her tiny baby and huge husband. Cast out from their families, she made it her business to welcome them into the community. The small corner shop on Church Street needed someone to do deliveries, but the owner had taken one look at Elliott and told him the job was already taken. Dot remembered the day she had marched into the shop and said to them that if they didn't employ Elliott, she would make sure half the town took their custom elsewhere. He started work the next day.

A few years later, Elliott and Babs had the lease on the shop and lived in the flat above it. The friendship between the three of them had grown from gratitude to a family love they all craved.

'You're out and about early, Dot.' Babs stood at the front of the shop stacking newspapers into a wooden stand.

'Have you got time for a brew? I need to talk to you about something.' Dot said.

'Elliott! Can you watch the shop for a bit? I'll get Albert ready for school, and me and Dot will walk him there.'

Elliott appeared in the doorway, filling the space with his massive frame. 'Good luck with that, Babs. He says he doesn't need to go anymore. He's only done a week.' Elliott smiled at Dot. 'Morning. Who knew such a small boy could be so strong-willed.'

'Hello, Elliott. Young Albert giving you the run around?' Dot chuckled at the sight of the big man holding a small shoe in one huge hand and a wriggling child tucked under his other arm.

Babs extracted the child from his gentle grip. 'We'll take it from here.' She stretched up and kissed her husband on the cheek.

They took Albert up to the flat to prepare him for the day. After some cajoling and a bribe of a sugary treat, they set off on the walk to school.

'Right,' Babs said. 'That's him finally dropped off, I thought he would never go in. Shall we have a walk through the park and you can tell me what's on your mind?'

The pair of them sat on a wooden bench looking out over the sea. The May sunshine dappled through the trees, as the damp grass sparkled with dew.

'I've got a small problem, Babs, and I need your help,' Dot said. 'But you must keep what I'm about to tell you to yourself. You can't tell anyone, not even Elliott. I know it's a terrible thing to ask a wife to hide something from her husband, but I'm not asking you to lie. I'm just asking that you keep it to yourself.'

Dot sat ramrod straight with her hands in her lap. 'You know you can trust me, Dot.' Babs turned to face her friend and took hold of her hand.

Dot told her the whole sorry tale, with no omissions. 'So,' she said. 'I need you to give Vincent some work in the shop. I'll pay his wages, but we don't need to tell him that. Just a few hours here and there. You look like you could do with an extra pair of hands in the mornings.'

'Blimey, Dot. Vincent is lucky to have someone like you. Are you sure he won't bring trouble to your door? What about this girl, will she come looking for him?' Babs frowned at Dot, genuinely concerned for her welfare.

'No, we have to make sure that no one can find him. He's a good boy really, he just got in with the wrong crowd. He's had a tough beginning. With his mother abandoning him and his dad in and out of prison.' Dot reached into her bag for a handkerchief and dabbed her eyes.

'Are you sure you need this bother after losing Geoff?'

Dot looked away. 'I never really got to know Geoff. I know I couldn't replace him. But I'm certain given the right opportunity … Well, let's just say I think Vincent is a decent lad deep down.'

Babs nodded. 'I haven't said anything to Elliott about Geoff. I swore I wouldn't.'

'Thanks,' Dot said.

Babs retook hold of Dot's hand. 'What happened to Vincent's dad?'

Dot sniffed. 'He got a proper job. The first one in his life. He was going to make a good living working as a labourer on a big construction site in Birmingham. He left Vincent with his grandmother, in London, to take care of him while he was away. He had only been working a month when he fell to his death on site. He and two others were killed.'

'Dot, you've never told me any of this.'

'No point raking up the past. We need to think of Vincent's future and get him back on track.' Dot straightened herself up and put away the hankie. 'First of all, we will have to stop calling him Vincent. I've had a daft idea. We'll call him Geoff. We can tell people he's the son of a good friend of mine and he's staying with me until he gets sorted. People around here know I often take in lodgers.'

Babs thought for a moment. 'Will the police be looking for him? Do they know where he was headed?'

'No, I don't think they're looking for anyone else now they have Mick and Barry in custody. Mick will keep Vincent out of it.'

'What about this Barry?'

Dot shrugged. 'Vincent's not sure. He's hoping he will.'

'Well,' Babs said. 'Let's keep our fingers crossed.'

'Mick and Vincent are like brothers. After his grandmother died, Vincent stayed with Mick's family. He's been there since he was sixteen-years-old and we would write to each other, but the letters became less frequent as he got older. Still, I wrote to him every month.'

'Come on, Dot. Let's go to your house and tell Vincent, I mean, Geoff, what we have planned.'

'Thank you, Babs. I knew I could rely on you.'

Babs smiled and swallowed back tears. 'You have always been there for me. This is the least I can do.'

The pair stood and briefly hugged before setting off to Haggerlythe Street. They walked in pensive silence. Babs thought of her family, the way they had cast her aside for not conforming to their rules, and of Dot, only too happy to accept her and Elliott.

CHAPTER FOUR

October 2018 ...

Brian and Elliott stood at the bar of their local pub, The Fallen Angel, waiting for the rest of the quiz team to arrive.

'Shall we get another pint of this?' Elliott said. 'We were here a bit early tonight.' He swirled the remains of his drink around his glass and held it up towards the barman.

Brian shook his head. 'I think I'd better go for something else, that was a bit strong. Anything above 5% seems to knock the hell out of me these days.'

Elliott chuckled at his friend. 'You're getting old. You can't take the pace anymore. Shandy perhaps?'

'Hey, I'm two years younger than you. I'll get these.' He got his wallet out and pulled out a ten-pound note. 'Another pint of the porter and I'll have the pale ale please, Michael.'

Michael looked around the room. 'There's a good turn out tonight. Where's the rest of your team?' He put the money in the till and handed Brian his change while the beer settled.

'They'll be here soon hopefully,' Brain said. 'They won't miss quiz night. Marion is bringing along her lodger. Isobelle she's called.'

Michael placed their drinks down on the bar. 'Is Marion taking in lodgers now?' he asked, as he wiped down the counter.

Brian took a long drink. 'It's a friend of hers from her school days on Teesside. Marion said she's recently widowed and fancied staying here for a few months.'

'Ah,' Michael said. 'She'll never leave. I came here years ago, and I've been here ever since.'

Elliott looked across at him. 'Yes, you have been here a while. You just lose track of time as the years gallop past. How long have you been running this place?'

'I've worked here for ten years, but I've only been manager for three.'

'Whitby is a difficult place to leave,' Elliott said. 'Look at my Babs and me. Came here over 40 years ago, after our families disowned us, and we've loved every minute of it.'

Michael pulled a pint for another customer. 'Forty years. That's a lifetime.' He served the customer and resumed wiping down the bar.

'What brought you here, Michael?' Brian said. 'I've never thought to ask.'

Michael stopped wiping for a second, then continued with the task. 'I came looking for my father. He left my mother when she was pregnant. She only told me who my real father is when I was twenty-five, and she became ill.' Michael rubbed his chin. 'She's a heavy drinker. She has liver disease, and the doctors told her she would die if she kept on drinking.' He shrugged.

'So, your mother's still alive?' Brian said.

'Yes, barely. She won't listen to me or anyone else. I couldn't stand watching her drink herself to death. I rarely visit these days.'

'Oh, I'm sorry, Michael.' Elliott said, and looked down at his pint as his mind drifted back to thoughts of Babs, his wife, and her death only twelve months previously.

'The man who you thought was your dad …?' Brian said.

'He died in prison.'

Brian glanced at Elliott and then back towards Michael. 'Did you find your real dad?' Brian said.

'No. I didn't really have any firm leads. I just knew he had family from Whitby, and my mother thought this is where he would come. She said he got letters from someone up here called Dorothy.'

'No return address on the letters?' Brian said.

Michael frowned. 'No. Just from Dorothy in Whitby. I asked around when I first got here, but no one knew Dorothy or my father, Vincent.'

Elliott looked down at his pint as Michael moved further down the bar to serve another customer.

'You ok, Elliott? You look like you've seen a ghost.' Brian placed his hand on the big man's arm.

'I remember Babs mentioning a—'

'Here they are at last.' Brian turned away from Elliott, as in walked Marion and Isobelle closely followed by Geoff.

Brian and Elliott joined the others as they sat at their usual table in the corner, near the fire, awaiting the final member of their team, Jason.

'Right, everyone.' Marion smiled broadly at them all. 'This is my good friend, Isobelle, who I've finally persuaded to join us.' She introduced them in turn, gazing adoringly at Isobelle as she did. 'Oh, and here comes Jonny-come-lately.'

Jason rushed in, waved at them all, and made his way to the bar. 'Michael, I'll have a large vodka and lemonade. What a day I've had.'

Geoff joined him at the bar and ordered drinks for the others. 'I'll get that,' he said to Jason.

'Cheers,' Jason said. He picked up his drink, walked over to his fellow quiz-mates, and sat down. 'Oh, am I glad today's over. I've had nothing but trouble from suppliers.'

'Jason,' Marion said. 'This is my oldest friend, Isobelle. Belle, to her friends. She saved me from a storm when we were twelve, and she's staying with me for a while.' Marion plucked her lucky quiz pen from her bag.

Jason smiled. 'You saved her?'

Isobelle laughed. 'It's a long story. Marion was the hero. She got the school closed.' She looked across at Marion, and they both giggled.

Jason looked between them. 'Hmm, I'd love to hear about Marion misbehaving.'

'You'll have to buy me another drink.' Marion chuckled.

Jason turned to Isobelle. 'I'll have to get your friend to tell me everything. Are you here on holiday?'

'No,' Marion said. 'Bill trouble.'

'Sorry, Isobelle, are you having money difficulty?' Jason said.

'Nice to meet you, Jason,' Isobelle said. She frowned at Marion.

'The Bills don't cause her trouble anymore.' Marion looked at Jason.

'What Marion means,' Isobelle said, and gave her friend a sterner look. 'Bill was my husband.'

Jason glanced at the others. 'Was?'

Geoff returned with the drinks and placed them down before taking his seat. 'I think I've got everyone's drink,' he said. 'Have I missed much?'

'Marion's friend ... Belle?' Brian said, as Isobelle nodded. 'Was just telling us about her husband.'

Marion sighed. 'You might as well tell them.'

'I had two husbands called Bill,' Isobelle said. 'They both died of heart attacks. So, Marion always jokes, I don't have any problem with my Bill's anymore.'

Jason spluttered his drink and snorted. 'God, I'm so sorry. I've put my foot right in it again.'

Marion laughed loudly. 'Don't worry, Jason. They left her plenty of money, so she really has no Bills and no bills!'

The group around the table laughed uncomfortably and looked at Isobelle. 'Ignore her,' Isobelle said. 'She had a couple of sherries before we came out.' But she smiled fondly at her oldest friend and squeezed her hand as Marion blushed.

'Right,' Geoff said, and slapped his hand down on the table. 'Settle down everyone. It's about to start.' He glanced around the table at the others but lingered longer on Isobelle, who sat opposite him. He remembered their brief encounter when he drove Marion to Middlesbrough for the funeral of Isobelle's second husband. It had been such a long time since Geoff had found anyone attractive, and he had given up hope, at his age, of meeting a companion. But he liked Isobelle. Funny with a sharp mind. It didn't hurt that she was attractive and well turned out too. *For her age*, he said in his head and then laughed.

'Are you ok?' Isobelle looked directly at him and smiled.

'Yes. I have a good feeling about tonight.' Geoff said, and raised his glass towards her. 'Here's to tonight's win.'

Later, as they ordered another round to celebrate their victory, Brian took Elliott to one side. 'Were you going to tell me something earlier? About Babs?'

'Nothing to worry about. Just something Michael said.' Elliott smiled at Brian. 'Look at Marion, I think she's had one too many.'

Geoff came over to join them. 'I'm going to give Isobelle a hand to get Marion home. She's a little worse for wear.'

Elliott and Brian raised eyebrows at each other. 'Ever the knight in shining armour,' Brian said.

Geoff pretended to straighten a tie around his neck. 'Watch and learn, boys.' He turned away from them, laughing.

'Here he is! Our hero to walk us home.' Marion slurred, and put her arm around Geoff's waist.

The trio left the pub and walked outside into the freezing air. The building and cobbles sparkled with ice. 'Careful out here, Marion.' Geoff said, and held on tightly to one arm, as Isobelle took the other. 'It's a bit slippery.'

'Do you have to do this every week?' Isobelle asked him, as they continued steadily along the road.

'Well, we always walk home together, with me living at the end of the road. I like to make sure she gets back safely. Isn't that right, Marion?'

Marion glanced at Geoff. 'He's a gentleman.'

They carried on walking with Marion propped up between them until they approached her house and stopped at the gate. 'Why don't you come in for a night-cap, Geoff?' Isobelle said.

'Don't mind if I do.' They led Marion in through the front door and settled her in an armchair. As gentle snores rose up, Isobelle draped a soft throw over her friend and tucked it in. Pip climbed up onto her lap and snuggled down with her owner.

'What's your poison, Geoff?' Isobelle said. She opened the bureau's cupboard to reveal an interesting selection of spirits. 'Let's see. Crème de menthe, Limoncello. Ah, here. You look like a single malt man to me.' She held up a half-full bottle of fine scotch.

Geoff nodded. 'That'll do nicely.'

Isobelle poured some of the amber liquid into a glass and handed it to him. 'Bill … Number one Bill,' she said, 'liked a whisky. I can't stand the stuff myself.' She rummaged in the cupboard again. 'Ah, here we are. Vodka. That'll do for me.'

Geoff sipped his drink, turned away, and grimaced. The spirit burned his tongue and throat, he wasn't a whisky drinker at all. He couldn't abide the stuff, but he didn't want to admit this to Isobelle and ruin the moment.

Geoff glanced at his watch. 'Have you seen the time?'

Isobelle stood. 'This has been lovely, Geoff, but I'd better put sleeping beauty to bed. I'll see you out.'

She moved to the front door and held it open for him. As he walked through, she caught hold of his arm and pulled him back in. 'Thanks, Geoff. I've really enjoyed tonight.' Isobelle put her hand to his cheek and reached up to kiss him. He responded by putting his hand on the back of her neck and kissing her firmly on the mouth. A loud snore from the front room jolted them back to reality, as they stood giggling.

'Sorry about that, I hope you're not offended.' Geoff released his grip on her.

Isobelle pushed her hands through her hair. 'Not at all. I think I'm going to enjoy living here. Goodnight, Geoff. I'll see you very soon.'

As Isobelle closed the front door quietly, Marion closed her eyes again and feigned sleep.

Michael bolted the door to the pub and tramped his way behind the bar. He took a glass from under the counter and half-filled it with whisky. He groaned as he caught sight of the pile of invoices under the counter. Snatching them up he pushed them inside a drawer, downed his drink in one, turned off the lights and headed to bed.

The next day …

Isobelle stood in the kitchen of Marion's house and poured boiling water into the teapot. The pot was one of the few things that she had brought with her from Middlesbrough. Not for sentimental reasons, just for the fact she liked her tea from this pot.

She looked out of the kitchen window and into the small yard as a fat seagull hopped around in the concrete space. 'You should look so cheerful, noisy bugger,' Isobelle muttered at the creature. Popping two paracetamols into her palm, she thought back to last night and her kiss on the doorstep with Geoff. She smiled to herself. Isobelle loved male company, but in the months since her second husband's death, this was the first time she had let her guard down. Back in her hometown, she sensed the widowers circling her like vultures. Ready to prey on the newly bereaved with her hefty inheritance. Isobelle found it difficult to trust anyone and often took someone's genuine concern as a cynical grab for her money. Marion had always been there for her. Suggesting she visit, and just have some time away from everything.

It had taken Marion a long time to persuade her to come, and Isobelle had hardly left the house. But, after last night, she felt that she would settle in and maybe even stay here for good. She would need her own place, though, and that wouldn't be easy to explain to Marion, her good friend and constant in her life. Isobelle knew that Marion's feelings for her ran deeper than friendship. They had never talked about it, of course, but they both knew it existed. Bubbling just beneath the surface.

Isobelle made her tea and carried the steaming teapot and bone-china cup into the front room of the house. It was freezing in here and needed the wood-burning stove lighting, but she didn't have a clue where to start. Kneeling in front of the grate, she banked it up with the dry logs from a basket next to it and scrunched up some newspaper. 'How hard can this be?' she said to herself. Isobelle took one of the long matches from the box and struck it on the side, guiding the flame gently to the paper. A large flame jumped and curled around the logs, burned briefly then fizzled to nothing.

'Let me do that.' Marion appeared in the doorway. Kneeling next to Isobelle, she had the flames raging in no time. 'It takes practice.'

'You're up early,' Isobelle said. 'I thought you'd be sleeping off last night.' Isobelle stood and got a cup for her friend.

Marion gratefully accepted the hot tea. 'I've got work today. I could have done with a sleep-in.'

'I don't know why you don't retire.'

Marion sighed. 'I would, but I'm hoping they'll offer me a redundancy package soon. Besides, it's only a couple of days a week.'

'I'll have a walk into town and get something to make us a nice meal later.' Isobelle looked out of the front window as Geoff walked by. Turning to look at her, he grinned and waved. She found herself blushing slightly as she smiled and waved back.

'Who are you waving at?' Marion sat with both hands around her cup.

'Your escort home from last night. Geoff, isn't it?' Isobelle busied herself with pouring more tea. 'Maybe I should invite him to eat with us. As a thank-you.'

'It would be nice if it was just us two tonight, Belle. Anyway, I'm not sure my friends are ready for your cooking.' Marion laughed.

'Fair point.' Isobelle conceded that cookery was not one of her strong suits. Her two husbands had been excellent cooks, and she had barely made a meal during the whole time of her marriages. Her first marriage lasting over forty years, but the second, to his best friend and best man at their wedding, lasting no more than their wedding night. Two dead husbands from heart attacks, and two large life insurance pay-outs later, meant Isobelle wanted for nothing. Except for the companionship and love of the opposite sex. She enjoyed spending time with her friend, Marion, but still, she craved the closeness of having a physical relationship with a man. When her second husband died, Marion had been there for her. Hinting, at their age, they should forget about that side of things. *'We just need each other now,'* she had said to a grieving Isobelle. *'Friendship is the most important thing at our time of life.'* It was the only time that Isobelle had wanted to slap Marion.

'Right, I'm off for a shower,' Marion said, and placed her empty cup down. 'Are you sure you'll be ok today? You won't be bored?'

Isobelle thought about Geoff. 'No, I'm sure I'll find something to keep me occupied.' She pulled the chair closer to the flames and closed her eyes.

CHAPTER FIVE

Marion sat at her till position and set everything out in front of her. Till stamp, sponge, pen and rubber bands. All neatly lined up and in their correct place. Her first customer was Elliott.

'Good morning, sir. What can I help you with today?'

'Very professional, Marion, considering the late night we had.'

Marion frowned. 'I know.'

'I said I'd get Jason some change for the shop.' He pushed a cloth bag across to Marion. 'There's a list of coins he needs in the bag.'

She started to count the money. 'I'm due a coffee break soon if you fancy one?'

'Haven't you just got here? Anyone would think you're trying to get fired.' He chuckled at his own joke. 'I'll nip up to Costa now and get us a table. I could do with a chat, to be honest.'

She leant closer to the glass. 'Oh, that sounds interesting.'

He took the filled bag from her. 'Latte?'

'Please. I'll be five minutes.'

Elliott left the bank and walked the short distance to the coffee shop, ordered their drinks and found a table. He glanced outside at the dozens of people passing by. Even at this time of year, the town bustled and moved with people and tourists. Not like when he and Babs had first arrived. Back then, it was only busy through the warmer months. Now, with all the different events going on, there wasn't really a quiet time. Despite this, he still loved the place. Even the loss of his beloved wife could not dampen his affection for Whitby. He adored the little fishing town and the people who meant so much to him.

Marion appeared a few minutes later and sat opposite him, adding two sachets of brown sugar to her drink and stirring carefully. 'What's on your mind, Elliott?'

'I don't really know if I should say, it's probably nothing ...'

Marion carried on stirring her drink, knowing that the best way to get Elliott to talk was to keep quiet herself.

'I was going to mention this to Brian,' he said. 'But I'll see what you think. You can't tell a soul. Promise me.' Marion crossed her fingers over her heart without speaking. 'Michael from the pub,' Elliott continued. 'Well, he came here years ago looking for his real father.'

Marion looked up from her coffee. 'How intriguing. Go on.' The urge to speak getting the better of her.

'When Babs and I moved up here we were taken under the wing of a woman called, Dot. She was good to us and made sure we had a warm welcome from the locals. She took in lodgers now and again. Geoff was one.'

'Hmm.' Marion took a sip of hot coffee.

Elliott took a mouthful of his own drink. 'Dot died a few years after Geoff moved in. He was the son of a good friend of hers, I think, and she became like a mother to him. Well, Dot was like that to me too. And Babs.'

'What does this have to do with Michael?'

'When Babs was in hospital, she told me that I needed to know about Vincent. A young man from London that lived with Dot. She kept going on and on about him.'

Marion frowned. 'Who's Vincent?'

'Michael said his dad was called Vincent and got letters from a Dorothy.'

'Dorothy, as in Dot?' Marion said.

Elliott shrugged. 'Maybe.'

'Did you know Vincent?'

'Babs was on so much medication that I didn't pay much attention to what she told me.' Elliott sniffed and looked down at his drink. 'But I can't remember a Vincent.'

Marion reached across the table and touched his arm. 'We all miss her. She was such a good friend to me. But I don't remember a Dot?'

'She died before you moved back here. Like I said, only a few years after she took Geoff in.'

'Maybe Geoff knows who Vincent is?' Marion rummaged in her pocket for a tissue and wiped a small spill of coffee from the table. 'Michael's from London, so I suppose his dad was too.'

'Possibly, Michael said he always believed another man was his dad. He said this man died in prison. But apparently, his mother told him about his real father when she was ill. She has a drink problem, ironic that Michael now runs a pub. That's why he came here. To look for his real dad.' Elliott shook his head. 'All these years Michael stood behind that bar listening to our problems, and not one of us thought to ask about his.'

'What did his dad go to prison for? I mean the dad he thought was his dad, not his real dad. If you know what I mean?'

Elliott laughed. 'I think I do. I never thought to ask.'

'I wouldn't worry about it. Just ask Geoff if he knows a Vincent.' She glanced at her watch. 'I have to get back. Let me know how you get on.' Marion picked up her gloves and shrugged into her coat. 'See you soon.'

Elliott sat for a while wondering what he should do. He missed Babs and her gentle, wise words. And he missed Dot. Both would have known what to do. So much time had passed since he arrived from London with all his belongings and a tiny baby boy. People had come and gone through his life, some had turned their backs on him and tried to make him feel ashamed for loving the wrong person. Life had been hard without his mother and father on his side, but he wouldn't change a thing. Elliott would give up the rest of his life if it meant he could have five more minutes with Babs.

Lost in his thoughts, he didn't notice Brian come into the coffee shop and stand in front of him. 'I said, do you want a refill, Elliott?'

Elliott looked up at him. 'Sorry, I was miles away. Or should I say, years away. I can't stop, mate. I must get this change back to Jason. I've been gone ages. But I might pop in The Angel for a pint later.'

'Ok. I'll be in there about seven. See you then,' he said, and ambled over to the counter to join the queue.

Marion sat in her favourite chair in front of the now raging wood-burning stove. 'Are you managing in there, Belle? It's gone very quiet.'

Isobelle stuck her head around the living room door, her dark, curly hair scraped back from her face, and her cheeks flushed. 'I won't lie, it's not my best effort. Does that pub do food? My treat, obviously.'

Marion stood and followed. 'Good grief. It's like a sauna in here.' Picking up a spoon, she prodded at the dish on the hob. Thick, brown globs of grease dripped from the utensil. 'What was it?'

'Coq-au-vin.' Isobelle pulled on the oven gloves and put the dish back in the oven. 'Let's leave it there and go out.'

'Good idea,' Marion said. 'I'm starving now.'

'I'll be five minutes, just got to freshen-up.'

Marion started to wash the mountain of pots that had been needed for tonight's creation. She laughed. 'Good thing Belle could rely on her looks and not her homemaking skills.' Marion thought to herself as she plunged the dishes into hot, soapy water.

'Leave that, Marion.' Isobelle said, as she entered the kitchen in a cloud of perfume. Her hair now loose and fresh lipstick perfectly applied. 'I'll do it when we come back.'

'I'm almost done. But we'll have to tackle the contents of the oven later. Probably best to throw the whole thing out. Dish as well.' Marion dried her hands and applied some cream to them. 'Good job we didn't invite Geoff.'

'Who?' Isobelle asked, innocently. 'Oh, the man from last night. Do you think he'll be in the pub tonight?'

'You'll find most of us frequent the pub quite a few times in the week. It can get lonely living by yourself.'

Marion pulled on a pair of thick socks and shoved her feet into her black, fleece-lined shoes as Isobelle found her own shiny, leather boots and zipped them up over her calves.

Marion raised her eyebrows. 'It's only the local, Belle.'

'Oh, these old things. I've had them years.' Isobelle checked her reflection in the hall mirror one last time and unhooked her thick, cream, wool coat from the back of the door. 'Ready?'

Marion picked up her front door keys, and they stepped out into the chill air to walk the few minutes down the hill to The Fallen Angel.

As they approached the welcoming lights of the pub, Elliott and Brian arrived from the opposite direction. 'Hello, ladies,' Brian said, holding the door open for them. 'First round on me.'

Geoff joined them as they stood at the bar. 'Take a seat, I'll help Brian with the drinks.'

They all sat at a large table in the corner of the pub. Pictures of Whitby and various fishing boats hung on the walls along with ancient sea maps. A large model ship, *The Fallen Angel*, stood proudly on the window ledge.

'It's lovely here. Very traditional.' Isobelle said, looking around the room. 'I can see why you all spend so much time in this place.'

'Marion.' Geoff chuckled. 'What have you been telling her about us? You make us sound like a right bunch of boozers.'

'We are a right bunch though,' Elliott chipped in. 'From all over England, all of us with a tale to tell. We've been through so much together. Tears, laughter, deaths ...'

'Ok, Elliott. We didn't come here to be maudlin.' Brian gently teased his friend.

Elliott let out a bellowing laugh. 'Well, we're not called the Whitby Wailers for nothing!'

Isobelle looked on as her new friends laughed together and smiled broadly.

Raising her glass of merlot high, she made a toast. 'To the Whitby Wailers, my new friends. I think I'm going to like it here.'

'Cheers!' They all cried in unison and touched glasses.

Marion rose. 'Right, my round next, and I'll get some menus.'

'I'll help you.' Brian slid round from the back of the table and tried to squeeze his way past Geoff. 'Budge up a bit, mate.' Geoff edged his way along towards Isobelle as Brian headed for the bar.

Isobelle could feel the warmth of Geoff's leg against her own.

'You ok there, Isobelle?' Geoff said.

'I'm fine, Geoff. And I told you, call me, Belle.'

Elliott excused himself and headed for the toilets on the other side of the room.

'Yes, of course. I'd almost forgotten after all that whisky I had.' Geoff turned to look at her.

'I hope you haven't forgotten everything from last night?' she smiled and tucked a curly strand of hair behind her ear.

He let his hand slip under the table and touched her fingers. 'Maybe you could remind me what happened. But not in here of course. What are you doing tomorrow, we could meet up … or you could come to mine?'

As the others came back from the bar, Isobelle curled her fingers around his and then released them. She looked down and spoke quietly. 'Shall we say one-thirty?'

'I'll look forward to it.' Geoff stood to let Brian sit back down.

Brian joined Elliott at the bar. 'What did you want to talk about?' Brian said.

Elliott turned to face him. 'Oh, yeah. I'd almost forgotten. Can you remember anyone called Vincent?'

'Vincent?' Brian shook his head. 'No. Geoff might. He's been here a long time.'

'Geoff!' Elliott shouted.

Geoff, deep in conversation with Isobelle, looked up. 'Yeah?'

Elliott waved him over. Geoff made his excuses and joined his two friends at the bar. 'I hope you two aren't going to rib me over Belle?'

Elliott frowned. 'Not at all. I wanted to ask you something. Can you remember anyone called Vincent, living in Whitby?'

Geoff, who was gazing across at Isobelle, turned to face Elliott and placed his glass down. 'Vincent? Why?'

'Something Michael said yesterday.'

Geoff shrugged. 'Yeah?'

Elliott rubbed his chin. 'He said the reason he came to Whitby in the first place was to find his real dad. Apparently, the man he thought was his dad wasn't.'

'Right,' Geoff said. He glanced across at Michael serving a customer. 'And his real dad was this …?'

'Vincent,' Brian said.

Geoff picked up his drink and took a large swig. 'I can't remember a Vincent.'

'How did you end up here?' Brian said.

'I visited Dot, a family friend, and just decided to stay.'

'That's the thing,' Elliott said. 'Babs mentioned something when she was dying. She said Dot told her a secret about someone called Vincent.'

Geoff eyed the other two. 'I see. And you think …?'

Elliott lowered his voice as Michael moved nearer. 'That Dot may have taken him in. She had regular lodgers, and maybe this Vincent, Michael's dad, was one.'

'Well,' Geoff said. 'I can't help you.'

'Maybe he left before you came?' Elliott said.

'Maybe,' Geoff said.

'How did you know Dot?' Brian said.

'Dot worked in London with my mother. They were good friends. She moved up here in the early fifties, I think. We used to visit occasionally when I was a kid. She was like an aunty.'

'Then you moved up here?' Elliott said.

'Yeah. I'd broken up with a girl in the Smoke. I lodged in Skinningrove for a while ...' Geoff paused. 'You know what it's like? I was broken-hearted. I thought a change of scenery would mend it.' He forced a laugh. 'Dot put me up, and I fell in love with the place.'

Brian narrowed his eyes. 'What on earth made you move to Skinningrove?'

Geoff shrugged. 'I can't remember. It was a lifetime ago.'

'Yeah. I remember you arriving in Whitby. You've never mentioned Skinningrove though.' Elliott said.

Geoff huffed. 'Maybe you just forgot.'

'I don't think so,' Elliott said. 'I'm sure I'd remember. I remember you starting work for Babs and me, but—'

'Until I got that job at the builders. What a funny bloke the foreman was, I—'

'But you can't remember a Vincent?' Brian said.

Elliott rubbed his chin. 'Do you know if Dot had any family? I can't recall—'

Geoff threw his arms open. 'Jesus. This is like a third degree.'

Elliott glanced at Brian, who raised his eyebrows.

He sighed. 'Dot didn't have any immediate family that I know of. When she died, she left the house to me. If she had family, I'm sure she would have left it to them.' Geoff folded his arms. 'Ok?'

'We're only trying to help Michael,' Elliott said.

Geoff turned his head away and gulped at his drink.

'I wonder who Vincent was?' Brian said.

Geoff shrugged and drained his pint. 'Look, this is all very interesting. But I've got an attractive lady waiting over there. Sorry, lads. I'll have to leave you to it.'

'Aye, ok.' Brian winked. 'We'll sort this out. You go and sit with Belle.'

Geoff headed across to Isobelle, Marion and Jason.

'Oh, well,' Elliott said. 'I suppose it'll remain a mystery.'

'Yeah,' Brian said, as he eyed Geoff across the room. 'Anyway, how about another pint?'

Geoff stared over at Elliott and Brian, and then at Michael. Isobelle nudged him. 'Penny for them?' she said.

He turned to face her and smiled. 'Nothing, really. Elliott asked me about something from years ago. Forget about it.' He lowered his brow. 'So,' he whispered. 'Tomorrow.'

Michael wandered outside into the yard and took out his phone. 'Davy,' he said. 'It's Michael. Michael from The Fallen Angel.'

'Yes, Michael. What can I do for you?'

Michael glanced back towards the pub and moved further away from the door. 'I need another loan.'

Davy laughed. 'You haven't finished paying off the other one yet.'

'I know, but ...' He looked skywards. 'I've had a few quiet months. I'm sure it'll pick-up.'

Davy sighed. 'How much this time?'

'Five-grand.'

Davy laughed again. 'Are you kidding? How the hell are you going to pay back five-grand on top of the two you still owe me?'

'You'll get your money. I promise.'

'Listen, Michael. I'm a little strapped myself. I've had to fork out for my daughter's wedding.'

'Why doesn't she have the reception at my place? I can do you a good deal on the food.'

Davy chuckled. 'You don't know the wife. No offence, but your boozer wouldn't cut it, mate. She's having the reception at Wreckton Hall. It's costing me over twenty-grand for the lot. Sorry I can't help, mate, you see how it is.'

'I do,' Michael said. 'Thanks anyway.'

'Let me have a think,' Davy said. 'I may be able to put you in touch with someone who'll loan you the money.'

'I don't want anyone dodgy.'

'Michael,' Davy said. 'If you don't want my—'

'Sorry, mate. Go on.'

'I'll make a call.'

'Cheers. I really appreciate it.' Michael rang-off and slid the phone into the back pocket of his jeans. He rubbed his face, then went back inside. A young woman came out of the bar. 'Johnston Brewery has just been on the phone.'

Michael briefly closed his eyes. 'Yeah, go on.'

'We can't have any more beer until you pay their bill from last month.'

Michael tutted. ‘I knew there was something I needed to do. I’ll get on to it tomorrow. They’re so bloody impatient.’

‘Everything ok?’ she said.

Michael forced a smile. ‘Yeah. Everything’s fine.’

CHAPTER SIX

The next morning Isobelle lay quietly in her bed staring at the peeling paint on the ceiling and listened to Marion clattering about in the kitchen downstairs. She wanted to wait until her friend had left for work to avoid any questions about what she was doing today. Isobelle felt a knot of anticipation in her stomach as she thought about Geoff and their secret meeting later.

At 8.45, she heard the front door close and the crunch of gravel as Marion headed down the path. Isobelle jumped from the bed and giggled. 'Right, old girl, let's see what we can do with this,' she said to herself, as she ran a hand through thick, dark curls. Wandering into the bathroom, she turned on the bath taps and added a considerable glug of her expensive, fragranced bubble bath. 'Lovely.' She inhaled the perfumed steam and let her silk bathrobe slither to the floor.

An hour later she emerged from the steamy bathroom pink-cheeked and with any superfluous hair dealt with. Removing the towel from her head, she combed her hair carefully. Blessed with thick curls, which she hated as a child, but now loved, she began the laborious task of drying it. Hair dry, she put on her glasses and dabbed at the grey roots with a stick designed to blend them in with her colour.

Sitting in front of the large dressing table mirror, she applied her make-up. Her eyes wandered over to the dark green dress hung on the back of the door, and a moment of doubt eased into her thoughts. 'Oh, what the hell. Give him a day to remember.'

Finally, at almost one-thirty, she was ready. Slipping on her coat, she gathered her bag, and with a last check in the mirror, set off on the short walk to Geoff's.

She was surprised to see him standing at the end of his path. 'Belle, you look beautiful. Come on, I'll take you in the back way.' They both giggled, and she linked her arm through his.

'That's the best offer I've had all day, Geoff.'

Inside the house, they stood in the small kitchen with its yellow painted walls and pine cupboards.

He opened the fridge and took out a bottle. 'Would you like a glass of champagne, gorgeous? Just to relax us. I don't know about you, but I feel like a daft teenager.'

'Champagne sounds perfect.' Isobelle raised her eyebrows. 'Shall we take it upstairs?' Geoff walked over and put his hands on her waist, then kissed her.

'You don't think I'm too forward?' she said.

'I think you're wonderful, Belle. Here, let me take your coat.' He waited as Isobelle turned and slid the garment from her shoulders. Geoff slung it over a kitchen chair and started to kiss the back of her neck.

She turned back to face him. 'There's something I need to tell you.' Isobelle placed her palms on his chest. 'The last man I had sex with died during the ... err ... action.'

Geoff flung his head back and burst out laughing, but seeing the look on Isobelle's face, he stopped. 'Bloody hell, you're serious.'

'Yes, I am. Bill got some dodgy blue pills from the internet because he said he was too embarrassed to go to his doctors. He was having a bit of trouble in that department and wanted it to be special for our wedding night. Unfortunately, unbeknown to both of us, he had a long-standing heart problem.'

'Your wedding night? Belle, that's tragic. Marion never told me that.'

'Well, yes, it is rather tragic,' she said. 'But also, quite comical.'

Geoff suppressed the urge to laugh. 'I suppose it is.'

She frowned. 'It's been a while since, you know. I just hope everything is in working order if you know what I mean.' Isobelle smiled.

'It's been a while for me too, but at least no one died the last time I did it. Be gentle with me. A smile might be the only thing I can raise.'

She laughed. 'I love a sense of humour.'

'I hope you don't need one too much when we get upstairs.'

She led him towards the door. 'Well, we won't find out standing down here.' They walked hand in hand to the bottom of the stairs.

'Wait,' he said. 'I've forgotten the champagne. You go up. First door on your left.'

She walked into the large bedroom and looked at the king-size bed and the crisp white bed linen. 'Come on, Belle. You can do this. It's meant to be fun,' she whispered to herself.

'What did you say?' Geoff said, as he entered and handed her a glass of bubbles.

Isobelle tipped the contents of the glass into her mouth and held out her hand for a refill. 'Nothing. Cheers.' She put down her drink and turned around. 'Will you unzip me, sir?'

Geoff re-entered the bedroom carrying a tray laden with items of food and a second bottle of champagne tucked under his arm. 'Wow.' Isobelle said. 'This all looks amazing. Smoked salmon, olives, bread, and … smoky bacon crisps?' She picked up the packet.

'Yeah, you struck me as a salmon and olives kind of woman but, you can't beat a good bag of crisps.' Geoff placed the tray between them and climbed back into bed. He refilled their glasses and made a toast. 'Here's to us, Belle. Whatever's around the corner, let's enjoy the here and now.'

'I'll drink to that.' She surveyed the bedroom. 'It's a lovely cottage you have. How long have you lived here?' She had slipped one of Geoff's shirts on and sat propped up in the bed holding a glass in one hand and picking at the food with her other.

'I moved here from London in the late seventies.' He placed his drink down on the bedside table and looked away from Isobelle.

'So, what brought you here?' she said.

'I felt fed up with life in London and always fancied living by the sea.' He scratched his chin. 'Enough about me, tell me about your life. I'm sure it's more interesting than mine.'

She frowned. 'There must be more to it than you just fancied living by the sea, it's a long way from London.'

'No, that's it. Very boring really. Came here, loved it, never left.' He reached over and topped her glass up. 'So, tell me about all the broken hearts you must have left in your wake?'

'Not many. I got married young and was married for forty years. Bill was a wonderful man, but he always regretted that we couldn't have children. He filled the void by having a million hobbies and doing charity work. He travelled a lot.' Isobelle sipped at her drink. 'He died doing the Boxing day dip in the sea at Redcar. Dropped down dead on the sand.'

'Oh. I don't know what to say, Belle. That must have been awful.'

'Well, yes, but much worse for him.' She laughed. 'Sorry, I'm not being flippant, but it's the way I deal with things. People think I'm heartless, but it's not the case. I'm a big softy really.'

'I look forward to finding out.' Geoff smiled at her. 'What about husband number two?'

'Bill's best friend, also called Bill, was so good to me after the beach incident. He helped me with everything. We married only ten months after the funeral. But it wasn't like the pages of a love story, we just needed companionship. Like I said, poor Bill had some issues with the physical side of things'

'Bill two?' Geoff asked.

'Yes, Bill two. He knew that Bill … Bill one … and I had enjoyed a great sex life. He felt he was letting me down. But, to be honest, I saw him as more of a friend and the sex wasn't that important to me.'

'Go on.' Geoff offered her a crisp from the packet in his hand.

'He ordered some pills to make our wedding night special. And, if you can call sitting in A and E for five hours special, he got his wish.' She reached into the packet. 'We should never have got together in that way. We should have stayed as friends.'

Geoff put down his crisps and took a sip from his glass. 'What about Marion? She used to talk about you but never really mentioned husbands.'

'We've been friends since we were twelve when she moved to Middlesbrough. She was incredibly jealous of my first husband and ended up moving back here.'

'Why was she so jealous?'

'Geoff, it's a bit delicate really.'

He turned to face her. 'Years ago, I asked Marion out on a date. She flatly turned me down.'

Isobelle sighed. 'The thing is Geoff, she's gay. Marion was, and still is, in love with me.'

'Ah, I can't say that's a massive shock. That she's gay, I mean.'

She playfully slapped his arm. 'Why, because she resisted your charms?'

He laughed. 'Well, yes. They worked on you, though. Seriously, there's never been any men in Marion's life. It makes sense now.'

'We've both always known, but we have never spoken about it. I think the world of Marion, and I would do anything for her, but I'm straight. It took her ages to persuade me to come here and live in her house. I'm still not sure it's the right thing.'

'Will she be jealous of this?' He made a gesture with his hand between the two of them.

'Geoff, we absolutely cannot tell her. At least not until we know where this is going.'

He reached over and took the glass from her. 'Your secret is safe with me,' he said, then kissed her on the lips.

Isobelle lifted the sheet and glanced down. 'Again? You definitely can raise more than a smile.'

'Whenever you're ready,' he said.

They lay together, sleeping soundly, after the best part of two bottles of champagne. Isobelle awoke to pins and needles creeping up her arm wrapped around Geoff's neck. She slipped her numb limb from his body and reached for her bag on the floor. Rummaging through the contents in the dark, she found her phone and held it in front of her. She squinted. 'Shit!'

Geoff jumped awake. 'What's up?' He bolted upright and flicked on the bedside lamp.

'It's half-five! Marion has rung me three times, but my phone's on silent. She's going to kill me.' She leapt from the bed, picked up her crumpled dress from the floor, and struggled into it.

He watched on in amusement. 'Belle, she's not going to kill you.' He pointed to the floor, laughing. 'Don't forget your underwear.'

'It's not funny.' But she couldn't hold back a giggle as she fought drunkenly with the dress zipper.

He walked over to her and fastened the dress. 'There you go.' He patted her on the bottom.

'Right, how do I look?' She smoothed down the dress and slipped on her shoes.

'Like you've been having amazing sex and drinking champagne all afternoon.'

Isobelle looked in her bag and took out a packet of mints, popping one into her mouth. 'I'll have to go.' She gave him a peck on the cheek and hurried from the room.

The next day …

Isobelle glanced about nervously and tapped on the back door to Geoff's cottage.

'Come in,' Geoff shouted.

She slipped inside and looked at Geoff sat at the table. 'I got away with it,' she said, breathlessly.

'What happened?' he said, and poured some tea into a cup for her.

'She was asleep in her chair when I got in, so I slipped upstairs and got changed. When I came back down, I convinced her I'd been on a long walk.'

'And she believed you?'

Isobelle laughed. 'I think so.'

He leant across the table and kissed her. 'Good. Our secret is safe.'

She looked at the photos in front of Geoff and sat next to him. 'What's all this?'

Picking up one, he pushed it towards her. 'That's Dot.'

'The woman who took you in?'

Geoff sighed. 'My aunty.'

'But I thought—'

'Listen, Belle,' he said, and took hold of her hand. 'I have something to tell you, but you must promise to keep it between us.'

'Of course. I won't tell anyone.'

'Not even Marion,' Geoff said.

She squeezed his hand. 'Especially not Marion.'

Geoff began. 'Dot was my aunty, my dad's sister. She moved up to Whitby in the fifties. My dad and I would occasionally visit. When he wasn't inside.'

Isobelle's eyes widened. 'Prison?'

'Yeah. Nothing bad, not really. Theft from shops, that sort of thing. Anyway, he promised to go straight ...' He shrugged and lowered his eyes. '... and might have done, but he fell on a building site he worked on and died.'

'I'm sorry, Geoff,' she said, and squeezed his hand again.

'Anyway.' He took a deep breath. 'They say the apple doesn't fall far from the tree. I lived with my gran and later some friends.' He rubbed his chin. 'This is such a long time ago, Belle. It's almost as if it happened to someone else.'

She moved closer and smiled at him as his eyes glistened. 'Take your time. I won't judge you.'

'I got into a bit of bother myself. So, I moved up here.'

'What sort of bother?'

'A mate of mine, Mick, and another bloke, Barry, robbed a security van. Barry shot a guard. I was the getaway driver.'

She looked at the photo. 'I see.'

'The guard survived. Mick and I had no idea Barry had a gun. I always worried one of them would come clean about it and tell the police I was there as well. I shouldn't have gone with them ...' He took another deep breath and continued as Isobelle nodded. 'Mick died in prison.'

'What about Barry?'

Geoff shrugged. 'I don't know. He must be out of prison by now. He got twenty-five years.'

'It was such a long time ago,' Isobelle said. 'I would just let sleeping dogs lie. You said that Mick's long dead and Barry may be too. It's no good—'

'Yvonne, Mick's wife, told me she was pregnant. She said it was mine.'

'Go on,' Isobelle said.

Geoff sighed. 'I thought she lied back then. We only had a one-night stand, and let's just say, I wasn't the only one. She was having an affair with Barry. Maybe I secretly hoped she was lying. Maybe she was. However ...'

'However?'

'Michael.' Geoff said.

'Michael? Michael from the pub?'

Geoff nodded. 'He told Elliott and Brian that he came to Whitby years ago looking for his real dad. Someone called Vincent.'

Isobelle frowned. 'Vincent? Do you know this Vincent?'

Geoff pointed at himself. 'I'm Vincent. Dot suggested I use the name Geoff in case anyone came looking for Vincent.'

'Right,' Isobelle said. 'And you think Michael is your son?'

'I don't know. His mother must have told him that, though.'

Isobelle picked up a photo of a young Geoff. ‘No one else knows? Not even Michael?’

‘No,’ Geoff said. 'I've kept this secret all these years, but I feel I can trust you. And it's good to tell someone. What do you think I should do?’

‘If you speak to Michael, it may reopen the case.’

‘I know.’ Geoff rubbed his face. ‘Maybe I *should* let sleeping dogs lie.’

Isobelle stood and hugged him. ‘Maybe you should.’

CHAPTER SEVEN

Barry stepped through the gate of the prison and headed across the road to the waiting car. He opened the rear door and tossed his bag onto the floor before climbing into the passenger seat next to a man. 'Nice motor …' he said.

The driver held out his hand. 'Frank,' he said. 'I work for your cousin Danny.'

'He said you'd be here.'

'What does liberty feel like?' Frank said.

Barry glanced back at the prison, his home for the last twenty years, and smiled. 'Great.' He turned back to face the driver. 'Take me to a boozer. I'm going to make up for lost time.'

'Your Danny wants to see you.'

'Yeah? What about?'

He smiled. 'He's got a job for you.'

'What sort of job?' Barry said.

'He's done ok since you went inside. He needs someone to go around and pick up money he's owed.'

Barry scoffed. 'I'm not a rent collector.'

The man laughed. 'There's a bit more to it than that. Danny looks after certain businesses, and he makes sure they don't come to any harm.'

'Protection?'

'Yeah. I'll take you to his house.'

The car pulled onto the drive of the huge property. Barry looked out of the window at the impressive building flanked by two stone lions.

'What do you think?' Frank said.

'Smart.'

'Come on, he's waiting.'

Barry followed him inside, through a marbled-floored hallway, and into the massive lounge. A man seated in a chair, stood and made his way over to Barry.

'Barry,' he said. 'Nice to see you.' He patted him on the arm. 'Looks like you've been working out.'

Barry slowly scanned the room and drank in the opulence of his surroundings. 'Not much else to do inside,' he said.

The man held out his hands. 'Aren't you going to give your cousin a hug?'

Barry smiled. 'It's great to see you.' The two men embraced.

Danny looked at the other man. 'Get the man a drink, Frank. I want to have a chat with him.'

'Ok, boss.'

Danny pointed to a chair, and the two men sat opposite each other. 'As you can see, I'm doing all right.'

'Protection, Frank said.'

He opened a box on the table next to him, pulled out a large cigar and offered it to Barry who took it from him, sniffed it before placing it in his mouth. Danny took a second from the box and lit both cigars.

'I need someone,' Danny said, blowing a thick plume of smoke into the air, 'to encourage some of the people to pay a bit quicker. Most are ok, but there's always one or two that need a little push.'

Frank returned with two drinks and placed them on the small table between the two men. 'Anything else, boss?'

'Yeah. Stacy wants to go down Regent Street.' Frank nodded at the pair and left.

'Stacy?' Barry said.

'My wife.'

'Ah,' Barry said. 'I heard you got married again.'

'You can meet her later. She has a friend. I thought the four of us could go for something to eat. I figured that you may be interested in a bit of female company.'

'Yeah. Sounds great.'

'My proposition,' Danny said. 'Are you interested?'

'What's the pay like?'

Danny laughed. 'We'll discuss that later, but I'm sure you won't be disappointed.'

Barry sipped his drink. 'It's a different world to when I went inside.'

'You'll adjust. You heard about Mick?'

Barry scowled. 'Heart attack, wasn't it?'

'Apparently.'

'Vincent,' Barry said. 'Where's he?'

'Vincent disappeared off the face of the earth in 1978. I haven't been able to trace him.'

'That bastard has got my money.'

Danny frowned. 'Well, he's long gone. He might even be dead.'

Barry growled. 'There must have been over twenty-grand.'

Danny smiled. 'Forget about it. You'll make plenty of money with me.' He held out a glass. 'Here's to your new life.'

Two weeks later …

Barry pulled the car up outside the block of flats, glanced up at the towering edifice, and jumped from his vehicle. He looked upwards again, then set off inside. Reaching a door, he knocked. A dog barked from inside, and the door opened.

A man in his twenties, holding a can of lager, stood there. 'Yeah?'

'I'm looking for someone called Yvonne,' Barry said.

The man looked him up and down. 'There's no Yvonne here. Now piss-off, I'm watching the racing.'

Barry placed his foot inside the door opening, preventing the man from closing it. He pushed at the door. 'Listen, mate.'

'Who the hell do you think you are—?'

Barry grabbed hold of the man who dropped his can, spraying foam across the carpet. He tried to wrestle free, but Barry punched him just below the ribs. The man folded onto the floor, gasping for breath and Barry pulled him towards the railings outside.

'I'm only asking a question,' Barry said. 'No need to get chewy with me.'

'I don't know any Yvonne.'

A woman appeared from inside. 'Leave him alone. I'll phone the police.'

Barry turned to face her and scowled. 'I wouldn't do that. It's a long way down, and I don't think he'll survive the fall.'

She brought a hand up to her mouth.

The man struggled to his feet as Barry grasped him by the neck and pushed him up against the wall. 'I was asking your husband if he knew an Yvonne.'

'We don't know any Yvonne,' she said.

Barry relinquished his grip. 'Ok.' He patted the man on his cheek. 'Next time be a little more polite. Then people don't have to resort to this.'

The man nodded, and Barry pushed him back indoors. Neighbours from nearby stood outside their homes.

Barry glanced left and right. 'Anyone remember an Yvonne living here?' he said.

A woman two doors away, arms folded, stepped closer. 'I do. Who's asking?'

He moved towards her, reached into his pocket and pulled out a note. 'You do?'

'She moved away years ago.' The woman pondered. 'Must be ten or eleven years now.'

'I don't suppose you know where she went?' He held the cash aloft.

'No idea. She left owning money and rent, though. Some fella came around looking for her.'

He handed her the note, the woman quickly depositing it inside her jeans pocket. 'Did she live alone?' he said.

'No. She had a son.' The woman pondered again. 'Michael.'

Barry nodded and handed the woman a second note. 'Thanks. Only takes a bit of manners,' he muttered to himself and hurried off.

2003 …

Barry pushed the man's head below the surface of the water. His victim spluttered, as he fought for breath.

'I told you what we'd do if you didn't have the money,' Barry said. He pulled the man's head free from the liquid, as water splashed over the side of the bath.

The man behind Barry laughed. 'Push him under again, Baz. Drown the bastard.'

Barry forced the man below the water.

'Please …' the man gasped as water sprayed from his mouth. '… I'll get the mone—'

His head disappeared beneath the surface again as he splashed about helplessly. The man behind Barry grabbed their victim's legs and lifted them off the floor, forcing him further under the water.

Helplessly, the man continued to thrash, then slowed and stopped altogether. The two men dropped the limp form, now lying motionless half in and half out of the bathtub. The drenched Barry stood and surveyed the dead man.

'What happened?' Barry's friend said.

'He must have had a heart attack or something.' Barry picked up a nearby towel and dabbed at his clothing. 'We hardly doused him.'

'Danny won't be happy. He owes him five-grand.'

Barry grunted. 'You leave Danny to me. I'll explain what happened. Have a look around and see if there's anything of value. I'll meet you in the alley out the back with the van.'

2010 …

Barry stood at the bar and waited to be served. A woman, close by, eyed him up and down. 'Barry?' she said.

He turned to face her. 'Who's asking?'

She smiled. 'Don't you remember me? Sheila. Sheila Fletcher.'

He furrowed his brow. 'From the estate?'

'Yeah. How are you?'

He smiled. 'Not bad. A lot older.'

'I always fancied you.'

He leant on the bar. 'You did? I was a bit better looking back then.'

'I don't know,' she said. 'You're still the same handsome Barry I remember.'

He rubbed his bald head. 'I had a bit more hair.'

She laughed. 'I remember that curly mop of yours.'

'What are you doing here?' he said.

'I moved away years ago. Brighton. But I've come back.'

He smiled. 'Sick of all that sea and sand?'

'Yeah. My old fella died a couple of years back, and ...'

'Sorry about that.'

She waved a hand dismissively. 'He was a waster. What about you, then? Any special lady in your life?'

'There's been a few over the years.' He shrugged. 'Did quite a long stretch in the nick.'

She nodded. 'I remember. Still, you're here now.'

'What did your old man do?'

She smiled. 'Bit of this, bit of that. Nothing too legal.'

The pair laughed. 'Can I get you a drink?' he said.

'I'd love one. Glass of white.'

'Who are you here with?'

She nodded towards the corner. 'A couple of girls from way back. Jackie, I don't think you'll know her. But you might remember Rita.'

'Her face seems familiar.'

Sheila smiled. 'She used to knock about with your mate's wife. Yvonne Tate.'

'Mick's missus?'

'Yeah, that's her.'

Barry eyed Rita. 'Shall we have our drinks over there?'

Sheila linked his arm. 'If you like, handsome.'

The pair sat. 'Do you remember Barry?' Sheila said to her friends. 'From the estate.'

'Bit of a bad boy, if I remember,' Rita said.

Barry smiled. 'I haven't changed. Talking of remembering things,' he said. 'Yvonne Tate ...?'

Rita sipped her drink through a straw. 'Yvonne? Yeah, I remember her. Wasn't she married to your mate ...?'

'Mick Tate.'

'Yeah,' she said.

'Mick died while I was inside, I was hoping to pop around and give her my condolences.'

Sheila linked his arm. 'I hope that's all you're going to give her? I can be very jealous.'

Barry smiled. 'Yeah, all right, Sheila. I only bought you a drink, not asked you to marry me.'

Sheila frowned, as her two friends stifled a giggle.

Rita pondered. 'She moved away a while ago with her boy. Clapham seems to ring a bell. I'm not sure though.'

2018 …

Barry pulled out his mobile. 'Yeah?'

'Are you still interested in Yvonne Tate?' a man's voice said.

Barry stopped outside his car and fumbled for his key. 'I am.'

'I ran into a mate of mine, and we got talking about the old times. I asked if he remembered Mick and his missus.'

Barry opened the door and slid onto the seat. 'And?'

'He said she lives over Walthamstow way.'

'Have you an address?' Barry said.

'I have. He did say that she's a piss-head these days.'

'The address …?'

Barry jotted it down and smiled. 'There's a drink or two for you next time I see you.' He hung up and started the engine.

Barry knocked on the door of a flat and waited, nothing stirred. He knocked again louder, as a muffled voice shouted some obscenity from within. He put the carrier he held on the floor and banged again with the side of his fist. As the door began to open, he picked up his bag. Barry stared at Yvonne as she pulled the cord of her dressing gown tighter around her small frame. Grey-hair and wrinkles replaced the youthful looks he remembered.

She squinted at him, bleary-eyed. 'What do you want?'

'Do you remember me?' Barry said.

Yvonne rubbed at her eyes. 'Who are you?'

'Barry.'

A flicker of recognition traversed her features. 'Barry.'

'Can I come in?'

She turned and padded along the short corridor and into the front room. He surveyed the squalor she lived in as Yvonne slumped onto a chair. She shakily pulled a cigarette from her dressing gown pocket and lit it.

'I was sorry to hear about Mick,' he said.

Yvonne looked away and took a long drag of her cigarette. She coughed as the smoke filled her lungs. 'History,' she mumbled. 'A lifetime ago.'

He moved forward and held out the carrier. 'I've brought you a gift. For old times' sake.'

'What are you on about?' she said, turning to face him.

'I need some information.'

She puffed greedily on her cigarette. 'Information? I don't know anything.'

'Vincent?'

Yvonne scoffed. 'Left me. You all left me.'

'Where did he go?'

She shrugged. 'I don't know.' She shook her head at him. 'That was the seventies. I can't remember what happened in the seventies.'

Barry pulled a litre bottle of vodka from his carrier and held it out. 'Look what I've got here.'

She rubbed her mouth with the back of her hand and grabbed at the bottle.

Barry pulled it away from her. 'Vincent? What happened to Vincent?'

'He left. I don't know where'.

'You must remember where he would have gone?'

'I …' She blew smoke from the corner of her mouth and closed her eyes.

'Think, Yvonne.' He pulled a second bottle from the carrier and allowed the bag to fall to the floor. 'Two bottles. All yours if you can just remember.'

Tears filled her eyes. 'I can't. It's all a blur.'

'Shame,' Barry said. He turned and moved towards the door.

Yvonne unsteadily got to her feet. 'Please,' she said. Her eyes locked on the bottles in Barry's hands. 'I don't know.'

Barry stopped at the threshold. 'Your lad?'

'Michael?'

'Yeah. Where is he?'

Yvonne's shoulders slumped. 'Left years ago. I lived with a bloke, and they didn't get on.'

'Did you ever find out who his dad was?'

Yvonne scoffed. 'Vincent.'

'Vincent?'

'Yeah. After you told me you couldn't have kids, I realised he had to be Vincent's. It couldn't be anyone else despite what you all thought about me.'

Barry laughed. 'You and Vincent. Poor Mick, he had no idea his two mates were shagging his missus.'

Yvonne looked away. 'It was a one-off with Vincent. We were drunk and …'

'Did you tell him who his father is?'

'Yeah.'

'Where's Michael now?'

'Whitby. He's been there years. Runs a pub.' She cackled. 'I've thought of going up there myself. All that free booze.'

Barry glanced around the room again and placed the bottles on a nearby table. 'Fill your boots.'

Danny looked at Barry. 'Whitby?' Danny said.

'Yeah. I fancy a change of scenery.'

He held open his hands. 'Come on. Why are you really going there?'

Barry sighed. 'There's a possibility that Yvonne, Mick's missus ...' He slumped onto a seat. 'She had a boy. He wasn't Mick's.'

Danny smiled. 'Yours?'

'Me and Yvonne had a thing back then. When she told me she was pregnant, I lied and said I couldn't have kids. I didn't want to be saddled with a nipper.'

'Are you sure he's yours?'

Barry rubbed his chin. 'Not totally. Yvonne had a one-night stand with someone else. He could be the father.'

'Who?'

'Vincent.'

Danny sighed. 'You're not still chasing Vincent, are you? Christ, Barry, it's been over forty years.'

'Vincent's history,' Barry said. 'I need to know if Michael is my son or not. If he's not, he has a pub.'

'I'm not following you?'

Barry grinned. 'His dad stole money off me. If I can't get it from Vincent, his son will have to pay.'

Danny folded his hands together on the desk. 'I can't say I'm happy losing one of my best men.'

'I'm getting too old for this. I'm in my sixties. You've got plenty of good lads.'

'What are you going to do for money while you're up there?'

'I'll manage.'

Danny opened a drawer in his desk. 'I'll give you the name of a good mate of mine who lives up north. Maybe he can help you out with a bit of work. Me and him go back a long way.'

CHAPTER EIGHT

One month later …

Elliott ambled along the cobbles towards the shop when he spotted Michael on the other side of the road. He crossed and intercepted him. 'How was your holiday?' Elliott said.

'It wasn't really a holiday. A relation in Leeds got married. I decided to make it a longer break. Did the stand-in do ok while I was away?'

'He's a funny bugger. We didn't really take to him.'

'Sorry to hear that. If I go away again, I'll ask for someone different. Are you off to the shop?'

'Yeah. I don't do a lot these days. Jason does the bulk of it. He wants to extend.'

'Really? Business must be good?'

'It's doing very well.'

'I've had a cash injection myself,' Michael said.

'What for? Is the pub struggling?'

Michael sighed. 'A little. I'm hoping it'll pick up. The money I've borrowed should tide me over.'

'But how—?'

'That was another reason I went to Leeds. I have a few contacts there. One guy, a friend of a friend, is looking to put money into the pub. A silent partner.'

'Oh, good,' Elliott said. 'Well, it's great to see you back. I'll be in with the rest of them tonight. See you then.' Elliott turned away and then spun back around. 'Your dad …?'

'What about him?' Michael said.

'You never found him then?'

Michael shook his head. 'Maybe he was never in Whitby in the first place. He could have moved anywhere. He might even be dead.'

'Yeah. Me and Brian asked around, but no one knew a Vincent.'

Michael shrugged. 'It's probably for the best. I don't know how I'd feel if I met him.' He winked at Elliott. 'See you tonight.'

Elliott marched into the shop and took off his coat. 'I'm back.'

Jason popped up from behind the counter. 'Great. I'm starving. I'm going to get a sandwich and a coffee.'

'Is there anything I need to do?'

Jason pulled on his coat. 'One of the suppliers is bringing some of those new artworks. They sold really well last time. I've put the money in an envelope to pay him. It's in the till.'

'I talked to Michael,' Elliott said.

'He's back, thank God. That stand-in boss was awful.'

Elliott chuckled. 'Yeah, I told him that. Do you remember he was looking for his dad?'

Jason stopped at the door. 'Who?'

'Michael,' Elliott said. 'Don't you remember me telling you about his dad?'

'Oh, yeah. I remember.'

'It's a shame we can't help trace him.'

Jason opened the door and paused. 'Maybe we can. I'll grab some lunch, and then we'll have a chat.'

Jason leant back in his chair and smiled. 'Elliott,' he shouted.

Elliott finished locking up and entered the storeroom. 'Have you found anything?'

Jason scoffed. 'I didn't have a lot to go on. Someone called Vincent.'

Elliott shrugged. 'You said you may be able to help.' He bent down and looked at the computer screen. 'Ancestry World? What's this all about?'

'Do you remember ...' Jason said. 'I traced my family back to the sixteenth century?'

'Yeah,' Elliott said. 'But we don't—'

'I know, I know,' Jason said. 'This is what I used.' He tapped the screen.

'How does this help us though?'

'Well,' Jason said. 'I got to thinking. The woman Geoff lodged with. The woman who left him the cottage.'

'Dot,' Elliott said.

'Dorothy Kinghorn,' Jason said.

'Yes. Dorothy Kinghorn.'

Jason spun around on his chair to face Elliott. 'I searched for a marriage certificate.'

'For Dot?'

'For Dot,' Jason said. 'She married a John Kinghorn in 1954. He died in 1956.'

'How does that help us, though?'

Jason pulled up another screen on the computer. 'Her maiden name was Fry. I thought that maybe this Vincent was a relation of hers.'

'Fry.' Elliott rubbed his chin. 'Geoff said Dot didn't have any relations though.'

'Stay with me,' Jason said. 'I checked for children and siblings on the census. She had no children, but she did have a brother. Robert.'

'Robert Fry?'

'Yeah. Robert Fry. He married a woman called Elizabeth, and they had one child, a boy.' He hit the keyboard and another screen popped up. 'And guess what his name was?'

Elliott popped on his glasses and stared at the screen. He grinned. 'Vincent Fry.'

'Vincent Fry,' Jason said. 'Michael's dad was Dot's nephew.'

'That makes Michael—'

'Dot's great-nephew.'

Elliott patted Jason on the back. 'Jason, you're a star.'

Jason folded his arms and pouted. 'I'm not just a pretty face, you know.'

Jason and Elliott entered The Fallen Angel and sat down with the rest of the Whitby Wailers quiz team.

'I got you two a drink,' Geoff said. He slid the glasses towards them.

Marion eyed Jason and Elliott. 'What are you two looking so pleased about?' she said.

The pair lifted up their drinks, took a swig, and thanked Geoff in unison. 'We have news,' Elliott said.

'Oh, yeah?' Brian said.

'Remember me telling you about Michael's search for his dad?'

Geoff glanced at Isobelle, and she looked down at her drink.

'Yeah,' Brian said.

'This boy …' Elliott put an arm around Jason's shoulder. '… is a genius.'

'Well,' Marion said. 'With all that private education, he should be.'

'Oh,' Jason said. 'A saucer of milk for the cat.'

'He used this Ancestry thingy,' Elliott said.

'World,' Jason said.

Elliott placed his drink down. 'Yeah, Ancestry World, to delve into Dot's past.'

'My Dot?' Geoff said.

'Your Dot,' Elliott said.

Isobelle picked up her glass. 'What about her?' she said.

Elliott grinned. 'She had a nephew called Vincent.'

'Ah,' Marion said. 'Michael's dad?'

'Exactly,' Jason said.

Elliott eyed Geoff. 'I thought you said Dot didn't have any relatives? Did I get that wrong?'

Isobelle surreptitiously squeezed Geoff's hand under the table. 'She didn't,' Geoff said. 'As far as I know. She told me that her only relations were distant cousins. She never mentioned a nephew.'

'But Vincent was her nephew,' Elliott said. "It said on the—'

'Yeah, ok. But I didn't know him.' Geoff huffed. 'She didn't tell me everything. You and Babs knew her as well as me.'

'I never said you did know,' Elliott said.

'She did leave the cottage to you though,' Marion said.

Geoff turned to face her. 'What are you implying?'

'I'm only joking,' she said.

'Come on.' Brian chuckled. 'Tell the truth. Did you get Dot to change the will in your favour and dupe her nephew?'

Geoff stood. 'I don't have to listen to this rubbish. Dot and I were very close. She was like a mother to me. And you lot are accusing me—'

'Geoff,' Elliott said. 'Brian's only kidding.'

'Yeah, Geoff,' Brian said. 'Just a bit of fun.'

Geoff rubbed his temple. 'I'm going to the loo.' He pushed his chair out of the way and stormed off.

Isobelle looked at the others. 'I hope you're all satisfied.'

'Come on, Belle,' Jason said. 'It was a bit of ribbing.'

'We'll apologise,' Marion said. 'We didn't mean to upset him.'

'Geoff's not feeling well. He doesn't need you lot having a go at him.'

'We didn't know,' Elliott said, as Isobelle stood and followed Geoff. She reached him before he disappeared inside the bathroom.

'Geoff,' she said.

He stopped and turned. 'Christ, Belle. They're going to find out.'

'I've told them you've been feeling unwell. Just play on that. Brazen it out.'

He took hold of her hand. 'Thank God I've got you,' he said. His eyes sparkled with tears as he rubbed his face. 'Christ, if they do—'

Isobelle squeezed his hand. 'They won't.'

Geoff returned moments later with Isobelle, and the pair slumped into their seats. Elliott looked around the table as silence deafened them. 'Listen, Geoff,' he said. 'I think we all owe you an apology.'

Geoff shook his head. 'It's ok. I've been feeling a bit under the weather today, and I … Well, let's just say I'm a little over-sensitive.' He picked up his glass. 'I couldn't be mad at you lot for very long. To the Whitby Wailers.'

'Yeah,' Brian said. 'Hear, hear. To the Whitby Wailers.' They all clinked glasses. 'Let's win this quiz and see if we can get into the next round.'

CHAPTER NINE

Brian glanced at the pictures from what seemed like light years ago. He paused at one, a photo of a house, it's garden full to overflowing with flowers of every colour, and allowed his mind to drift back in time.

Scarborough, 1997 …
Brian stood at the basin and splashed cold water onto his face. He felt terrible as an icy shiver wrapped around his body despite the warmth of the day. His reflection looked back at him – hollow-eyes and grey skin. He groaned and let his forehead rest on the mirror.

'You ok, mate?' A male voice from beside him said.

'No, I'm not too clever. Think I'm coming down with something.'

His colleague stood beside him at the sink. 'There's a sickness bug going about. Get yourself home, I'll clear it with the boss.'

'But we've got that job in Pickering today,' Brian said. 'We promised him we'd have it done.'

His friend patted him on the shoulder. 'Don't worry about it. I'll finish the jointing. I should be able to get it done by the end of today. I'll do an hour or two overtime if I have to.'

'Cheers, Billy. I owe you one.'

'You shouldn't have come in. You look awful.'

'I know. Thanks again.' Brian picked up his keys and crossed the yard to where he had parked his BT van. He grabbed his bag from the passenger seat and locked up, then headed for his own car. He paused outside the vehicle as nausea swept over him. The pain in his stomach intensified as his mouth filled with saliva. 'Hold it down, only a short drive home,' he said to himself.

Fifteen minutes later, he turned into the cul-de-sac where he lived with his wife of almost twenty years and his nine-year-old son. Brian frowned as he saw Valerie's car parked on the drive. Maybe she has got this virus too, and left work early, he thought as he pulled to a stop across the pavement.

He put his key into the front door, but the key was in the lock from the other side and wouldn't turn. 'How many times, Val? Take the bloody key out,' he muttered. Opening the wooden gate to the back of the house, he plodded down the path. Sweat soaked his body and ran down his back, the pain and feeling of queasiness increasing with every step. Turning the corner to the rear of the house, he dropped his keys, and as he bent to pick them up, he heard a crash from the kitchen.

He stood back up, looked through the window, and gasped. There on the kitchen table lay his wife, naked. And between her legs ... 'Oh, my, God!' Brian let out a shout and banged his fist against the glass.

As he fumbled with his key in the lock, Valerie opened it from the inside. She stood there holding a tea-towel with a map of the Isle of Man over her naked body. 'Brian, it's not what it looks like,' Valerie spluttered.

'Where is he?' Brian ran inside the house and into the living room. 'There you are! You bastard.'

'Brian, it's ...'

'Not what it looks like? Val has already tried that.' Brian clutched his stomach as a needle of pain shot through him.

'Are you ok? You don't look well.'

Brian scoffed. 'Finding your wife and brother at it on the kitchen table can have that effect, Ian. I eat my meals at that table, you filthy pig!' He turned as Valerie walked into the room now dressed in a tracksuit.

'Calm down. We can talk about this sensibly,' she said, holding up her hands in front of her.

'There was nothing sensible going on in the ... in my ... kitchen! My God woman, have you no shame? I could've been the window cleaner!' He walked towards Valerie, and Ian grabbed his arm to stop him. Brian faced him, bent double with the cramps in his heaving guts and vomited over the half-dressed Ian.

Brian, shaken from his reverie, placed the photograph back on the table, stood and made his way to the front door.

Elliott knocked again. 'Elliott,' Brian said, as he opened it. 'What are you doing here?'

Elliott followed Brian through into the kitchen. 'Just a chat, Brian. If you can spare a minute?'

'Yeah. Have a seat. I've only just brewed up.'

Elliott glanced down at the pictures on the table. 'What are all these?' he said, easing himself onto a seat.

'Ah,' Brian said. 'Just thinking about the past. It must have been the discussion we had in the pub last night.'

'About Michael's dad?'

Brian popped a mug in front of Elliott and filled it from the pot. 'Yeah.' He picked up a picture of a boy. 'Our Oliver.'

Elliott took the photo from him and studied it. 'Do you still hear from him?'

Brian joined his friend at the table. 'Yeah. I had an email the other week. He keeps asking me to go out to Australia and visit.'

'Why don't you?'

'Too far, Elliott. I couldn't sit all those hours on a plane.' Brian smiled. 'He still calls me Dad.'

'Well, you were his dad for all those years. Just because he's not biologically yours doesn't make him any less of a son.'

'I know. He's my nephew anyway.'

'Your brother, Ian. Ever hear from him?'

Brian sighed. 'Occasionally. The odd card on birthdays and Christmas. He's still living with my ex.'

Elliott nodded. 'In Scarborough?'

'Yeah.' Brian gathered the photos together and dropped them into the shoebox on the table. 'Anyway, you were talking about Michael's dad?'

'Yeah. What was your take on Geoff's reaction?'

Brian rubbed his chin. 'I thought it a little odd, but we did give him a hard time.'

'Yeah, I suppose we did.' Elliott looked out of the window.

'You don't think,' Brian said, 'that he did get Dot to change her will, do you?'

Elliott turned to face Brian. 'Good God, no. Dot treated Geoff like her own son. It didn't come as a surprise when she left everything to him. It's just ...'

'Vincent?' Brian said.

'Yeah. If Dot had a nephew, why did she never speak about him?'

Brian shrugged. 'No idea. Maybe they fell out.'

'Michael said she used to write to Vincent. That doesn't sound as if they fell out.'

'No, I suppose not.' Brian lifted his mug and took a drink.

'I'd love to find out what happened to him. If only for Michael's sake.'

'How can we do that?'

'I've already got Jason working on it now. He's checking stuff on the internet.'

Brian grinned. 'We're going to do a bit of sleuthing, are we?'

'And Marion.'

Brian frowned. 'Marion?'

'Yeah. I ran into her this morning near the harbour, on her way to work.'

'What about Geoff and Belle?' Brian said.

Elliott placed a finger on his upper lip and thought for a moment. 'Geoff seems a little off lately. He seems to get upset when we mention Dot, so, maybe we should leave him out of this. Besides, there's enough with us four.'

'And Belle?'

Elliott raised his eyebrows. 'You do know Geoff and Belle are having a thing?'

Brian laughed. 'I suspected. Do you know for sure?'

'Not for sure, but I'll be amazed if they're not.'

Isobelle walked along the footpath and past the Abbey. She halted by the side of the road and sat on a bench. She didn't have to wait long before Geoff's car pulled to a stop next to her.

Geoff lowered the window. 'How much for a good time?' he said.

Isobelle stood, ambled over and leant on the door popping her head inside the passenger window. 'It depends what you want, luv,' she said, mimicking chewing gum. 'I don't do anything kinky.'

Geoff held up a £5. 'I've only got this, darling. Will it be enough?'

Isobelle wiped her nose and sniffed. 'I'll see what I can do.' She pulled the door open and climbed inside.

Geoff laughed. 'What did you say to Marion?' he said.

'She's at work. I feigned being asleep until she left the house. Couldn't be bothered with her third degree.'

'Third degree?'

Isobelle turned to face him. 'Last night at the pub.'

'Oh, yeah. I was trying to forget that. Did she mention anything about it when you got home?'

Isobelle sighed. 'She tried to, but I told her I was too tired. It'll only hold her off for so long though.'

Geoff rubbed his chin. 'Yeah.'

Isobelle nudged him. 'Let's forget about that for now. You were going to show me this house.'

Geoff smiled. 'I was. What about a kiss first?'

Isobelle looked away and dramatically fanned herself. 'Why, sir,' she said, in her best deep south drawl. 'You are forward.'

'I find you get nothing unless you ask,' he said, attempting his own accent.

Isobelle burst out laughing. 'That's the worst accent I've ever heard in my life.'

Geoff laughed with her. 'I can do an Irish one.'

'No, you're ok,' Isobelle said, and planted her lips on his.

They pulled apart, and Geoff stared into her eyes. 'That's worth a fiver of anyone's money,' he said.

'Wait until I get you home,' she said. 'You'll need more than a fiver.'

'What do you think?' Geoff said, as he drew the car to a halt. The pair got out.

Isobelle stared at the dilapidated property. 'It's not how I imagined it.'

Geoff chuckled. 'Why?'

'There's a lot that needs doing.'

Geoff stepped closer. 'I've been inside. Most of it is cosmetic. Structurally ...' He gazed at Isobelle. '... it's sound. I can do most of the work myself.'

Isobelle raised her eyebrows. 'You're not getting any younger.'

Geoff flexed his arm muscles. 'Nonsense. I'm as fit as a flea.'

'Can you afford it?'

'Yeah. With what I'll get for the cottage, and what I've managed to tuck away over the years.'

'Well,' Isobelle took hold of his hand, 'if it's what you want.'

Geoff smiled. 'It's a little bigger than the cottage, and look at the size of the back garden.'

She followed him as he walked around the side of the property. 'Wow,' she said. 'What a view.'

'It's magnificent, isn't it?' he said. 'Imagine waking up to that every morning.'

'The garden is huge.'

'I might have some chickens. Fresh eggs every day. I make a mean poached egg.'

She turned to face him. 'Enough for two?'

'Certainly.'

Isobelle took hold of his hands and kissed him. 'Go for it.'

Geoff pulled her towards him. 'We could be happy here, Belle. I've never felt like this with anyone else.'

Isobelle brushed a stray wisp of hair from his face and kissed him again. 'You don't think we're going too fast?'

'Come on, Belle. At our age we can't be messing about. Unless you're having second thoughts, that is?'

Isobelle gazed at the cliffs in the distance. 'I've never been more certain of anything in my life.' She turned to face him and grinned.

Elliott entered the shop. 'Any luck?' he asked Jason.

'Give me a chance, Elliott. I've been rushed off my feet all day.'

'Sorry. If you want to have a look now, I'll watch the shop.'

Jason folded his arms. 'I will if you make me a cup of tea first. I'm spitting feathers here.'

'Ok,' Elliott said. 'I'll put the kettle on, and you can get cracking.'

Elliott locked the door to the shop and joined Jason at the desk in the storeroom. 'Anything?'

Jason sat back in the chair and stretched. 'A little. Vincent lived with his grandmother.'

'What happened to his mother?'

'I haven't been able to trace her. She disappeared off the electoral roll when Vincent was about eight.'

Elliott pulled a seat closer to Jason and sat. 'It sounds like there was some family difficulty,' Elliott said. 'If he lived with his grandmother, maybe his mother died?'

Jason scratched his head. 'I haven't been able to find a death certificate for her. But it's possible, I suppose.'

'So how long did he live with his grandmother?'

Jason picked up a death certificate, he had printed off, and handed it to Elliott, who studied the document. 'His grandmother died in 1970,' Elliott said.

'Yeah. Vincent would have been sixteen.'

Elliott pondered. 'He wouldn't have been old enough to get a place on his own.'

'No,' Jason said. 'His grandmother lived in Islington, so I checked the electoral rolls starting from two years later. He first appeared on the electoral roll in 1974. He was still living in Islington, but had moved addresses.'

Elliott raised his eyebrows. 'And?'

'The last time he appears on the records is 1978. He was living at an address ...' Jason picked up a piece of paper. 'Flat 1A, 62 Queens Road.'

'Right,' Elliott said. 'And you lose contact with him then?'

'Yeah. I've searched other boroughs, but nothing. If he did come north, he could be anywhere.'

Elliott rubbed his chin. 'We know that Michael's mother told him that his dad left London in the late 70s, which tallies with this.' Elliott studied the paperwork again. 'Have you been able to locate a Vincent Fry around Whitby from that time?'

Jason shook his head. 'I've searched Whitby and other areas, but I've found nothing.'

Elliott sighed. 'So, we've hit a dead end?'

'Well,' Jason said. 'Not entirely.' He picked up a small notepad. 'At the time Vincent was living at flat 1A, 62 Queens Road, there was a couple who lived at the same address.' He showed Elliott their names. 'Mr and Mrs Walton. And according to the current electoral roll, they still live there.'

Elliott patted Jason on the arm. 'You're a genius, Jason.'

'I know. You've already said.'

'So, I need to talk to Mr and Mrs Walton and see if they remember Vincent.'

Jason nodded. 'You could write.'

'Bugger that,' Elliott said. 'I'll go down there.'

'To London?'

Elliott grinned. 'Yeah. Why not?'

Jason raised his eyebrows. 'When was the last time you were down there?'

Elliott shrugged. 'Not since Babs and I left.'

'Won't it feel a bit strange?'

'Yeah, I suppose. But my parents are long dead. It's not like I'm going to run into them. I haven't seen any of my family for years. I've had the odd letter or two, though. And London is a big place.'

'What happened back then?' Jason said. 'You never really told me.'

'It was a different time. My parents were just trying to protect me, I suppose. Folk were a lot more prejudice in those days. Dad said people would be angry with Babs and me. Her family felt the same way. You must know all about prejudice, Jason?'

'Yeah. When I told my parents I'm gay, they went ballistic. Dad was so … homophobic. Queers and puffs, he called us. So, you can imagine how he felt having a son who was one of them.'

'People are so petty,' Elliott said. 'What's colour, sexual orientation, religion, or anything else got to do with what's in a person's heart.'

'Exactly.'

'Have you never been tempted to get in touch over the years?' Elliott said.

'What's the point. They would never change. I couldn't stand having someone put up a façade for me.'

Elliott put an arm around Jason. 'I think you're a smashing lad. Babs and I thought so the first time we met you.'

'Thanks.'

'I mean it. I changed my will last year,' Elliott said.

'Right …'

'I'm leaving the shop to you.'

Jason's eyes filled with tears. 'What about your Albert?'

'He's a big-time lawyer. He doesn't need the money. They'll still be a little for him and the grandkids if he ever has any, but you've built this shop up. You deserve to reap the rewards.'

Jason stood, and the two of them hugged.

'I could even kill two birds with one stone,' Elliott said, in an effort to lighten the mood.

Jason frowned. 'What do you mean?'

'I have a niece on my mother's side who lives in Clapham. I've been in correspondence over the last few months. She's compiling a family tree. Maybe I could meet up with her.'

'Why haven't I heard about this before?'

Elliott laughed. 'I don't tell you everything.'
'Would you like me to come?' Jason said.
'Who'll look after the shop?'
'I suppose.'
Elliott rubbed his chin again. 'I'll ask Brian. He's into all that Egyptology stuff. I'll entice him with the British Museum. He once told me he would love to go there.'

CHAPTER TEN

Isobelle rushed back from Geoff's before Marion was due home, carrying some ready meals and vegetables for their tea. Even with her rudimentary culinary skills, she felt pretty confident it wouldn't be ruined this time.

She glanced at the clock and tutted. 'Where the hell are you?' she muttered. Marion usually arrived home around twenty-past five, but it was now six o'clock. She glanced at the sad-looking ready meal, with its blackened plastic curling at the edges, and sighed. 'Trust Marion to be late when I had decided to cook.' Pip padded in and looked at Isobelle. 'I know, Pip,' Isobelle said. 'You'll be waiting for your tea too.'

She patted the dog's head and walked into the front room as Marion finally arrived home. 'Where the hell have you been?' she said.

Marion stopped in the hall, slid off her coat, pulled off her shoes, and pushed on her slippers. 'Why?'

Isobelle nodded towards the kitchen. 'I cooked tea.' Marion frowned. 'Don't worry,' Isobelle said. 'It was a ready meal.'

'Was?' Marion said.

'Yeah. It was ready at twenty-past five. It was still ok at twenty to, but at …' Isobelle glanced at the clock. '… five-past six, it's probably past it's best.'

Marion followed Isobelle into the kitchen. 'Let's have a look,' Marion said. 'See what we can salvage.'

Isobelle pushed her half-eaten meal away from her. 'I think I'll have a sandwich,' she said.

'What did you get up to today?'

Isobelle stood and picked up the plate. 'I went for a long walk.' She scraped the leftovers into Pip's bowl. 'Robin Hoods Bay.'

'That's a good walk,' Marion said.

'About five or six miles,' Isobelle said.

'Did you walk back?'

Isobelle sat back at the table and took a sip of wine. 'No, I got the bus.'

Marion pushed the last forkful of food into her mouth and slid the empty plate away. 'That wasn't so bad.'

'You still haven't told me why you were late.'

Marion emptied her glass. 'I ran into Elliott.'

'How is he?'

'He's well. Remember Michael's father?'

Isobelle stood again, collected Marion's empty plate and along with her own, placed them in the dishwasher. 'Not that again.' Isobelle sighed.

'It's interesting,' Marion said. 'Michael's a nice lad. It would be good to help him out.'

Isobelle picked up the bottle and topped up their glasses. 'I suppose. What did he say?' She sat down and took a large gulp of wine.

'He's on about travelling down to London.'

'London?' Isobelle said. 'What for?'

'He has a lead on Vincent.'

'Remind me who Vincent is again?' Isobelle said, feigning ignorance.

'Michael's dad.'

'Oh, I see. So, what's he going to do in London?'

'Well,' Marion said. 'He has an address for where Vincent used to live. Apparently, there's a couple that lived in the flats, back in the seventies. They still live there now. Elliott is hoping they remember what happened to him.' Marion stood. 'I'll have to go for a pee.'

Isobelle watched her friend leave, picked up her mobile and texted. *"We need to talk."*

She received a text back. *"What about?"*

"Michael's dad. I'll phone later.'

"Ok x," Geoff replied.

Marion returned and sat at the table. 'That's better.'

'What does Elliott hope to achieve?' Isobelle said.

Marion held up her glass. 'Shall we have these in the living room? I need my comfy chair.'

Isobelle followed her friend. 'You didn't answer my question.'

'I'm not sure,' Marion continued. 'According to Michael's mum, Vincent may have come north. I think Elliott is hoping this couple know if he did, and if so, where.'

Isobelle yawned. 'Sounds like a wild-goose chase to me.'

'Yeah, maybe. But it's fun nonetheless. Don't tell Geoff, though.'

Isobelle frowned. 'Why?'

'Elliott thinks that it upsets him talking about Dot.'

Isobelle frowned again. 'What's Dot got to do with it?'

'Ah, that's the thing.' Marion grinned. 'Michael's dad, Vincent, was Dot's nephew.'

'Do you want me to take Pip for a walk?' Isobelle said.

'Would you? I'm all in.' Marion popped her feet onto the footstool. 'I'll finish my wine, and then I'll have a shower.'

Isobelle raced away from the cottage with Pip, and towards Geoff's. His silhouette appeared in the distance, and she hurried to meet him. They made their way down to the beach and let the dogs off their leads.

'What's happened?' Geoff said.

'Elliott's going down to London.'

'London? Why?'

Isobelle sighed. 'Marion told me she spoke with him earlier. He has a lead on Vincent.'

'What sort of lead?'

'Where he lived in London. An address.'

Geoff bit on his bottom lip. 'Islington.'

'She never mentioned the area. Only that Elliott has a name of two people who lived in the same flats as him.'

'Me, Belle. As me. I'm Vincent, remember.'

Isobelle took hold of his hand. 'As you. Can you remember them?'

Geoff nodded. 'Stan and Betty Walton.'

'Will they remember you?'

Geoff shrugged. 'Probably. We were quite friendly.'

'But they can't tell him anything?'

Geoff sat on a large rock and looked towards the sea. 'Not really. After the robbery, I left. I grabbed a few things and headed north.'

'Can you remember if you left anything there that would tell them where you went?'

'Yeah,' Geoff said. 'Letters and postcards from Dot, but nothing they don't already know.'

She threw open her arms. 'Well, there's no need to worry.'

He rubbed at his temple. 'Why don't they just leave the past alone? Why interfere?'

She sat next to him and took hold of his hand. 'They'll lose interest eventually.'

'What happens if they put two and two together and realise that I'm Vincent?'

She lowered her head. 'I don't know. Surely they won't.'

'Maybe I should tell Michael the truth?'

'Are you sure?' she said.

Geoff turned to face her. 'It would be better coming from me.'

'I suppose. Your surname ... How did you say you decided on the name?'

'Dot suggested the name.' Geoff rubbed at his temple again. 'She had a son called Geoff who lived In Skinningrove.' Geoff shook his head. 'He was killed in a motorcycle accident before I moved up. I assumed his identity. Back then it was easy. I got a driving licence, and the rest was a piece of cake. I wasn't keen, but Dot insisted, and I didn't really have a choice.'

'They won't be able to trace Dot's son?'

Geoff rubbed his chin. 'No. I'm sure they won't.'

Isobelle stood and threw a ball for Pip. 'You'll just have to brazen it out.'

He stood and faced her. 'Although ...'

'Although?' she said.

'I told Brian and Elliott that I lived in Skinningrove for a while. They were asking me questions about my past. I just blurted it out in the pub. I thought it would be a bit more believable.'

'They probably won't remember.'

'Hopefully not,' Geoff said. 'But if they do?'

Isobelle stared into the distance. 'Let's cross that bridge when, and if, we have to.'

He followed her stare. 'Yeah.'

The next day ...

Brian sang along merrily to the radio as someone knocked on the door. He put down the plate he'd been drying, wiped his hands with the tea towel, and answered.

'Elliott?' he said. 'What are you doing here?'

'Fancy a pint?'

'Oh, yeah. I do.'

Elliott stepped inside the hall as Brian turned off the radio and pulled on his coat. 'The Angel?' Brian said.

'How about The Feathers, for a change.'

Brian shrugged. 'Ok. The Feathers.'

'Are you still into your Egyptology?' Elliott said.

'Yeah. There's a documentary on The History Channel tonight. I'll be watching that.'

The two men walked the short distance to the pub and went inside. 'I'll get the drinks in,' Elliott said, as Brian found them a seat.

Elliott joined his friend and handed him a beer. 'Have you ever thought of visiting The British Museum?'

Brian took a swig of his pint. 'Loads of times. I never fancied going to London on my own, though.'

'How about I come with you?'

Brian's eyes widened. 'Why?'

'I have a lead on Michael's dad. That's why I suggested coming here and not The Fallen Angel.'

'A lead, eh? Tell me more.'

Elliott explained Jason's discovery about Vincent and Mr and Mrs Walton.

'Sounds like a good idea,' Brian said. 'When are you thinking of going?'

'Next week?' Elliott said.

'You do know the quiz quarterfinals are next week?'

'Yeah, I know. I thought we could travel on Thursday morning, after the quiz night.'

Brian nodded. 'Fine by me. We'll need to book a train and hotel. I take it we're staying longer than one night?'

'I thought Thursday and Friday night. If we get an early train, we can go straight to Islington and speak to the Waltons. Then on Friday, we can have a day at the museum.'

'Sounds good to me.'

'Also,' Elliott said. 'I need to meet up with a niece of mine.'

'The one you've been emailing?'

'Yeah. I said we'd meet her near Kings Cross for a coffee before we travel back.'

Brian clasped his hands together. 'Looks like you've got all this planned.'

Elliott smiled. 'Yeah. I'm finding this sleuthing exciting. Hopefully, we can find out some information that will help find Michael's dad.'

'Have you told Geoff?'

Elliott rubbed his chin. 'I'm not sure we should.'

Brian frowned. 'Why?'

'His reaction when we mentioned Vincent and Dot was a little …'

'Yeah, I know what you mean. I think he misses Dot a lot more than he lets on.'

'Yeah, that's what I thought. Better keep him out of this for the moment.'

'Hey, what are you two doing in here?' Marion said.

The two men looked up. 'Hi, Marion,' Brian said. 'Just discussing a little trip of ours.'

'Oh, yeah?' Marion said. 'London. Elliott told me.'

Elliott sipped his drink. 'Have you told Belle?'

'Yeah,' Marion said. 'I don't like keeping things from her. But I did ask her not to let on to Geoff.'

'I suppose it's ok if she knows,' Elliott said. 'But we'll keep Geoff in the dark for the moment.'

Marion sat. 'Of course.'

'If anyone asks,' Brian said. 'We're visiting The British Museum.'

'No problem.' Marion looked at the two men and glanced towards the bar. 'I'll have to go. One of the girls from the bank is leaving today. We're having a little send-off.'

'Don't get too drunk,' Brian said.

'As if. When are you going to London?'

'Next week,' Brain said. 'After the quiz.'

'I'll see you two later,' she said, and wandered off.

Geoff pulled his car to a halt around the corner from The Fallen Angel, looked across at Isobelle, and blew out. 'Well, here I go.'

'Do you want me to come in with you?' she said.

He glanced out of the window at the pub. 'It's probably better if I go on my own.'

She took hold of his hand and kissed him on the cheek. 'Good luck,' she said. 'I'm sure it won't be as bad as you think.'

He forced a smile and returned her kiss. 'I'll leave the keys in the ignition,' he said. 'In case I have to make a quick get-away.'

She laughed. 'I'm sure there won't be any need for that.'

'Hopefully not.' Geoff got out, steadied himself, then went inside. She sighed and watched him disappear.

Geoff headed for the bar where Michael stood reading a paper. He looked up. 'Hi, Geoff. Usual?'

'Can I have a word?' Geoff said.

'You can have as many as you like,' Michael said, and pointed around the bar. 'I'm not exactly rushed off my feet, here.'

Isobelle sat nervously waiting, as a red BMW pulled up behind her. She watched through the mirror as the driver took out his mobile, and made a call.

'It's a bit delicate,' Geoff said.

Michael frowned. 'This sounds—' His phone rang in his pocket, and he pulled it out. 'Can you give me a couple of minutes, Geoff,' he said, and pointed to the phone.

'Yeah, no problem.'

Michael answered it and walked into the back. 'Yeah,' he said.

Isobelle watched as a tall, well-dressed man wearing mirrored sunglasses got out of the car. He spoke briefly on his mobile and hung up. The man glanced up and down the street as if watching for someone. He moved towards the wooden door leading to the back of the pub and waited, his demeanour anything but casual. Isobelle turned in her seat, and hiding behind it, watched as Michael popped his head outside. They spoke briefly, before Michael looked left and right, then beckoned the man inside.

Michael closed and locked the gate behind them before turning to face the man. 'Toby,' he said. 'You wanted a word?'

'Hey,' Toby said. 'Why the sad face. I've got your money.' He pushed a hand inside his pocket and pulled out an envelope. 'As promised.'

Michael took hold of the package, but Toby held onto it. 'I need another favour,' Toby said.

Michael sighed loudly. 'I told you selling that dodgy booze was a one-off. The people I sold it to don't need anymore.'

'We're not talking booze, mate,' Toby said. 'We want you to do us a favour.'

'Like what?'

Toby pulled a small packet from his trouser pocket and held it out to Michael. 'Tabs.'

'No way,' Michael said. 'No way am I dealing in drugs.'

Toby stepped forward and gently patted Michael's cheek. 'I don't think you understand, Michael. The booze was just a tester, to see if you could be trusted.'

'Listen, Toby—'

Toby pushed Michael in the chest, causing him to stumble backwards. 'I don't think you get this. The people who helped save this dump of yours …' He sneered as he surveyed the pub. '… don't take no for an answer.'

'But, Toby,' Michael pleaded. 'I don't want to get in trouble with the law.'

Toby smiled. 'You won't if you do what I say.' He turned and looked at the pub again. 'It would be a shame, after all your hard work, if it went up in flames.' He faced Michael. 'Especially if you're inside it.'

The colour drained from Michael's face. 'What do you want me to do?'

'There's a shipment coming in from Holland on a boat. All you have to do is be there to meet it. I'll phone you, and give you an address to take it to.'

Michael rubbed his face. 'Ok.'

Isobelle ducked down in the car as the gate opened again. The man stepped outside with Michael. Brief words were exchanged before he climbed into his car and roared off. Michael put his hands over his face and slowly pulled them down. He shook his head, and then stepped back through the gate, closing it with a bang. He raced back through into the bar, snatched up a tumbler and half-filled it with vodka.

'Everything all right?' Geoff said.

Michael drained the glass and turned to face him. 'Fine, Geoff. Fine.'

'About that word?' Geoff said.

Michael stared down at the bar, then looked up. 'Sorry, mate. It'll have to wait.' He turned and put his head into a room behind him. 'I'm off out, Dave,' he said. 'Look after the bar.'

Geoff watched as Michael pulled on his coat and hurried off. 'Another one?' Dave said to Geoff.

Geoff picked up his half-glass and drained it. 'No thanks,' he said, and left. He made his way around to his car and climbed in.

'I take it that didn't go well?' Isobelle said.

'You could say that.'

'I bet you never even spoke to him.'

Geoff turned to face her. 'How do you know that?'

'A man turned up after you went in.'

'A man?'

Isobelle nodded. 'He drove a BMW. He parked over there.' Isobelle indicated behind Geoff's vehicle.

'What's this got to do—?'

'I watched this guy on the phone. He looked very shifty.'

'Shifty? What do you mean?'

Isobelle pondered. 'He looked up and down the road nervously. As if worried someone might see him. Then Michael opened the gate to the yard and let him in.'

'Right. What was this guy like?'

'Tall, six foot three, maybe. Blonde hair. Late-twenties, early-thirties. Very well dressed.'

Geoff glanced towards the gate. 'How long was this bloke in there?'

'Minutes.'

'And when he came out?' Geoff said.

Isobelle tapped her chin with an index finger. 'Michael didn't look happy.'

'I see.'

'You didn't manage to speak to him then?' Isobelle said.

'No. Michael was fine when I went in, but he had to take a call. When he came back, his mood had altered. He just stormed off.'

'So, you didn't mention …?'

'Never got a chance to.'

'I took this,' she said, and held up her phone.

Geoff stared at the photo of the car, it's licence plate clearly visible. 'Well done.'

'Do you think Michael's in trouble?' she said.

Geoff glanced back at the pub. 'I don't know.' Geoff turned on the ignition. 'Which direction did the car go in?'

'You're not thinking of following it?' she said.
'Why not?'
'It could be miles away.'
'Worth a try,' Geoff said. 'It shouldn't be hard to spot.'

Toby pulled into the supermarket car park and turned off the engine. He took out his phone and dialled.
'Wayne,' Toby said. 'I've just spoken with Michael.'
'And?' Tavistock said.
'He wasn't exactly keen, but he'll play ball.'
'Good. This is the biggest shipment yet. I don't want any cock-ups. Keep an eye on him, just in case.'
'Will do.' Toby rang off and then called another number.
'Yeah, Toby?'
'Tavistock has taken the bait. We have our patsy, too.'
'The guy who runs the pub?'
'Yeah,' Toby said.
'Doesn't Tavistock suspect anything?'
'No. He's happy for me to organise it from my end. I take it you're still interested in the shipment?'
'Yeah. Price as agreed?'
'As agreed,' Toby said.
'Keep me in the loop.'

Isobelle and Geoff watched from a distance as the car moved off again. Geoff started the engine and followed.
'That was a stroke of luck,' she said.
'There's not many bright-red BMW's around. Thank God.'

They trailed the vehicle all the way to Middlesbrough. The car finally turned off onto a new estate in Nunthorpe and pulled onto a drive. Geoff and Isobelle watched as the man got out of the car and headed inside.
'So, we know where he lives,' Isobelle said.
'We need a name.'
'We don't know he's done anything wrong. It could all be innocent.'
Geoff rubbed his chin. 'I remember Michael telling me he had money problems. Yet now, he doesn't appear to have.'
'You think someone has lent him money?'
'People do desperate things when they need cash,' Geoff said. 'He may have borrowed it from the wrong person.'
'Maybe we can help in some way?'
'But what can we do?" Geoff turned to face her. 'He could be my son. I need to know if he's done something silly.'
'I know.' Isobelle said, softly.

'I can't let him dig himself into a hole. My dad went to prison, so did Mick. I very nearly did as well. I don't want him to make the same mistake.'

Toby came out of the house, jumped into his car and drove off.

'Aren't you going to follow him?' Isobelle said.

'No. We need his name.'

Isobelle grabbed hold of the handle on the passenger door. 'Where are you going?' Geoff said.

'To find out his name.' She wandered over to the house next to the man's and knocked. She waited a few moments before a woman carrying a baby answered.

'Sorry to trouble you,' Isobelle said. 'I'm looking for a friend of mine. She lives on this estate. I think it's next door, but I've knocked, and there's no answer. Have I got the right house? She's called Mary Peters?'

'No,' the woman said. 'There isn't a Mary Peters living next door. A man lives there alone. He's called Toby Newton.'

'Ah,' Isobelle said. 'I'll have to try and ring her again. Sorry to trouble you.' She hurried back across to the car and climbed inside.

'Toby Newton.'

'How?'

'I told her I was looking for my friend's house. Mary Peters.'

Geoff raised his eyebrows. 'Like the Irish athlete?'

She laughed. 'It just came to me.'

'Now we have a name,' Geoff said. 'What do we do with it?'

Isobelle held up her finger. 'I may have a solution.'

CHAPTER ELEVEN

The next week ...
Isobelle tapped on Geoff's door. 'Come in,' he shouted.

She pushed open the door as Geoff stepped across the threshold and kissed her full on the lips. 'I thought you'd never get here,' he said.

'Bloody Marion. I said I'd follow her to the pub. I thought she would never leave.'

'We'd better get going,' he said. 'We don't want to miss the start of the quiz.' Geoff locked up, and the two of them hurried along the street. 'You said you had something to tell me?'

'Yes,' she said. 'Remember I told you about that retired policeman I know?'

'Yeah.'

'He's back from holiday. I've arranged to have coffee with him.'

'Right. To what end?'

She smiled. 'He has a soft spot for me. I thought I might ask him about our friend, Toby Newton.'

'He'll be suspicious, won't he?'

'I'm going to tell him that a friend of mine has a son who is mates with Toby Newton, and she thinks he may be getting into trouble. I said I would try and find out if this Toby Newton is dodgy and let her know.'

'Dodgy?' Geoff laughed. 'You've been watching too much television.'

Isobelle laughed as well. 'Maybe Newton is wrong a 'un from down south,' she said, in a mock cockney accent.

'You're good at these voices,' Geoff said. 'Have you ever thought of going into acting?'

'I was part of an am-dram group. It just comes naturally.'

'This ex-copper ...?'

'Anton,' she said.

'Yeah, this Anton. You're planning to sweet-talk him?'

'That's what I'm hoping.'

Geoff stopped a couple of hundred yards from the pub. 'You go ahead. We don't want the others to suspect.'

Isobelle moved forward. 'Give me a kiss, handsome.'

Geoff obliged and watched as Isobelle wandered off. He waited a few more moments, then set off towards the pub himself as Marion, hidden behind the corner of a shop, watched him go inside.

'I knew it,' she muttered under her breath and followed after him.

Isobelle joined Elliott, Brian and Jason at the table. 'Where's Marion?' Isobelle said, as she looked around the room.

'She isn't here yet,' Brian said.

She frowned. 'She set off before me.'

Geoff entered. 'Anyone want a drink?' he said.

'We've just got them in, thanks,' Brian said. 'Belle needs one, though.'

Marion came through the door and shrugged her coat off. 'Evening.'

'Where have you been?' Isobelle said. 'You set off before me.'

'I nipped to the shop to get some lozenges. My throats a bit sore.'

'You didn't say.'

Marion dropped onto a seat opposite Isobelle. 'I don't tell you everything, Belle, and I'm sure you don't tell me everything.'

Isobelle frowned. 'What do you mean by that?'

Marion waved a hand and looked away. 'Never mind. I could murder a drink.'

Geoff returned from the bar and lowered the drinks onto the table. He placed a glass of wine in front of Marion and one in front of Isobelle, then raised his glass. 'To the Whitby Wailers,' he said.

'The Whitby Wailers,' they all said in unison.

Brian moved forward in his seat. 'Are we all ready for tonight?' They all nodded. 'Because,' he continued, 'we're playing The York Minsters, and they won it two years ago.'

'We know,' Elliott said. 'But they haven't got *Marcus*, and he's like a walking encyclopaedia.'

'What happened?' Isobelle said. 'Have you nobbled him?'

Geoff laughed. 'No. He's been picked to appear on Mastermind, and it's filming this week.'

'Even without him,' Brian said. 'They're still a good team. We'll have to be on our mettle.'

'If we keep our heads we'll win,' Geoff said. 'Get over this hurdle, and the trophy is in our sights.'

'Just think for a second or two,' Jason said. 'Don't rush in with an answer.'

Geoff looked at everyone in turn and rubbed his hands together. 'Let's do this.'

The quizmaster tapped a spoon on the side of his glass to attract everyone's attention. 'That completes the quiz. Winner of the North Yorkshire Brainmaster 2019 quarter final is The Whitby Wailers, by 27 points to 26.' The customers in the packed pub let out a cheer and clapped.

The Wailers shook hands with the gallant losers and, as tradition dictated, bought drinks for them.

Brian patted Elliott on the back. 'Where did you get the answer to that tie-break question from?' he said. 'I hadn't a clue.'

'Stroke of luck, that. I heard it on radio four last week.'

Brian chuckled. 'I'm going to have to stop listening to my normal station and tune in to something a little more highbrow.'

Elliott moved closer to Brian. 'Still on for tomorrow?'

'Yeah. I'm all packed.'

'Good. I'll pick you up at nine.'

Geoff joined them. 'What are you two plotting?' he said.

'Just discussing our brilliant win,' Brian said.

Geoff blew out. 'It was close. Great last answer from you, Elliott.'

'They're all easy when you know them,' he said.

'The semi-final is away,' Brian said. 'Ripon.'

'We'll have to sort out a minibus,' Geoff said. 'I'm not driving.'

Elliott patted Geoff on the back. 'We'll have plenty of time to worry about that, it's not until next month.'

Brian nodded towards Isobelle, sat with Marion and Jason. 'How's your relationship going?' he said.

Geoff raised his eyebrows. 'What relationship?'

Elliott chuckled. 'Come off it, Geoff. We know you and the lovely Belle have been seeing each other.'

'Is it that obvious?'

'I'm afraid so,' Brian said. 'But I don't think Marion knows yet.'

Geoff glanced across to Marion. 'No. Belle is a bit reluctant to tell her.'

'You ok?' Isobelle said to Marion.

'I'm fine.'

'Are you sure? Because—'

'Isobelle,' Marion said. 'I told you, I'm fine.' She picked up her glass and walked across to the bar.

Jason put a hand on Isobelle's arm. 'I think she may know,' he said.

Isobelle turned to face Jason. 'May know what?'

'About you and Geoff.'

Isobelle pulled a face. 'Ah. Does everyone know? I thought we were being discreet.'

Jason laughed. 'Not in this town.'

She frowned and glanced across at Marion. 'I probably should have told her.'

'Yeah. She may be a bit upset. I think she sees you as more than just a friend.'

Isobelle ran her finger around the rim of her glass. 'I didn't mean—'

'I know, I know, but Marion thinks a lot of you.'

'You know she's gay then?' Isobelle said.

Jason nodded. 'She confided in me a few years ago. She thought I'd understand. I suggested the name for her cottage. She said she wasn't bothered who knew.'

'But I'm not gay, Jason.'

'I know. But I've had similar feelings for straight people. So, I know how she feels. I think you two need to talk.'

She looked towards her sullen friend again. 'I think we do.'

Isobelle came out of the ladies' and headed over to where the others sat. She looked towards Marion's empty seat. 'Where's Marion?'

'She's just left,' Brian said.

'Oh,' Isobelle said. 'I better go after her.'

Geoff stood and followed Isobelle towards the door as Brian, Elliott and Jason rolled their eyes.

Geoff took hold of Isobelle's arm as she got outside. 'Belle, is everything all right?'

She turned to face him. 'Marion knows.'

Geoff sighed. 'I see. What are you going to do?'

'Talk to her.'

'I'll walk you home,' he said.

Isobelle kissed him. 'You go back inside and celebrate our victory. I'll ring you in the morning.'

'Are you sure?' he said.

She placed a hand on his cheek. 'I'm sure.'

Geoff watched as Isobelle raced off and disappeared into the distance, then headed back inside.

Isobelle arrived at the cottage and paused to view the nameplate above the door. *Two Hoots!* it read. She took in a deep breath and headed indoors.

Marion sat in her armchair, cradling a brandy. 'Hi,' Isobelle said.

Marion drummed her fingers on the arm of the chair. 'Why didn't you tell me?'

'I didn't want to hurt your feelings.'

Marion scoffed. 'You think everyone else knowing before me doesn't hurt my feelings?'

'No, of course not. I just—'

Marion scoffed again. 'Looking for the right time?'

Isobelle dropped onto the seat opposite her friend. 'I'm sorry.'

'How long has this …' She turned away as tears queued patiently in her eyes. '… been going on?'

Isobelle swallowed a lump. The sight of her friend upset, difficult to take. 'Not long after I came here.'

Marion shook her head. 'How didn't I see it?'

'Perhaps it would be best if I left.'

'You can't leave now, it's past ten o'clock.'

'I meant in the morning.'

Marion lowered her head. 'I waited for you, Belle. A lifetime. I knew you weren't gay, but foolishly …' Her words dried up to nothing. 'I can't help how I feel.'

'I know you can't. You're my oldest and dearest friend. I've never wanted to hurt you. I'd do anything to avoid that, but Geoff and I …'

'I know.' She looked directly at Isobelle, then looked away and sighed. 'I will get over it. I just need a little time, that's all.'

Isobelle nodded and took hold of Marion's hand. 'I'm off to bed. Don't have too much to drink.'

Marion forced a smile. 'Just this one.'

Isobelle left, and Marion picked up the box next to her seat and began looking through the contents. She took hold of a photo of her younger self and allowed her mind to drift back through the years.

Middlesbrough, 1968 …

Marion undid the buttons on her school blazer. 'It's too small, Mum. Do I have to wear it?' she grumbled as her mother re-fastened the buttons.

'You look very smart, Marion. Very grown-up. Your dad would've been so proud.' Her mother sniffed and wiped her eyes.

And there it is, Marion thought. The one thing her mother could say that meant she had to stop behaving like the twelve-year-old that she was and pull herself together, to remember her dad, and be strong for the pair of them.

They had moved here from Whitby only two weeks earlier and only three short weeks since they had buried her father after his sudden and unexpected death from pneumonia.

Marion was furious at him. He had left them so quickly and with no provision made to keep the life she knew in her home town. Here they were in Middlesbrough. Wrenched away from the school and pals that she loved. Forced to rent a room in a terraced house that belonged to a family friend. Her mum had got cleaning work at a large council office near the town centre and worked from four a.m. until half-past seven. This allowed her to come back to see Marion off to school and then go to her second job as a dinner lady in a local primary.

'Sorry, Mum. It's fine, really.' Marion felt anything but fine. She felt fat and hot in her too-small second-hand blazer. Her red-hair, poker straight and scraped back into a high ponytail, showing her pale, freckled face. She knew she would hate this place with its dirty air and small, cramped houses with no gardens.

'I've made you paste sandwiches for your dinner, and there's a little biscuit in there too.' She handed Marion her lunch wrapped in paper. 'Right, off you go. How lucky you are that the school is only a five-minute walk. When I was your age, we walked for two hours. I'll walk with you to the end of the street and then you can see the school gates.'

They set off towards Marion's new school in the already humid July heat. Marion saw other children coming out from their houses and felt the flush of embarrassment that her mother walked with her. 'You go back, Mum. I'll be ok.' She walked with her head down, and her shoes scuffing the pavement.

'Are you new?' A voice called from behind them said, and they both turned around. 'I'm Isobelle.'

Marion stared at the pretty girl before them. Her shiny, black curls held in place with a green velvet ribbon that matched the colour of her eyes. The school blazer, a perfect fit and brand new. Black leather shoes polished and gleaming with two brilliant white socks rising from them.

'Say hello, Marion.' Her mother's words broke the spell that the other girl had cast over her.

'I'm, um, Marion.'

'Ok, um Marion.' Isobelle laughed. 'I'm going to look after you.' She linked her arm through Marion's, and they set off towards the school gates.

Marion, aware of stares from other pupils, walked with Isobelle across the yard, through the door and into the school. 'They said we had a new girl joining us from the seaside. Are you from the seaside?' Isobelle fixed her green eyes on Marion. 'I bet you lived on fish and chips. I love them.'

'Err, yes. I'm from Whitby.' Marion felt her skin redden under Isobelle's intense gaze.

'Here we are,' Isobelle said. 'Room 2R. Miss Randolph is our form teacher. She's the art teacher. Do you like art? I love it. Miss Randolph says I have a real talent.'

Marion gaped in awe at Isobelle and her confident manner. Her hair and her perfect face. The new clothes and the smell of fresh laundry.

'So, do you?' Isobelle cocked her head to one side.

'What?'

Isobelle wagged her finger at Marion. 'Do you like art? You're not listening to me.'

'I'm not very good at art. But I'm good at maths.' Marion managed to answer.

'Good, you can help me.' Isobelle grabbed Marion's arm and led her to a desk at the back of the classroom. 'I'm rubbish at maths.'

The other children filed into the room, followed by the willowy figure of Miss Randolph. 'Right, children, settle down. We have a new pupil today all the way from Whitby. Come up here and introduce yourself to the class.'

Marion squirmed down in her chair. This was her worst nightmare. All those eyes looking and scrutinising her. She turned to Isobelle, who smiled and nudged her. 'Go on. They don't bite.'

As she walked to the front of the room, sudden darkness blocked the light. The children looked out of the windows to see the sky turning an ominous sludge green and almost splitting into two separate halves. Then there was blackness and a howl of wind like a missile falling to earth.

A child screamed from somewhere in the class. 'What is it, Miss, is it a bomb?'

'Children, children, get under your desks now!' Miss Randolph dropped to her knees and pulled Marion with her under the large, oak, teacher's desk.

Outside the sky was as black as jet. A yellow streak of electricity forked its way up from the earth and crackled overhead. Balls of hail plummeted down as the winds clashed in a swirling vortex that rattled the window panes and lifted roof tiles.

They cowered under their desks. The children frightened but excited by this sudden interruption to their day. The inky darkness began to lift, and the hail subsided. Miss Randolph emerged from the floor and brushed herself down. 'Children! Can you get up, please? There's no need to be frightened. Just a little storm.'

The door opened, and the headteacher marched in. 'Everyone ok in here?' he asked. 'The power is off, so we'll have to close the school until we know what's happened.'

Marion made her way back to Isobelle, who took her hand. 'Wow,' Isobelle said. 'That was some entrance you made. And you've got school closed. This is the best day ever.'

Relieved at not having to introduce herself to the rest of the class, Marion grinned at Isobelle. Perhaps, she thought, Middlesbrough wouldn't be so bad after all.

'Come on, Marion. We'll walk home together.' Isobelle linked Marion's arm and led her friend from the classroom, into the once more humid July air.

Marion topped up her drink and picked up more pictures. She smiled and allowed her mind to drift back to another time.

Middlesbrough, 1976 ...

Isobelle and Marion sat on the bed in Isobelle's bedroom as they had done thousands of times before over the years. The room decorated in the latest fashion of bright orange wallpaper with matching bedding and purple velvet cushions.

Isobelle liked everything to be the best quality and the newest trend. She resented that she now worked in a bank instead of putting together interiors for a top-end designer in London. Her parents would never have allowed her to follow her dream.

'This looks great, Belle.' Marion swept a hand around the room. 'You'll have to help me makeover my flat. It's so boring compared to your room.'

Isobelle smiled at her friend. 'Yes, I'd like that. I can't wait to have my own place and move out of here.' She bit on her bottom lip.

'Is everything all right?' Marion said.

'Why?'

Marion narrowed her eyes. 'It's just you seem a little distracted.'

'I'm fine. I was just thinking about what dress I'm going to wear to the disco on Saturday.'

'Oh, yeah,' Marion said. 'I can't wait. Are you going to stay over at my flat?' Marion sighed. 'It's so much cheaper living at home. But I'm on a good wage at the bank and, with Mum going back to Whitby, I didn't have much choice. When I've saved a bit, I'm going to get a bigger place. Maybe one with two bedrooms, so you can stay more often.'

Isobelle stood and walked to the window. 'Your flat's fine,' she said. 'You've done well to get a place of your own.' Isobelle turned to face her. 'I need to ask you something.'

Marion sat smoothing out the new bedding where Isobelle had sat. 'Is it about work? I know you thought you should have got the promotion, but I really need the extra pay.'

'No, it's not that. You deserve that job. You work so much harder than me. It's just, well ...' Marion looked directly at Isobelle as her friend closed her eyes and took a deep breath. 'I've been seeing Bill,' Isobelle said.

Marion sat up straight. 'Bill? Bill, the manager's clerk? Seeing him about what?'

Isobelle frowned. 'Don't be thick, Marion. We've been going out.'

Marion's shoulder's slumped. 'I see. This is Bill Duffy? Bill engaged to be married to Jennifer?' She picked up a magazine from the floor and began flicking through it. Pictures of wedding dresses filled the pages. 'Well, I hope you're going to stop seeing him?'

Isobelle sat back down on the bed and snatched the magazine from Marion. 'I can't. We've been together a few months, and he's going to tell Jennifer today.'

'A few months! Why didn't I know about this?'

'I, we, just wanted to see where it was heading before going public.'

Marion jumped up. 'I'm not just public, I'm your best friend. So, where is it *heading?*' Tears stung her eyes and threatened to spill out.

'He's asked me to marry him. And I've said yes.'

Marion turned away as tears tumbled down her cheeks.

'Please be happy for me, Marion. I want you to be my bridesmaid. This won't change anything between us, I promise. You're like the sister I never had.' Isobelle placed a hand on Marion's arm. 'It would mean so much to me.'

'Are you pregnant?' Marion sniffed.

'No, we've always been careful.'

'Well, you've had enough practice in that area.'

Isobelle turned her friend around to face her. 'Don't be nasty, Marion. I really want you to be happy for me, but I'm marrying Bill with or without your blessing.'

Marion winced at the anger clouding Isobelle's face.

'Ok, it looks like I have no choice then.' Marion forced a smile. Her words caught in her throat as she almost had to cough them out. 'Can I choose my dress?' She picked the magazine from the floor and pointed to a pink, ruffled creation. 'I'm definitely not wearing that.'

'Yes, yes, of course, you can.' Isobelle grinned. 'We'll pick you a beautiful one. You'll look gorgeous. I'll even help you with your hair.' Isobelle pulled Marion in close for a hug. 'As long as it matches the colour scheme.' Isobelle laughed and held her friend tightly as Marion melted into the embrace while tears slowly trickled down her cheeks.

Marion dropped the photos back into the box and pressed on the lid. She drained her glass, picked up the bottle, and poured herself a considerable measure.

Isobelle hadn't been able to sleep. Her thoughts drifting from one low point in her life to another. Bill, her first husband, entered her consciousness. At first, resisting the temptation, she finally succumbed, opened the drawer, and pulled out his photo. Sighing heavily, she pushed it back inside. Her phone beeped. She had received a message from Geoff. *"Hope everything is ok?"*

She texted back. *"Yeah. I'll see you tomorrow."* Except it wasn't ok. She felt guilty for not telling Marion. Felt awful that she had to find out from someone else. Isobelle looked at the clock. It had been nearly an hour since she had come upstairs, and Marion was still downstairs. She climbed out of bed, pulled on her dressing gown, and tiptoed down. Marion sat fast asleep in the armchair, Pip, curled up on her lap. The brandy bottle half-full an hour ago, lay empty on the coffee table.

CHAPTER TWELVE

After enduring a fitful night, Isobelle had finally fallen asleep in the early hours. She wearily opened her eyes and viewed the clock next to her. 'Ten o'clock,' she said to herself. 'How the hell could I sleep so long?'

Pulling her tired limbs from the bed, she showered and quickly changed before descending the stairs. Marion was nowhere to be seen.

'Pip,' she shouted, as she entered the kitchen. Isobelle filled the kettle, placed two slices of bread into the toaster, and slumped onto a seat. Her phone in her pocket sounded. Yawning, she answered.

'Hi,' Geoff said. 'How did it go?'

Isobelle sighed. 'She's upset that I hadn't told her.'

'Well, I can understand that. It's as much my fault as yours though.'

'Yeah, but she's my oldest friend.'

'At least it's out in the open now,' he said.

'She's not here. She must have taken Pip for a walk.'

'Do you want me to have a word with her?'

Isobelle groaned. 'I'm not sure that will help. She'll get over it.'

'Are you meeting your policeman friend today?'

She groaned again, as the toast popped up. 'I'd forgotten about that.' Isobelle pulled the browned bread from the toaster and lavishly buttered it. 'Two o'clock in Guisborough,' she said, and took a bite.

'Do you want me to take you?'

Isobelle poured the boiling water over the tea bag in her mug. 'No, I'll be fine.'

'Are you sure?' Geoff said. 'We could have tea out somewhere?'

'I thought I might treat Marion to a Thai,' Isobelle said.

'Not a bad idea. Let me know how you get on.'

'I will. We can meet tomorrow, though. I might have some information by then, and Marion will be at work all day, so ...'

'So?'

'The day is ours,' she said.

'I'll look forward to that.'

'Me too,' she said, and rang off. Isobelle squeezed the teabag against the side of the mug with a spoon then fished it out.

Pip came running into the kitchen. 'Hello, fella,' Isobelle said.

Marion appeared at the threshold. 'Morning,' she said.

'Morning,' Isobelle replied.

'Is there one of those for me?' Marion nodded towards Isobelle's drink.

Isobelle stood. 'Of course.'

Marion plucked the second piece of toast from the plate and took a bite. 'Bring it through, will you?'

'Marion,' Isobelle said. 'Are we good?'

Marion smiled. 'We're good.'

'I was going to book a table for us at the Thai restaurant tonight. Fancy it?'

'I do. Is Geoff coming?'

'Just us two,' Isobelle said.

'I'd like that.' She turned, but then spun back around. 'I do like Geoff.'

Isobelle smiled. 'I know you do.'

Isobelle hung up and put down her mobile. 'Right, that's the table booked for seven-thirty.'

'What are you doing the rest of the day?'

'Do you remember Anton Mackenzie?' Isobelle said.

'The policeman?'

'Retired policeman now. Well, I'm meeting him for a coffee in Guisborough.'

'Does Geoff know?'

Isobelle smiled. 'It's not like that. He's starting up the amateur dramatics again. He wants me to join.'

'I see. Why are you meeting in Guisborough?'

'He lives there now. Moved last year, I think.'

'If I remember Anton correctly, he had the hots for you.'

Isobelle drained her teacup. 'Unfortunately, I haven't the hots for him.'

Marion laughed. 'He's bound to give himself the leading man parts, and you the leading lady part so he can snog you.'

Isobelle pulled a face. 'I hope not. He has awful breath.'

'Oh dear,' Marion said. 'Before I forget.' She reached over to the table and picked up a photograph. 'Look what I found.'

Isobelle joined her friend and viewed the picture. 'Oh, my,' Isobelle said. 'Look how young we are.'

'About fifteen,' Marion said. 'Look at you, so pretty.'

'Look at your freckles,' Isobelle said, and took the snap from her.

'I've got some others photos.' Handing Isobelle the box they began sifting through them.

Elliott and Brian reached Kings Cross station at twelve. They dropped their luggage off at the hotel, before continuing on the tube to Islington and covering the remaining half-mile on foot. Finally, they reached their destination, and Elliott pulled out a piece of paper to check the details. 'This is it,' he said. 'Flat 1.' He pressed the bell and waited.

The door creaked, and a small, grey-haired woman peered at them as the door opened fully. 'Yes?' she said.

'Mrs Walton?' Elliott said.

'Yes.'

'My name's Elliott Walker, and this is my friend, Brian Shawcross. It's a bit of a longshot, Mrs Walton, but do you remember a gentleman who used to live here. Vincent Fry?'

She pondered a moment. 'The name seems familiar. My husband might know. His memory is better than mine. Stan,' she shouted.

A man appeared at the door. 'What is it?'

'These two gents are looking for someone who used to live here.' She frowned and looked towards her husband.

Stan looked at Elliott and Brian. 'Yeah, who?'

'Vincent Fry,' Brian said.

Stan's eyes widened. 'Vincent Fry? Yes, I do remember him.' Stan glanced back at his wife, who shrugged.

Brian nudged Elliott. 'Can we have a chat about him?' Elliott said.

'Come on through. Betty, put the kettle on.'

Brian and Elliott were joined by Stan and Betty. She poured out the tea and pushed a plate towards them. 'Help yourself,' she said.

Brian added milk to their drinks and sat back. 'Vincent Fry?' he said.

'Vincent Fry,' Stan said, and glanced at his wife again. 'He lodged with us in the seventies.'

'I remember him now,' Betty said. 'Nice lad. Despite what anyone else thought.'

Stan smiled at his wife. 'As my wife says, gentlemen,' he said, 'Vincent was a nice lad.'

Elliott glanced at Brian. 'Do you know where he went?' Elliott said.

Stan continued. 'Vincent rented a bedsit off us for a couple of years. Never caused us any trouble. We became good friends. He used to help repair my car, and I'd help him with his. He had a battered old Escort. Blue, if I remember right.'

'You've got a good memory,' Brian said.

'Ah, well,' he said. 'That's because he had a mate called Mick who got into bother. This Mick was arrested for robbing a security van with another bloke.'

'He shot a guard,' Betty chimed in. 'Not Mick, the other bloke. He never died, though. Made a full recovery.'

'This Mick ...?' Elliott said.

Stan rubbed his chin. 'Mick Tate.'

'Would visit Vincent?' Elliott said.

'Yeah,' Stan said. 'He seemed like a nice bloke too. Just goes to show. Anyway, Mick and the other bloke ... Barry, I think he was called, robbed the van and shot the guard. The police caught Barry at the scene, and Mick the next day. He confessed to everything.'

'What about Vincent?' Brian said.

'Well,' Stan continued, 'the day after the robbery, the police came calling. There was no answer at his flat, so, I had to let them in. He'd gone. Legged it.'

'Right, I see,' Brian said, and picked up his cup. 'And you never heard from Vincent again?'

Betty nudged her husband, who held a hand up. 'We might as well tell them, Betty. It was years ago.'

Elliott leant forward. 'What was?'

Stan's eyes widened. 'An eyewitness said he saw Mick getting into a car after the robbery. There was obviously a third man, and, well ...'

'Vincent?' Brian said.

'Yeah. One of the policemen said that they were interviewing people Mick knew.'

'So, you've never seen Vincent from that day?' Elliott said.

'No,' Stan said, and dipped his biscuit into his tea. 'He'd taken some of his gear, and left.'

'Still owing a week's rent,' Betty said.

'That's right,' Stan said. He glanced at his wife. 'Times were hard back then. We barely kept our head above water.'

'We understand,' Elliott said. 'We just want to find Vincent.'

'What did you do with his things?' Brian said.

'I'm coming to that,' Stan said. 'It was mostly clothing he'd left. The odd item of value, but nothing much. Anyway ...' Stan took a deep breath. 'A few days later, we received a letter from—'

'Vincent?' Brian said.

'With our rent money and a little extra,' Betty said.

'He thanked us for looking after him and told us to dispose of his things. He said the money was a thank you.'

'How much did he send you?' Elliott said.

'Two-hundred pounds.' Stan sighed as the end of his biscuit plopped into his drink. 'We thought it might have been from the robbery. Vincent didn't have a lot of money.'

'We resisted spending it at first,' Betty said. 'But you know what it was like in the seventies.'

Brian nodded. 'We're not here to judge, Betty.'

'So,' Stan said, 'we did what we were asked. We kept anything of value for so long, then sold it. We gave the clothes to a jumble sale.'

'This letter?' Brian said.

'I burned it,' Stan said. 'I didn't want the police finding it. Despite what he did, I had a lot of time for Vincent.'

'I don't suppose you remember where it was posted from?' Elliott said.

'Hull,' Betty said. 'It's surprising the things that stick in your mind.'

Elliott glanced at Brian. 'Great,' Elliott said. 'It looks as if Vincent was making his way up north.'

'What about your box?' Betty said.

'Oh, yeah, my box.' Stan stood and disappeared.

Elliott and Brian looked at Betty. 'He has a box,' Betty said. 'He keeps bits and pieces that people have left. Photos, letters, stuff like that. He's a big softy.'

Stan returned with a large box and began searching through it. 'I'm sure there's something. Aha,' he said. 'What have we here?' Stan pulled out a small, brown-paper wrapped package and held it up. On the top was written: *Vincent, 1978.*

'What's inside?' Brian said.

'Photos and letters, I think.' Stan handed it to Elliott.

'How do you know Vincent?' Betty said.

'We're friends with his son, Michael,' Brian said. 'We're trying to help him trace his dad.'

Elliott opened the package and took out pictures, postcards and letters. 'Can we keep these?' he said to Stan.

Stan glanced at his wife. 'Can't see why not. Give them to his son.'

'You don't know what happened to Vincent?' Betty said.

Brian paused with a postcard in his hand. 'No. Michael thought he may have headed up north. The letter you received confirms this.'

'Where are you from?' Stan said.

'Whitby,' Brian replied.

'That's where the postcards are from,' Stan said.

'It's very kind of you,' Elliott said, and reached into his pocket and pulled out his wallet. 'Let me give you some money for your trouble.'

Stan scoffed. 'Wouldn't hear of it.' He waved away Elliott as he held out some notes. 'I hope you find Vincent, no matter what he did ... For his son's sake.'

'Are you sure?' Elliott said, still holding the money.

'No, no,' Betty said. 'We're a good deal better off than we were in the 70s. We're glad to help. Now, how about another cuppa. We don't get many visitors, do we, Stan?'

'Not these days,' her husband said, picking up another biscuit.

Elliott and Brian waved at the couple, standing on the step of their property, as they walked off.

Elliott held up the package. 'Like Michael said, Vincent wrote and received messages from Dot.'

Brian looked at the parcel. 'It sounds as if Vincent was involved in this robbery.'

'Yeah, looks that way.'

'Well,' Brian said. 'We know he and Dot corresponded regularly. But, did he travel from Hull to Whitby? And if so, when?'

Elliott pondered before walking on, closely followed by Brian. 'We'll have a good read of these on the train, and I'll ask Jason to look into the robbery. Maybe he can search the local papers and find out when it took place.'

'That'll tell us when Vincent left.' Brian said.

'Exactly.'

Isobelle entered the coffee shop and looked around. Her friend, Anton, sat in one of the corners, waved at her. Isobelle waved back, then made her way over to him. He stood as she reached him and kissed her on either cheek.

'Hi,' he said. 'How are you?'

She smiled. 'I'm good, Anton.'

He took hold of her hands and looked her up and down. 'Still as beautiful as ever.'

The pair sat, and Anton pushed a cup of coffee towards Isobelle. 'I got you a skinny latte. It's still your preferred drink, I hope?'

'It is. How good of you to remember.'

Anton clasped his hands together. 'So, Belle, what have you been getting up to?'

'Well, I'm living in Whitby at the moment.' Anton nodded. 'With my friend, Marion. Do you remember Marion?'

'I do,' he said. 'How is she?'

'Very well.'

'Is this a permanent arrangement?'

Isobelle smiled. 'Probably not. I'm renting my own home in Middlesbrough to a lovely family, but they're moving away shortly. I may sell it and buy my own place in Whitby soon. Who knows?'

'You've been seduced by the sea air?' he said.

'I have. What about you?'

'As I told you on the phone, I've moved to Guisborough.'

Isobelle sipped her coffee. 'Anyone I know?'

Anton smiled. 'How perceptive of you, but then you could always read me well. Audrey.'

Isobelle smirked. 'Audrey Faulkner?'

'Yes,' Anton said.

'How is dear Audrey?'

Anton laughed. 'She's very well.'

'Her usual self?'

'Indeed. I know what you're thinking.'

She sipped her coffee again. 'You don't. Does she know you're here with me?'

Anton frowned. 'She's visiting family in Bristol. I neglected to tell her we were meeting. I thought it for the best. Given how you two feel about each other.'

'Probably a wise decision.'

Anton smiled. 'What about you? Anyone special in your life?'

'There is someone. He's called Geoff.'

'Does he know you're here with me?'

Isobelle smiled. 'I have no secrets from Geoff. It's not as if we're conducting an affair or anything.'

'True.'

'Am-dram?' Isobelle said.

'Nicely swerved. I'm hoping to start it up again next month.'

'So soon?'

'We're not getting any younger, Belle.'

'True.'

'Are you interested? Only last time we spoke about it, you said …' He smiled. *'Never again. Only if hell freezes over.* I think that was about the size of it.'

'Near enough.' Isobelle drained her cup. 'I've had a change of heart. With all the spare time I have, I thought it would be good to give my thespian side an airing.'

'I'll email you the address and meeting times,' he said. 'You do have an email?'

'I do.' Isobelle took out a pen and jotted it onto a napkin.

'Anything else?'

She smiled. 'What do you mean?'

'I was a copper for forty years, Belle. Let's just say I have an inkling.'

She put her pen away and zipped up her handbag. 'There is a favour you could do for me. Well, it's not actually for me.'

'Go on.'

'A friend of mine has a son. She's worried he's getting into bad company. Coming home late, being evasive, etcetera.'

'Typical lad in my experience. There'll be a woman on the go or an angry husband.'

'That's what I told her,' Isobelle said. 'But you know how mothers and sons are?'

'Yes. I do.'

'There's one particular guy he's been knocking around with.' Isobelle pulled a piece of paper from her pocket and handed it to Anton. 'I promised her I'd see what I could do.'

'Toby Newton?' Anton said. 'I'll phone up an old colleague. See if he has any previous.'

'Thanks, Anton.'

He gazed at Isobelle. 'Does your partner know about our past?'

'He does. He's not the jealous type.'

He nodded. 'Sorry to hear about Bill.'

'One or two?'

'Two. I was quite shocked when I heard. I thought of phoning, but, well …'

'I know. It's all history now.'

Anton pushed the paper inside his pocket. 'How about another coffee?'

She glanced at her watch. 'Yeah. Go on then. I'll get them.'

Brian and Elliott came out of The British Museum. 'That was great,' Brian said.

Elliott pulled out his phone as it rang. 'Jason. Anything?'

'The robbery took place on May fourteenth, 1978,' Jason said.

'Right. So, we have a date?'

'I checked the papers thoroughly,' Jason said. 'Two guys admitted to the robbery – Vincent's mate Mick and a bloke called Barry Hunt. Hunt was charged for shooting the guard. He got twenty-five years, and Mick got fifteen.'

'No one else mentioned in connection?' Elliott said.

'Not by name. It said the police were looking for the whereabouts of a friend of Mick's but didn't mention a Vincent.'

'Thanks, Jason. We'll be back home tomorrow.'

Brian looked at Elliott. 'Jason?' Brian said.

'He says the robbery took place on May fourteenth, 1978.'

'We can assume,' Brian said. 'That if Vincent travelled up north then, or the day after, he'd have been in Whitby on the fifteenth.'

'Yeah, probably. According to Stan, he did have a car.'

'We could be barking up the wrong tree here,' Brian said. 'He might never have come to Whitby.'

'No. But we know he travelled as far as Hull. We won't give up yet.'

'When did Geoff arrive?' Brian said.

Elliott rubbed his chin. 'Earlier, I think.'

'I'll ask him.'

Elliott frowned. 'Geoff is a bit touchy at the moment. Maybe we won't have to.'

'What do you mean?'

Elliott sat on a bench. 'Babs gave Geoff some work. I remember him starting. He used to run errands to the wholesalers and that.'

'But how would—?'

'I kept all the paperwork.'

'From 1978?'

Elliott chuckled. 'Yeah. Babs would have gone mad if she'd have known. I promised her ages ago I that I would throw them out. I just never got around to it.'

'You think from those that you can tell when Geoff arrived?'

'I can tell when he started work for us, but if I remember rightly ...' He rubbed his chin. 'Babs said he had moved in with Dot the week before.'

'Are you sure?'

'Not a hundred per cent. I wouldn't have bothered with any of this if it hadn't been for what Babs said when she lay dying.'

Brian looked at his friend. 'She was dying, Elliott. It may have been ... Well, you know.'

'I know,' Elliott said. 'But ...' He pondered. 'There was something Babs wanted to get off her chest. I just know it. Something important.'

Isobelle climbed into the car next to Geoff. 'Everything ok?' Geoff said.

'Yeah. Anton's going to get a friend to check on this Toby.'

'Good.' Geoff stared outside.

She placed a hand on Geoff's arm. 'There's something I need to tell you.'

Geoff turned to face her. 'Yes?'

'Anton and I had a fling, years back. I'm not proud of what I did, but I thought you ought to know. No one knows, not even Marion.'

'You don't still harbour feelings for him, do you?'

Isobelle took hold of Geoff's hand. 'No,' she said. 'Never really did.' She squeezed his hand. 'It was ill-judged, and I never forgave myself for betraying Bill.'

'Why tell me now?'

She forced a smile. 'I don't want any secrets between us.'

Geoff laughed. 'Well, you know all mine.'

'I really like you. I like you a lot.'

Geoff held out his hand, and she took it. 'I'm glad you accepted my offer of a lift.'

'I couldn't face the bus journey.'

He smiled. 'I've never felt like this about anyone.'

'Ever?' she said.

He kissed her. 'Ever.'

'Me neither.'

‘Shall we have a spot of lunch?’ he said.
‘I’m going out with Marion tonight. So I don’t want much.’
‘I know just the place,’ he said. ‘And then back to mine?’
She raised her eyebrows. ‘That sounds lovely.’

CHAPTER THIRTEEN

Elliott entered the shop pulling his suitcase behind him. 'It's great to be home.'

'Good time?' Jason said.

'Yeah, not bad and Brian loved the museum.'

'I've printed out the info on the robbery,' Jason said. 'It's in the back.'

'Good lad. I've got to check something myself. I'll get rid of this case first, make us a cup of tea and then I'll crack on.'

'Do you need my help?' Jason said.

'No, I'll be back in a few minutes.'

Elliott pulled open the box and took out the paperwork. He placed it on the table in front of him and began sifting through it. After several minutes he pulled out a piece of paper, held it up and smiled to himself.

Jason poked his head around the corner. 'I've locked up. I'm off home.'

'Ok, I won't be too long.'

'Aren't you coming?'

Elliott stood. 'I'm going to nip round to Brian's.'

'Ok, see you later.'

Elliott shoved the piece of paper into his trouser pocket, pulled on his overcoat, pushed on his hat and headed off.

Brian sat opposite Geoff and picked up his mug of tea. 'The British Museum was great,' Brian said. 'Have you ever been?'

'Years ago.'

'The Egyptian exhibits were wonderful.'

Geoff sipped his tea. 'How did you get Elliott to go to London with you? I didn't think museums were his thing.'

'I think he enjoyed it.' Brian placed his mug down. 'Besides, we had another reason to go.'

Geoff looked at him. 'Oh, yeah?'

'Michael's dad.' Brian allowed the words to sink in as he viewed his friend.

Geoff rolled his eyes. 'Are you still messing about with that? You need a hobby.'

'Elliott is convinced we can find him.'

Geoff drained his cup and placed it down. 'I would have thought you two had more interesting things to do than this. It's over forty years ago.'

'Are you sure you can't remember Dot saying anything about Vincent?'

Geoff sighed. 'Like I said, she never mentioned anyone with that name. She never mentioned she had a nephew either. I don't know what else to say.'

'We know he reached Hull.'

Geoff folded his arms. 'Hull?'

'Yeah. We spoke to the people who owned the flat where he lived.'

'I see.' Geoff glanced at his watch. 'Listen, I have to be somewhere.'

'I thought we were going for a pint?'

Geoff stood and pulled on his coat. 'I've remembered something I need to do. Maybe later.'

'Ok,' Brian said, and watched him disappear through the door.

Geoff raced to the road and took in a lungful of air. He leant on the gatepost for support and allowed the beating inside his chest to subside.

'You all right?' Elliott said.

Geoff spun around. 'Oh, hi,' he said. 'Fine, mate. Just stood up a bit quickly, that's all.'

'Brian inside?' Elliott said.

'Yeah. Listen, I'm in a rush. I'll see you later.' Geoff hurried off as Elliott watched then made his way up the path and tapped on the door. Brian opened it. 'Elliott,' he said. 'You've just missed Geoff.'

'I saw him.' Elliott followed Brian inside. 'He seemed a little shaken. Is he ok?'

Brian pointed to a seat, and Elliott sat. He pulled a mug from the cupboard and plonked it in front of his friend. 'He's acting a bit strange if you ask me.'

Elliott poured himself some tea. 'Strange?'

'I asked him about Vincent.'

Elliott shook his head. 'I thought we agreed not to.'

'I know, I know,' Brian said, and held his hands up. 'I just asked him if he remembered anything Dot might have said.'

'What did he say?'

Brian rubbed his chin. 'The same as before, but then he made up some excuse and left. All a little strange.'

'I spoke to him outside. He seems preoccupied.'

'He'd agreed to come for a pint with me, but when I mentioned Vincent … well, let's just say, he couldn't get out of here quick enough.'

'He knows something,' Elliott said. 'I'm certain.'

Brian frowned. 'What though?'

Elliott pulled the paper from his pocket and pushed it across the table.

Brian examined it and stared at Elliott. 'He started work with you the week after the robbery.'

'That's right. I remember now, Dot told Babs that he had arrived the week before.'

'About the same time as we think Vincent may have arrived?'

'Yeah. If Vincent did arrive.'

'Geoff said he lived in Skinningrove,' Brian said.

'Yeah,' Elliott said. 'That's right.'

'You think he's lying?' Brian said.

Elliott rubbed his beard. 'Dot said he was the son of a friend from London. I can't remember her mentioning him before he arrived though.'

'Would you remember if she had?'

'Probably not,' Elliott said.

'Are you thinking what I'm thinking?' Brian said.

'That Geoff had something to do with Vincent's disappearance?'

'Yeah. Babs told you there was a secret she promised Dot she would keep.'

'That's right.'

Brian raised his eyebrows. 'What if Geoff was staying at Dot's when Vincent arrived?'

'Yeah,' Elliott said. 'That's what I thought. Something might have happened between Geoff and Vincent,'

'And Vincent goes missing.' Brian said.

'But what could have happened? And why would Dot side with Geoff over her own nephew?'

'He was a desperate man. On the run from the police, maybe Dot wanted to inform them. Maybe Vincent tried to stop her, and …?'

'By all accounts,' Elliott said. 'Vincent sounds like he was a nice lad.'

Brian scoffed. 'Nice lads don't rob security vans.'

'I suppose not.'

'Maybe Dot—'

'Killed him?' Elliott said. 'I can't believe that.'

'She confessed something important to Babs.'

'She did. But what about Geoff?'

'Maybe Geoff helped dispose of Vincent,' Brian said. 'Maybe that's what he had over her. It seems a little strange that she should leave everything to him.'

'I can't believe he blackmailed her.'

'Maybe he just helped her,' Brian said.

'Dot and Geoff were very close. Like Mother and son. But if Dot did something ... Something she told Babs. Something she regretted. Maybe Geoff did help her in some way?'

Brian tapped his chin with a finger. 'I'm popping over to our Brenda's tomorrow. I'll call into Skinningrove on my way, see if anyone remembers Geoff.'

'That's a bit of a longshot.' Elliott said.

'Worth a try though. People live in places like Skinningrove all their lives. Someone may remember him. Someone may remember Dot.'

Elliott looked at his friend. 'There is another possibility.'

Brian rubbed his chin. 'You think Geoff could be Vincent?'

'Yeah. I'll get Jason to check for a Geoff Brown in Skinningrove.'

'Not a bad idea. But it's all getting a bit out of hand.'

Elliott frowned. 'We've come this far. We need to know.'

Geoff sat on a bench inside Pannett Park as Isobelle hurried towards him. He stood as she approached, and the pair hugged.

'What's up?' she said.

'Elliott and Brian are back from London.'

'I heard. Marion told me they visited The British Museum, and ...'

Geoff sighed. 'As well as doing a bit of sleuthing.'

'Yeah. They visited where you used to live.'

The pair sat. 'They know I travelled up as far as Hull.'

'How come?' Isobelle said.

Geoff puffed out his cheeks. 'I sent a letter to Stan and Betty, the people who owned the flat I lived in, with the rent I owed them. They must have looked at the postmark.'

'I see. It still doesn't mean they know who you are?'

'It's only a matter of time.' Geoff gazed at the different shades of green surrounding them. 'Why can't they keep their noses out?'

'What can we do?' Isobelle said.

'I don't know,' Geoff said. 'If they find out that I'm Vincent, they may tell the police.'

'Surely they wouldn't.'

'I don't know, Belle.'

'Anton phoned,' she said.

Geoff huffed. 'Why do I get the impression this is not good news?'

'Toby Newton has a string of offences, mostly for smuggling contraband and violence.'

Geoff put his face in his hands. 'How is Michael involved?'

'I don't know.'

'Maybe I should speak to him?' Geoff said.

'And say what? If you tell him who you are, he'll have something on you.'

'Christ, Belle. What a mess.'

She took hold of his hand. 'First things first. Vincent is dead. He needs to stay that way.'

'But how?'

'Marion.'

He furrowed his brow. 'How is Marion going to help us?'

'Marion can't keep a secret to save her life. She told me Elliott and Brian were going to London and said they were checking on where you lived.'

'And?'

'I'll get Marion drunk,' Isobelle said. 'She'll spill the beans after a few drinks.'

'I don't see—'

'Have you still got any of the letters you sent Dot?'

Geoff shrugged. 'I put Dot's personal stuff in the loft.'

She squeezed his hand. 'Don't you see? If there are any of the letters you sent to Dot still there, you can forge another and use the old envelope.'

'What for?'

'If you date it weeks, or better, months after you moved to Whitby, and Marion sees it …'

'But, how will she?'

Isobelle smiled. 'I'll concoct a story that I'm suspicious of you.' Geoff nodded, and Isobelle continued. 'Then while you're away—'

'Away? Away where?'

'We'll think of that later. Marion and I will search through your house.'

'And find the letter?'

'Exactly.'

Geoff smiled. 'No one will believe it was sent in the seventies. It'll look too new.'

'We'll look it up on the internet. I saw a programme once about forgeries. You can age paper to look much older, and if it's in the original envelope—'

'I'm not sure about this.'

'Geoff,' Isobelle said. 'If we can convince Marion, she'll tell Brian and Elliott I'm sure. Then they'll just believe that Vincent disappeared.'

'There's so much that can go wrong.'

'But if it works?' she said.

'What about Michael, though?'

Isobelle pondered. 'We'll follow him.'

'Are you mad? Toby Newton sounds dangerous. These people don't mess about.'

'When we gather enough information, we'll tell the police.'

'And Michael?' Geoff said.

'We'll try and keep him out of it. From what I saw and heard at the pub, I don't think he's a willing accomplice.'

'I must be mad,' Geoff said. 'But …' He huffed. 'We'll give it a go.'

Isobelle filled Marion's glass and handed it to her. 'There's something I wanted to ask you,' Isobelle said.

Marion took a sip. 'Yeah?' she slurred.

'How long have you known Geoff?'

'Ages. When I moved to the same road. Why?'

Isobelle sat opposite her. 'He seems a bit preoccupied of late.'

'Really? This has nothing to do with Michael's dad, has it?'

Isobelle furrowed her brow. 'Michael's dad? Why should it?'

'Like I told you, Elliott and Brian went to London—'

'I know,' Isobelle said. 'To the British Museum.'

'That wasn't the only reason. They were trying to find some information on Michael's dad, Vincent.'

'I know all this, Marion. How does this concern Geoff?'

Marion sipped her drink. 'Geoff said he had never heard of Vincent.'

Isobelle shrugged. 'Maybe he hasn't?'

Marion sat forward in her seat. 'Vincent was Dot's nephew.'

'I know all this, but—?'

'Don't you think it's a bit strange that Dot left her cottage and stuff to Geoff, and not Vincent? Blood is thicker than water.'

Isobelle shook her head. 'Geoff said Dot was like a mum to him.'

'Mm,' Marion said. 'Still a bit strange. And you did say he's a little preoccupied.'

'That could be anything. He may be ill and keeping it from me.'

Marion drained her sherry glass and held it out to Isobelle. 'Geoff's always struck me as a deep pool. There's a bit of a mystery there.' Isobelle replenished her glass.

'You're making up daft stories here,' Isobelle said.

'That's not what Brian says.'

'What did Brian say?'

Marion leant in closer. 'They think Geoff is an imposter. That he's not who he says he is.'

'Is that what Brian actually said?'

'Well, not in so many words.'

'I'll have a word with Brian myself.'

'No,' Marion said. 'You mustn't. He swore me to secrecy.'

'Who do they think Geoff is then?'

Marion sipped her drink. 'Vincent.'

'Michael's dad?'

'Yeah. And a robber to boot.'

Isobelle laughed. 'Ok, Miss Marple, you've been watching too much television.'

'Well,' Marion said. 'We'll see.'

Isobelle stood. 'I'm off to bed. You can manage to turn the lights off, can you?'

Marion lifted her glass. 'Yes, of course.'

Isobelle climbed the stairs and slipped into her bedroom, closing the door behind her. *'I've sown the seed,'* she texted to Geoff.

Brian knocked on the door of Elliott's house. 'Come in,' Elliott shouted from inside.

'Did Jason get any information?' Brian said. He pulled open his coat and loosened his scarf.

'We may have been wrong about Geoff being Vincent,' Elliott said.

'Why?'

Elliott handed his friend a piece of paper. 'A Geoff Brown lived in Skinningrove in 1978. Here's his address.'

Brian sighed, and took the paper. 'I'm glad. At least Geoff hasn't been lying to us all these years.'

'Are you going soon?'

Brian checked the clock. 'Yeah. I promised our Brenda that I'd meet her for lunch, so I was hoping to check on where Geoff lived first.'

'Is it even worth going now?' Elliott said.

Brian pondered. 'It won't do any harm. People probably don't remember him anyway.'

'Not even time for a cuppa? I've just brewed up.'

'Better not.' Brian re-fastened his coat and tightened his scarf.

'Ok, we'll catch up later.' Elliott said, as Brian left.

'Yeah,' Brian said over his shoulder. 'For a pint.'

Elliott sat and rubbed his chin. 'Where did you go, Vincent?'

Brian pulled his car up outside the house and checked the address. Satisfied, he climbed out and knocked on the door.

A young woman holding a baby opened it. 'Yeah?'

'Sorry to bother you, miss, but I'm looking for someone that used to live here. Geoff Brown.'

The woman shook her head. 'Don't know anyone with that name.'

'Ah, I see.'

'You could ask Agnes,' she said.

'Agnes?'

'Agnes Grant. She moved into a bungalow around the corner. Number four Cramer Close. We bought this house from her. She'd lived here for donkeys' years. If anyone would know, Agnes would.'

‘Thanks,’ Brian said, and headed off.

Isobelle looked about before slipping inside Geoff’s cottage. ‘What did she say?’ he said.

‘Elliott and Brian think you’re an imposter.’

Geoff clasped his hands together. ‘Well, that’s it then.’

Isobelle joined Geoff at the table and took hold of his hand. ‘No, it’s not. That gives us the edge.’

‘How?’

‘I was a bit offhand with Marion when she told me, and again this morning. Next, I’ll soften her up.’

‘Go on,’ Geoff said.

Isobelle opened her handbag and took out some writing paper. ‘It helps when you’re a bit of a hoarder. This papers quite old.’

‘1970s?’

Isobelle shook her head. ‘Not quite, but it’s a good twenty years old. I got Marion to take me across to my house.’

‘I thought you had people living there?’

Isobelle shook her head. ‘They’ve moved out. New job, or something.’

Geoff picked up the paper and examined it. ‘Basildon Bond. I’ve not seen this for years’

She snatched it from him. ‘We’re not here to admire it.’ She reached into her bag again and unfolded a sheet of paper. I printed this off the internet.’

‘Not at Marion’s, surely?’

‘Marion hasn’t got a printer or the internet. She’s a proper Luddite. I did it at the library.’

Geoff scanned the sheet. ‘Will this ageing method work, though?’

‘We’ll try a blank sheet first. If that works, we’ll do it on your letter.’

‘The letter I’m going to write? The one from Vincent to Dot?’

‘That’s right.’ Isobelle reached into her bag and pulled out a pen. ‘Use this Bic biro. They’ve been about forever.’

‘And,’ Geoff said, ‘once I’ve written the letter, and we’ve aged it successfully. Then what?’

‘We entice Marion here.’

Geoff lowered his brow. ‘Here?’

‘Yeah. You told me she has a key to the cottage?’

‘That’s right. For when I’m away.’

‘So,’ Isobelle said. ‘I’ll feign that I believe you’re an imposter. I’ll encourage her to come to the cottage with me and look for evidence.’

‘What about me?’ Geoff said.

‘You need to go away for a couple of days.’

Geoff held out his hands. ‘Where?’

Isobelle pulled a set of keys from her pocket. 'At my house in Middlesbrough. As I said, the tenants have recently left. Tell any of my nosey neighbours, and there are quite a few, that you're house-sitting.'

'You've thought this through, haven't you?'

'I love a good mystery novel. It's marvellous the ideas they can give you. When we get through this, we'll write a book.'

He laughed. 'Where am I going if any of the others ask?'

'You're visiting relatives.'

'Ok. I can make someone up, I suppose.'

'Now you're talking.' Isobelle smiled. 'Did you find any letters?'

Geoff leant across and plucked some sheets of paper from the sideboard. 'I found these.'

Isobelle read through them. She took hold of his hand and squeezed it tightly. 'You obviously loved her very much.'

'Like a mother,' Geoff said.

'Let's get started.'

'Will this work, Belle?'

She forced a smile. 'Here's hoping.'

CHAPTER FOURTEEN

Barry climbed from his car and pulled a folded sheet of paper from his pocket. He studied the address and made his way towards the shutter-covered front of the building. Heading along the concrete alleyway to the back of the nightclub he found himself inside a car park with several high-range cars dotted about. A black door, with *staff only* painted on it, located to the left-hand side of the building, lay slightly open. He looked about, extinguished his cigarette against the wall, and strode toward the door.

A large, thick-set man approached him as he entered. 'Can I help you?' he said.

'I'm here to see Mr Tavistock. Barry Hunt.'

The man looked him up and down. 'Wait here.'

Barry nodded and watched as the man disappeared through a door marked NO ENTRY. He surveyed the huge night club, similar to many he had been in before. Mirrors, stainless steel and surfaces that look pristine at night appeared a little grubby and tired during daylight. He turned as the door the man had left by reopened. The man motioned for him to follow.

The pair climbed a flight of stairs, through a heavy-oak door, and into an office. A large desk stood at the far end of the room, its legs sinking into an ocean of plush, deep, carpet.

A well-dressed man sitting behind the desk looked up. 'Get the gentleman a drink,' he said.

Barry held up a hand. 'I'm not much for tea, Mr Tavistock, and it's a little early for anything stronger.'

Tavistock smiled. 'Call me Wayne.' He looked towards the man 'That's all, Charlie. Make sure no one disturbs us.' The man nodded and left.

Tavistock leant back in his chair. 'How's Danny?'

'He's doing well.'

'How do you know him?'

'He's my cousin,' Barry said.

'Ah, I see. He didn't mention that.'

Barry smiled. 'I told him not to. I didn't want you thinking it was the only reason he recommended me.'

Tavistock steepled his fingers. 'How old are you, Barry?'

Barry grimaced and glared at him. 'Does it matter? I can do my job. I know how to take orders and, more importantly, I know how to keep my mouth shut.'

Tavistock laughed. 'I suppose so. Cards on the table. You come highly recommended by Danny. I run a tight ship, but lately, I've had my suspicions.'

'Suspicions?'

Tavistock stood and wandered over to the corner. He picked up a bottle and half-filled a tumbler as Barry glanced at the clock on the wall and frowned. It was just after ten o'clock in the morning. He slowly shook his head.

Tavistock turned and sat back down. 'My takings are down. Someone is skimming.'

'You have someone in mind?'

'Let's just say ...' Tavistock sipped his drink, 'I hope to confirm it soon.'

Barry settled back in his chair. 'Where do I come in?'

'I have shipments of booze, cigarettes and tobacco smuggled into the country. Someone who works for me has persuaded me to bring in something a bit stronger.'

'Drugs?'

Tavistock nodded. 'Ecstasy.' He studied Barry. 'That's not a problem, is it?'

Barry shrugged. 'Not to me.'

'I'm shelling out quite a bit of money here. I want to make sure I'm not being taking for a ride.'

'How are you getting them in?'

'By boat. We've identified a good location. We've also got someone to take the fall if it goes wrong.'

'What do you want me to do?'

'Toby Newton,' Tavistock said.

'Who's he?'

'He works for me. He's the guy who's organising this. He's also the guy I don't trust.'

Barry frowned. 'Use someone else.'

Tavistock sipped his drink again. 'The police are on to me. They're watching my operation closely, that's why I've left it to Toby. I'm not really happy about it though.'

Barry rubbed his chin. 'Ok. Do you want me to keep an eye on this Toby?'

'Yeah,' Tavistock said. 'The guy he's supposedly using could be working with him for all I know. I want to know everything Toby is doing, and I also want you to check out this guy.' He pulled a piece of paper from his drawer and pushed it across the table.

Barry studied the name, then looked up. 'Where does he live?'

'Whitby,' Tavistock said. 'He runs a pub there. I loaned him some money, and he got rid of some dodgy booze for me.'

'Leave it with me,' Barry said.

Tavistock opened his drawer again and pulled out a bundle of notes. 'Expenses.'

Barry stood and pushed the paper and money into his pocket. 'If I find out Toby is screwing you …?'

'Make him disappear.' He stared at Barry. 'Not a problem?'

Barry smiled. 'Not at all. My speciality.'

'And the pub owner …' Tavistock said.

Barry raised his eyebrows. 'Yeah?'

'He doesn't need to be around when this is all over either.'

Barry moved towards the door and paused. 'I'll need a shooter.'

'I'll organise one for you. Where are you staying?'

'Premier Inn up the road,' Barry said.

'I'll get it dropped off for you today.'

'Ok. I'll head off up to Whitby tomorrow. I'm staying in a caravan there.' Barry said, and Tavistock nodded.

Barry left and walked back along the alleyway. He pulled the piece of paper from his pocket and viewed the name before he crumpled it up and tossed it into a bin.

The next day …

Barry pushed the empty plate aside and stared out the caravan window. He could just make out the sea in the distance. His phone sounded.

'Danny,' he said.

'How did it go with Tavistock?'

'He seems ok. He wants me to keep an eye on someone who works for him.'

'Right,' Danny said. 'Doesn't he trust him?'

'Apparently not. I'm in Whitby now.'

'Any luck finding—?'

Barry laughed. 'You wouldn't believe the stroke of luck I had.'

'Why?'

'Wayne Tavistock has a smuggling operation going. He usually brings in ciggies and booze. His normal route is being watched by the police, so he had to look for another way to get them in.'

CHAPTER FIFTEEN

Brian knocked for the third time, sighed and headed back out of the gate.

'Can I help you?' A woman's voice called from the side of the house.

'Agnes Grant?' he said.

'Yes.'

'Sorry to bother you. I'm looking for an old chum of mine. Geoff Brown. I believe he used to live around these parts.'

She moved closer. 'How do you know Geoff?'

'He was a pen-pal of mine. I was in the area, so I thought I'd look him up.'

'Oh, I didn't know he had a pen-pal.'

Brian smiled. 'It was a long time ago. We haven't corresponded in years. We had similar hobbies at the time.'

'I see. Motorbikes, I suppose?'

'Erm, yes. Do you know where he lives now?'

She lowered her head. 'Geoff died some time ago.'

Brian's eyes widened. 'Oh, I'm sorry to hear that.'

'Geoff and I had only been married a couple of years.'

'You and Geoff were married?'

'Yeah. He was my childhood sweetheart.' She smiled as she remembered. 'He died on the road to Helmsley. Lost control of his motorcycle and … well, you get the picture.'

'I'm so sorry.'

She waved a dismissive hand. 'It was such a long time ago. I remarried and had three kids, so it wasn't all bad news.'

'I suppose. Oh, well. I'd better get going.'

She smiled. 'Would you like to come in for a cup of tea, mister …?'

'Call me Brian. If it's not too much trouble, I'd love to.'

'What do you think?' Isobelle said, and held up the letter.

Geoff took hold of it. 'It's fantastic. It looks old.'

'I told you it would work. But …' she said. '… we have to fold it a few times to look authentic, and then get Marion to find it.'

'And put it in one of the old envelopes I found?' he said.

'Yes. That's the idea.'

Geoff shook his head. 'The postmark will give it away.'

Isobelle sifted through the letters and stopped at one. She beamed. 'What about this?' She opened the letter and read it. 'It's from a friend of Dots in Newcastle.'

Geoff accepted the envelope from her and examined it. 'The postmark's smudged,' he said. 'I suppose ... But what about the writing on the front?'

Isobelle compared Geoff's letter to the writing on the envelope. 'It's not that different. It'll fool Marion.'

'But will it fool Brian and Elliott?' he said.

'We have to make sure they don't see the envelope. I'll get Marion to photocopy the letter. That should be enough.'

Geoff sucked in air. 'Let's hope so.'

Brian entered the pub and made his way over to Elliott in the corner. 'I got you one in,' Elliott said.

Brian slumped onto his chair and took a large swig. 'Cheers.'

'How did it go in Skinningrove?'

'I found where Geoff Brown lived, and even met with his wife.'

Elliott's eyes widened. 'His wife?'

'Or should I say, widow.'

Elliott frowned. 'I'm not following you.'

'Geoff Brown married a woman called Agnes. He died in a motorcycle crash in 1978. Agnes even showed me a photo of him.'

'It can't be our Geoff.'

Brian looked at him. 'Were there any other Geoff's living in Skinningrove in 1978?'

Elliott shook his head. 'No.'

'Well,' Brian said. 'There you go.'

Elliott rubbed at his beard. 'So, Geoff, our Geoff, has lied to us?'

'Yeah, looks that way.'

Elliott picked up his pint and took a thoughtful drink. 'Geoff could be Vincent then?'

'He has to be. There isn't another Geoff Brown in Skinningrove, and he definitely told us he lived there in the seventies. What are we going to do now?'

Elliott sipped his pint. 'I'm not sure. You can see why Dot thought so much of him. He was her nephew. That's why she left the cottage to him. It still doesn't add up. Why lie to us?'

'Geoff's our mate. He hasn't done us any harm, but he was obviously involved in the robbery, and didn't want the police to find him.'

'That's right.' Elliott fixed Brian with a stare. 'Perhaps we should let sleeping dogs lie?'

Brian sighed. 'I think so. It was years ago, and obviously, Geoff is a different man now.'

'What do we tell the others?'

'Jason, Marion and Belle?'

'Yeah,' Elliott said.

Brian slapped his head. 'And Michael?'

Elliott bit on his bottom lip. 'I forgot about him.' He glanced across at Michael, busy serving a customer.

'Geoff must know that Michael is his son,' Brian said. 'It's up to him to speak with him. We can't do anything about that.'

'Yeah.' Elliott rubbed his eyes. 'We shouldn't have started digging into the past. I'm regretting it now.'

Isobelle sat cradling a mug of tea as Marion came downstairs. 'Is there one of those for me?' Marion said.

Isobelle picked up a cup and filled it with tea. 'What you were saying the other night.' Marion sat opposite her, and Isobelle continued. 'About Geoff.'

'Listen, Belle. I was out of order. I'd had a bit to drink, and—'

'Geoff is hiding something.'

Marion added milk to her tea and took a sip. 'Hiding something?'

'He's been distant of late. There's something on his mind. And with what you said Elliott and Brian found out ...'

'That they think Geoff could be Vincent?'

'Yeah.'

'Belle.' Marion cradled the cup in her hands. 'Even if he is, it was such a long time ago. We may be—'

'I have to know, Marion. After what happened in my previous relationships, I need to know the real Geoff. I've fallen for him, but I can't be with someone who isn't totally honest with me. I've told him everything about my past.'

'What do you want to do?'

'He's gone away for a few days. He said he's visiting family.'

Marion pondered. 'I can't remember him mentioning any family. And I can't remember him visiting any before.'

'Have you still got that key to his place?'

'Belle,' Marion said. 'You're not suggesting ...?'

'I need to know that the man I've fallen ...' She stared at Marion. 'I need to know. You understand?'

Marion nodded. 'I do.'

'Today,' Isobelle said. 'We'll go today.'

Marion placed her cup onto the table. 'This afternoon would be best for me.'

'Ok.' Isobelle drained her cup. 'This afternoon.'

Marion waited for the front door to close and raced across to the window. She watched as Isobelle and Pip made their way up the street and disappeared out of sight. Marion took out her mobile and called Brian.

'Hi, Marion.'

'I need a chat,' she said.

'Yeah, ok.'

'With you and Elliott.'

'About Geoff?'

Marion slumped into her seat. 'Yeah.'

'What about meeting us in Costa?'

'This morning,' Marion said. 'It has to be this morning.'

'10.30?' Brian said.

'See you then.'

Isobelle stopped at the top of the 199 steps and caught her breath. Even though it was early, there was still a number of people about. She sat down on a bench, tied Pip to the arm, took out her phone and called Geoff.

'Hello,' he said.

'Did you get there ok?'

'I did. A lovely house you have, Belle. Thanks for letting me bring Freddie.'

She smiled. 'Both of you make yourselves at home.'

'What about Marion?'

'Everything is going to plan,' she said. 'We're going over to your place this afternoon. Did you put the letter where we agreed?'

'I did. I put it with a few more old documents to add an air of authenticity.'

'Good. You're getting the hang of this. I'll see you on Thursday.'

'You will.' Geoff coughed. 'Belle …?'

'Yes?'

'I really appreciate what you're doing for me. I don't know …'

'Geoff,' she said. 'Don't worry. This will soon be over, and we can concentrate on Michael.'

'Yeah,' he said. 'Michael.'

Brian smiled as Marion joined him at the table in Costa. 'Great timing,' he said. 'I've just got them in.'

'Where's Elliott?'

'He's at the shop. He'll be here soon.'

Marion sat and placed her hands on the table. 'About Geoff …'

Brian looked around the shop and moved closer to Marion. 'I checked him out.'

'What do you mean? I thought you said …' Marion paused as a woman passed nearby. 'Do you and Elliott still think he's Vincent?'

'Yes and no.' Brian fidgeted with his cup and spoon. 'A Geoff Brown lived in Skinningrove in the seventies. Jason found him on the electoral roll.'

'Geoff is telling the truth then?'

Brian shook his head. 'Geoff Brown died in a motorcycle accident in 1978.'

Marion frowned. 'I don't understand.'

'Don't you see? Geoff, our Geoff, can't be from Skinningrove. He must have assumed his name.'

Elliott arrived and joined them at the table. 'Sorry I'm late. What have I missed?'

'I was telling Marion about Geoff,' Brian said.

'If Geoff assumed the name of this man,' Marion said. 'Then he has to be Vincent.'

'It looks that way,' Elliott said.

'I told Belle we think he's Vincent,' Marion said. 'Sorry.'

Brian huffed. 'It's done now. What did she say?'

'She wasn't convinced at first. However, she thinks Geoff is holding something back from her. She's asked me to find out what.'

Elliott looked at Brian then back to Marion. 'How are you going …?'

Marion held up a key. 'Geoff's away for a couple of days. Visiting family. I have his house key.'

'Are you thinking of searching his house?' Brian said. Marion nodded.

'He's never mentioned having any family,' Elliott said.

Marion shrugged. 'I know. He's never mentioned any to me. But, well, that's what he told Belle.'

Elliott pondered. 'What are you thinking?' Brian said to him.

'I don't think it's a good idea,' Elliott said. 'I was deciding whether to confront Geoff on my way here. I just can't let it lie. It would be good if we could get some other evidence without breaking into his house.'

Brian scoffed. 'It's over forty years ago, Marion. What are you expecting to find?'

'No idea, but Belle is insisting on it. She wants us to go this afternoon.'

Elliott leant forward and sighed. 'Ok. Be careful. Make sure you leave the house as you find it.'

'We will.'

'What about Geoff?' Brian said. The other two focussed their attention on him. 'I mean if he is Vincent.'

'I think at the very least he owes us an explanation,' Elliott said. 'I know we said that we would let sleeping dogs lie …'

'He's still our friend,' Brian said. 'But …'

'You're not suggesting we inform the police, are you?' Elliott said. 'Because I wouldn't be in favour of that.'

'No,' Brian shrugged. 'I—'

'It's Belle I'm concerned about,' Marion said. 'I'm sure she wouldn't want him getting into trouble.'

Elliott looked at Brian. 'I'll have a word with him when he returns,' Elliott said. 'But over forty years have passed. Geoff, I'm sure, is a different man to the one he was.'

Brian lowered his head. 'He's never done me a bad turn. But I agree with you.' They both looked at Marion.

'As I said. Belle is my priority. I'll let her decide.'

Elliott blew out. 'I'm getting a coffee. Can I buy you two another?'

Marion entered her cottage to find Isobelle standing in front of the fire. 'Where the hell have you been?' Isobelle said.

'Sorry about that. I lost track of time.'

'Have you got the key?'

Marion held it up. 'Yeah.'

'Ok,' Isobelle said. 'Let's go.'

The two of them hurried along the road and stopped at Geoff's gate. Marion glanced around and pulled her collar up high.

Isobelle nudged her. 'Stop looking so guilty. You're just checking on a good friend's house while he's away.'

Marion nodded. 'I suppose.'

She followed Isobelle around to the back of the property, and the pair stopped at the door. Marion fumbled for the key in her pocket but dropped it on the cinder path.

Isobelle tutted and stooped to retrieve it. 'Marion,' she said, and took hold of her friend's shoulders. 'Pull yourself together.'

Marion nodded. 'Sorry, Belle.'

Isobelle opened the door and entered, closely followed by her friend. 'I'll look upstairs, and you concentrate down here.'

'Shoes!' Marion pointed at her feet.

'What?'

'Take your shoes off, Belle. We'll leave footprints everywhere and then the police will know we were here.' Marion bent and undid her shoes.

'Marion, calm down. No one is calling the police.' Belle held her boots up in front of her. 'Happy?'

'What am I looking for?' Marion said.

'I don't know. Photos, letters, that sort of thing. Anything that gives us a clue to who Geoff is.'

Marion took hold of her arm. 'You believe me that Geoff is really Vincent?'

'I don't know,' Isobelle said. 'Let's just say I'm keeping an open mind.' She moved to the foot of the stairs.

'Elliott said we have to …' Marion said.

Isobelle stopped and spun around. 'You told Elliott we were coming here?'

Marion looked at the floor. 'I'm sorry, Belle. I …'

Isobelle shook her head. 'I suppose Brian knows too?'

Marion nodded, and Isobelle sighed. 'I don't suppose it matters.' Isobelle waved a hand around the room. 'Just have a look.'

Isobelle climbed the stairs and entered the bedroom. She feigned searching as her friend checked through drawers and cupboards downstairs.

'Come on, Marion,' Isobelle said to herself. 'How hard can it be to find.' Finally, she could stand it no longer and descended the stairs. But as she reached the bottom, she spotted Marion through the mirror – which hung on the chimney breast – searching the drawer where Geoff had hidden the letter. She smiled to herself and quietly climbed back up the stairs.

Isobelle waited another couple of minutes before she walked down the stairs once more. Marion stared out of the window, deep in thought.

'Nothing,' Isobelle said. 'What about you?' Marion continued staring outside, and Isobelle made her way over to her and placed a hand on her shoulder. 'Marion?'

Marion turned. 'Sorry I was miles away.'

'I said, did you find anything?'

'Erm, no,' Marion said. 'Some old photos, but nothing exciting.'

'So, we still don't have any evidence that Geoff is Vincent?'

Marion shook her head. 'Listen, Belle,' she said. 'I'm not really comfortable doing this. Creeping around a friend's house.'

'But—'

'I know I said I was ok about it, but I'm not really happy being here. Can we just go?'

'Yeah, of course.' Isobelle frowned and put on her boots.

Marion hurried toward the door and outside. Isobelle narrowed her eyes, then followed her around the side of the house and along the path. They reached Marion's cottage in silence.

'Pip needs a walk,' Marion said.

Isobelle brought a hand up to her mouth. 'We didn't lock the door.'

'Oh, no,' Marion said. 'I need to go back.'

Isobelle took hold of her friend's arm. 'I'll do it. I'll take Pip with me. Kill two birds with one stone.'

'Are you sure?'

'You get yourself a sherry,' Isobelle said. 'I won't be long.'

'Thanks, Belle.' Marion said. 'I'm a bag of nerves. Maybe you should wipe down the handles?'

Isobelle clipped the lead onto the dog's collar and made her way along the road, down the side of Geoff's cottage, and around to the back. She secured Pip to the fence and went inside. Isobelle fumbled for the light in the gloom and flicked on the switch. She raced for the drawer, opened it, and pulled the bundle of letters out. The letter Geoff had left there was gone. Quickly gathering the papers together, she pushed them back inside and closed the drawer again. Isobelle locked the door, untied Pip, and wandered off.

Marion looked out of the window and along the road as she made a call.

'Hi, Marion,' Brian said.

'I need to talk to you and Elliott.'

'Tonight?'

'No. Tomorrow will do,'

'Is everything all right?' Brian said. 'You sound a bit agitated.'

'Fine, fine. I have some information, that's all.'

'Ok. I'll give Elliott a call.'

'Yeah, do that. Can we meet at yours?'

'Are you sure everything's ok?'

'Yes. Isobelle will be coming back at any moment. I don't want her to know.'

'I see,' Brain said. 'What time in the morning?'

'Ten?'

'Yeah, ten's fine. See you then.'

Isobelle sat on a bench a little way up the 199 steps and caught her breath. Her mobile rang.

'At last,' she said.

'Sorry about that,' Geoff said. 'I was taking a bath. That's got to be the biggest tub I've ever been in.'

'I do like my luxury. You and I will have to share one.'

'It is big enough for two. I'll look forward to that.'

Isobelle laughed. 'It is. Maybe we can test the theory out tomorrow.'

'Tomorrow?'

'Yeah. I thought I'd pop through. I'll tell Marion I have some paperwork to sort out at home.'

'How are you—?'

'Train. Can you pick me up at Nunthorpe station?'

'Yeah. What time?'

Isobelle swapped the phone to her other ear. '11.30.'

'No problem. How did—?'

'She was a nervous wreck, but she took the bait and the letter.'

'Good,' Geoff said. 'What did she say about it?'

'Nothing. At first, I thought she hadn't found it, but I went back and checked. It's definitely gone.'

'Strange that she didn't mention it.'

Isobelle laughed. 'I think it may have come as a bit of a shock. She's probably going to show it to Elliott and Brian.'

'Yeah. I'm sure she will.'

'Hopefully, they'll believe it's genuine,' Isobelle said. 'I think they will, then we can forget about all this Vincent stuff and focus our attention on Michael.'

'Yeah. I thought about him earlier. Maybe I should have a talk with him when I get back to Whitby.'

'Maybe,' Isobelle said. 'We'll discuss our plan of attack tomorrow.'

'Thanks for this, Belle. It's a wonderful thing you're doing.'

'Don't mention it. Just make sure there's some bubble bath for when I arrive.'

Geoff laughed. 'I will.'

CHAPTER SIXTEEN

Marion hurried along the footpath and tapped on Brian's door. 'Come in,' he shouted. 'Have a seat, I've just brewed up.'

'Morning, Brian.' She nodded towards Elliott. 'Morning, Elliott,' she said, as she sat down at the table with the other two. Marion pulled off her fur gloves and laid them carefully on her knees.

Brian placed a mug in front of her and poured some tea into it. 'So,' he said, and handed her the milk. 'You said you have some information?'

Marion poured a small amount of milk into the cup and stirred the tea. 'We're pretty sure that Geoff is Vincent, are we?' She huffed.

'Yes,' Elliott said. 'We told you that. The real Geoff Brown, from Skinningrove, died in 1978.'

'Well.' She pulled the letter from her pocket and tossed it onto the table. 'How do you explain this then?'

Elliott picked up the piece of paper and studied it before passing it to Brian.

'It's from Vincent.' Brian said.

'I know.' Marion tapped the letter. 'Look at the date.'

'It's dated six months after Vincent, I mean Geoff, arrived in Whitby,' Elliott said. 'Why would Vincent send a letter to Dot when he was already living with her? I don't understand.'

'Where did you get this?' Brian said.

Marion took a gulp of tea. 'From Geoff's. I photocopied it and put the original back this morning.'

Elliott took the letter back from Brian and rubbed his beard. 'Right, Geoff can't be Vincent.'

'You don't say,' Marion said, and glowered at the pair of them. 'So much for your detective work.'

'It appears Brian and I were wrong,' Elliott said.

'Does Belle know about this letter?' Brian said.

'No. I discovered it yesterday while we were searching the house. Isobelle was upstairs at the time. It was together with a load of old letters and postcards. She's oblivious, and I'd rather it stayed that way.'

'Do you know where it was posted from?' Elliott said.

'The postmark was smudged, but I'm pretty sure it was Newcastle. What does it matter anyway? It proves that Geoff isn't Vincent.' Marion glanced between Elliott and Brian. 'I'm not happy about this.'

'What?' Brian said.

Marion huffed again. 'All this creeping around, and I hate keeping things from Belle.'

'But it just confuses the situation more,' Elliott said.

'Don't you think I know that.' Marion drained her cup and stood. 'I want no further part in this … duplicity. You two do what you want, but keep me out of it. Have you thought that Geoff Brown is his real name? Brown is a very common surname.' Marion pulled on her gloves and moved towards the door. She stopped and faced the two men. 'If Belle finds out about this, she'll never forgive me,' she said, before leaving

The other two watched as she left, and Brian turned to Elliott. 'She could be right, Elliott.'

Elliott reread the letter. 'We were so sure …'

'It appears we're not as clever as we thought,' Brian said.

'Who the hell is Geoff, then?'

Brian rubbed his face with his hands. 'I don't know. Maybe he really was Dot's nephew. Maybe she had another.'

Elliott shook his head. 'She only had one nephew, *Vincent*. And why use a dead man's name?'

Brian shrugged. 'We don't know he did. Like Marion said, it's a common surname.'

Elliott rubbed his chin. 'He told us he moved to Whitby from Skinningrove. Why would he do that? He must have known a Geoff Brown lived in Skinningrove.'

'I don't know,' Brian said. 'But we have the semi-final of the quiz coming up. We can't afford to let this cloud that. And we can't afford to fall out with our teammates either.'

'Yeah. You're right.'

Brian collected the mugs and placed them in the sink as Elliott stroked his beard and studied the piece of paper again.

Geoff and Freddie waited on the platform at Nunthorpe station. He blew into his hands to keep warm. The day grey and full of drizzle, but his mood lifted as he spotted Isobelle. He strode over to her, and the pair embraced and kissed.

'How are you?' she said, patting the dog. 'You should have waited in the car, it's miserable out here. You'll catch your death.'

'I'm all the better for seeing you.'

She took hold of his hand as they walked back to Geoff's car. 'Have you eaten?'

'I had a spot of breakfast hours ago,' he said. 'But I thought we could have lunch together. My treat.'

'You read my mind. I know a lovely little Italian.'

They reached the car and climbed inside. 'Point me in the right direction, madam.'

'I'll do better than that,' she said, and took out her mobile. 'I'll put the address into my phone.'

'Everything all right this morning?'

Isobelle paused with the phone in her hand, then popped it on the dashboard near to Geoff. 'Marion was a little quiet.'

Geoff put the key in the ignition. 'Do you think they'll believe it?'

'I think so. It looks authentic to me. Hopefully, this will stop them delving into Vincent's past anymore.'

'Hopefully,' he said. 'But we still have the problem of Michael.'

'Yes.' Isobelle fastened her seatbelt. 'Have you given it any thought?'

Geoff stared out of the windscreen. 'I think I should come clean to him about who I am.'

'Right,' she said.

He turned to face her. 'What do you think?'

'Whatever you decide, Geoff, I'll support you.'

He leant across and gave Isobelle a peck on the cheek. 'Let's put it on ice until we get back to Whitby, shall we?' Isobelle nodded. He started the engine, turned, and winked at her. 'I've bought some champagne. It's in the fridge.'

She laughed. 'Oh, you have, have you?'

'I thought, after our meal, we could share it.'

Isobelle pulled down the visor and checked her lipstick. 'While luxuriating in a warm bath?'

Geoff raised and lowered his eyebrows quickly. 'I've checked the bubble bath situation …'

'And?'

He laughed. 'We may need to buy some more.'

'Oh, I see. You've been wallowing in my tub, have you?'

'I certainly have. But it'll be more fun with the two of us.'

'That was Marion,' Isobelle said. 'Asking how I am.'

Geoff frowned. 'Strange?'

'Yeah.' Isobelle slipped off her dressing gown and climbed in the massive bath opposite Geoff. 'She sounded a little weird.'

Geoff handed her a glass of champagne. 'Weird?'

'Yeah. As if she is missing me terribly.'

'Maybe she is.'

She clinked glasses with Geoff's. 'Well,' she said. 'I told her I won't be back until tomorrow. It'll be nice to have some time to ourselves without having to worry about Marion.'

'It will.' Geoff grinned.

Isobelle took a sip of her drink. 'Let's forget about Marion and all that lot back in Whitby. Even if it is just for tonight.'

'I'll drink to that.'

Jason sat back in his chair and puffed out his cheeks as Elliott finished telling him the events of the day.

'Bit of a surprise, then?' Jason said.

'That's the understatement of the year,' Elliott said.

'It still leaves us with a mystery.'

'Yeah. But where do we go from here?'

Jason held up a finger. 'Maybe we need to check into Dot's background a little more?'

'Why?'

'It's obvious from what you've told me,' Jason said. 'That Dot was very fond of Geoff.'

'Yes, she was.'

'Maybe it's Dot that had the secrets, and not Geoff.'

'I'm not following you.'

'Geoff Brown,' Jason said. 'The one from Skinningrove.'

'Yes.'

'Maybe we should look into his background as well.'

'Why?'

Jason smiled. 'I can't believe that Geoff would use a random name. Maybe Dot knew the Skinningrove Geoff? Maybe that's why *our Geoff* used his name.'

'We don't know he did,' Elliott said. 'Like Marion said, Geoff Brown, our Geoff Brown, could really be called Geoff Brown.'

'You believe that, do you?'

Elliott rubbed his chin. 'Not totally. There's something not right here, and Dot certainly told my Babs something.'

'It won't harm to run some checks,' Jason said. 'We may find nothing. If we don't, we haven't done any harm.'

'So …' Elliott leant in closer. 'What are you going to do?'

'I'll research his family.'

'Skinningrove Geoff?'

'Yeah,' Jason said. 'See if that throws any light on this mystery. See if we can link him to Dot.'

'That's a huge leap.'

Jason shrugged. 'We'll see.'

Elliott pondered for a moment. 'We'll have to keep it from Brian and Marion unless we find anything.'

'That's fine. We'll keep it between you and me.'

Geoff ushered Isobelle into his car and climbed in beside her. 'What's the plan?' he said.

'You'll have to drop me off somewhere near town.'

'The bus station?'

Isobelle shook her head. 'No. Marion's at work today, she may see me.'

'The end of Church Street?'

'Yeah, that's better.'

'Shall we stop for something to eat on the way?' Geoff said.

'That'll be nice.'

'I was thinking,' Geoff said. 'I may invite Michael up to my cottage.'

'Right,' she said. 'To tell him?'

'Yeah.' He glanced at her. 'What do you think?'

'What are you going to say?'

Geoff sighed. 'I thought I would keep it cryptic.' He glanced at Isobelle again, who nodded for him to continue. 'Drop a note off saying, *I know where your dad is.*'

'Ok. That's sounds fine. Then what?'

'Well,' Geoff said. 'I'll invite him to the cottage and tell him I suppose.'

'I thought we were going to gather some information on Michael and that Toby bloke?'

Geoff rubbed his eyes. 'It's eating away at me, Belle.'

She placed a hand on his. 'I know, but you have to time this right. Patience is the key.'

'How will we approach this, then?'

Isobelle pulled down the visor and checked her make-up. 'We follow Michael.'

Geoff sighed. 'But we don't know what he's going to do, and where or when.'

'I can get away a couple of nights a week, for a few hours, so that we can discuss our plan of action. I'll tell Marion that I'm going to amateur dramatics with another friend from Ruswarp.'

'Amateur dramatics which hasn't started up yet?' Geoff said.

'Which hasn't started up yet. She doesn't know. Unfortunately, you'll have to do the bulk.'

'Like I said, we don't know when or where?'

'It'll probably be at night,' she said. 'If you were doing something illegal, you'd do it at night.'

'I would.'

She tapped his arm. 'Here looks nice for lunch.'

Elliott served a customer and popped his head into the storeroom. 'Any luck?' he said.

'Some,' Jason said. Lifting his head up from the computer, he sat back in the chair. 'I've found Skinningrove Geoff's birth certificate. His mam and dad were Marjorie and Robert Brown.'

'Ok. Where do you go from there?'

He turned to face Elliott. 'I can find out if either of them is still alive.'

'We can't very well go around there and ask them about their dead son,' Elliott said. 'They must be quite old if they're still alive.'

'I'm just trying to build up a picture,' Jason said.

The bell on the door sounded, indicating they had another customer. 'I'll be back shortly,' Elliott said.

Jason studied the computer screen and typed in the address for a new website.

The next day ...

Brian stepped out of the paper shop, holding a pint of milk and a newspaper. He ambled along the road as he read the headlines. He stopped as he felt a hand on his shoulder and turned.

'Hello,' a voice said. Brian glanced between the woman who had spoken and a much older woman next to her.

'It's Brian, isn't it?' she said.

Brian narrowed his eyes. 'Yes.'

'Agnes ... Agnes Grant.'

'Of course,' Brian said. 'From Skinningrove.'

She placed a hand on her companion's arm. 'This is Brian, the gentleman I told you about. Geoff's pen-pal. Brian, this is Geoff's mother, Madge.'

'Oh, hello,' Madge said. 'Agnes said you had come looking for Geoff.'

'Yes,' he said. 'I was sorry to hear of your son's death.'

The old lady frowned. 'It's such a long time ago.'

'Do you live close by?' Agnes said.

'Yes. Not far away.'

Madge narrowed her eyes. 'I can't remember Geoff telling me he had a pen-pal in Whitby.'

'I was brought up near Scarborough,' Brian said. 'I moved up here years ago. I fell in love with the place.'

'We love coming here.' She looked up. 'Don't we, Agnes?'

'We do. Madge and I stayed good friends after Geoff's death. We often come here.'

'Are you off for something to eat?' Brian said.

'A cup of tea first,' Agnes said. 'Then maybe some fish and chips.'

The three of them walked on, over the bridge.

'I live up here,' Brian said, and pointed along Church Street.

'I knew someone who lived nearby,' Madge said. 'Haggerlythe Street.'

Brian narrowed his eyes. 'Haggerlythe Street?'

'Yeah,' Madge said. 'She's long gone. I hadn't seen her for a long time when she died. We had a bit of a fallout.' Madge pulled a tissue from her pocket and blew her nose. 'Sad really.'

'What was her name?' Brian said.

'Dot Kinghorn,' Madge said. 'She lived in the very end cottage. How long did you say you've lived in Whitby?'

'Twenty years.'

'Oh,' Madge said. 'Way before your time.'

Brian knitted his brow. 'A friend of mine knew her, I think. I've heard him mention her name.'

Madge pulled a fresh tissue from her handbag and blew her nose again. Briefly closing her eyes, she turned her head and stared along the road.

'Are you ok, Madge?' Agnes said.

'Fine,' Madge said and looked towards Brian. 'Anyway, Brian. It's been lovely to meet you.' She looked back at Agnes. 'I'm spitting feathers here. I could do with that cuppa.'

Agnes widened her eyes. 'Erm, yes.' She turned to Brian and shook his hand. 'Lovely to meet you again.'

'Lovely to meet you too,' Brian said. He watched as the two women made their way along the footpath and into a café. He took out his mobile and dialled.

'Hi, Brian,' Elliott said

'Are you at the shop?' Brian said.

'Yeah.'

'I'm coming around. I've got some news.'

Elliott turned to Jason. 'That was Brian. He said he has some news.'

'About what?' Jason said.

'Geoff, I think.'

Isobelle made her way downstairs and into the kitchen where Marion sat at the table.

Marion glanced at the kitchen clock. 'You must have been tired?'

Isobelle yawned. 'I was.'

'Did you sort out your business in Middlesbrough?'

Isobelle popped two pieces of bread into the toaster. 'Yeah. It was to do with the house. I've put it up for sale. I just wanted to check the previous tenants had left it ok.'

'And had they?'

'Yes. Spotless. I won't have to do anything before I inform the estate agents.'

'I thought you were going to rent it out, again?'

Isobelle slumped onto a seat. 'No. I think it needs to go.'

'Will you move up here permanently?'

Isobelle stood again and plucked the toast from the toaster. 'Yeah. I love it up here.'

Marion smiled. 'You can stay here as long as you like. You know that.'

Isobelle sat back at the table with her buttered toast. She placed a hand on the side of the teapot, then poured herself a cup. 'I know. You've been wonderful, Marion. But if I did move up here, I would probably get a place of my own.'

Marion frowned. 'And Geoff?'

'Geoff?' Isobelle took a bite of toast.

'Would you and he …?'

'Oh, I don't know. Two dead husbands. I'm not sure I could cope with a third.'

'Have you still got doubts about him?'

Isobelle lowered her brow and sipped her tea. 'No. I was being silly the other day. I don't know what I was thinking of.' She turned and stared out of the window.

Marion replenished her cup and studied her friend. 'It's a lovely day out there,' Marion said.

'It is.' Isobelle said.

'How about we put on our boots and have a good walk?'

Isobelle pondered for a moment. 'Yes.' She smiled at Marion. 'I'd like that.'

Michael answered his phone and stepped outside into the yard. 'What is it, Toby?'

'No need to be so snappy,' Toby said.

Michael sighed. 'You phoning can't be good news.'

'I'm just checking everything's ok your end?'

Michael sneered. 'Just great.'

'Look,' Toby said. 'Do this thing, and it gets Tavistock off your back. Then you can go back to your life pulling pints.'

'Can you promise that this is a one-off?'

Toby laughed. 'You have my word. I'll ring when I know more.'

Michael pushed the phone back inside his pocket and puffed out his cheeks.

CHAPTER SEVENTEEN

Brian bounded into the shop and over to the counter.
Elliott looked up. 'Morning,' he said.

'Morning.'

'You said you have news?'

Brian edged closer. 'Geoff Brown.'

'Our Geoff?' Elliott said.

'No. The one from Skinningrove.'

Elliott shrugged. 'What about him?'

'I met his mother.'

'Where?' Elliott said.

'Here, in Whitby. This morning. Geoff's widow, Agnes, was with her. Madge, she's called … But—'

'Brian,' Elliott said. 'Get to the point.'

'She knew Dot.'

'Who did?'

Brian huffed. 'Madge. Geoff's mother. She knew Dot. Not only that, but she also spoke with a southern accent. It was subtle, but it was definitely there.'

'How did she—?'

'She didn't say. She said she knew her, but they had a big fallout. When I tried to get more information, she couldn't get away quick enough.'

Elliott slumped onto the chair behind him and rubbed his beard. A customer came into the shop. 'Go into the back and make us a cup of tea,' Elliott said. 'Jason should be back soon.'

Geoff pushed the vacuum cleaner around the room. He stopped and turned it off, straining to listen, as his mobile rang.

'Hi, gorgeous,' Geoff said.

'Hi, yourself,' Isobelle said.

He sat on the sofa. 'Sleep ok?'

'Like the dead. I think all that energy I expended yesterday wore me out. I didn't get up until 10.30.'

'I overslept too. I'm normally up before daybreak.'

'Listen,' she said. 'I can't talk long, Marion's in the shower. I've promised her I'll go for a long walk today.'

'That's all right. I was going to nip round to Brian's and see how the land lies.'

'She's at work tomorrow. Maybe we could …?'

'Maybe we could.'

'Have you thought any more about Michael?'

Geoff sighed. 'I've thought of nothing else.'

'I've an idea.'

'Oh, yeah?' he said.

'Why don't we get a private detective.'

Geoff's jaw dropped open. 'A detective?'

'To help with finding out what he's up to,' she said.

'I'm not sure. That would involve a stranger knowing our business. It could even get Michael into deep trouble.'

'I know that, but we'll struggle to do it on our own. I could have a word with Anton again. He might know of someone.'

'Can I give it some thought?' Geoff said.

'Of course. I'll ring later.'

'Ok. Enjoy your walk, Belle.'

Jason eyed Elliott and Brian from behind his laptop. 'Madge married George Brown in 1952 at a registry office in Islington. Madge was eighteen, and George twenty-one.'

'That's where Dot was from,' Brian said. 'It's obvious they knew each other from back then.'

'Do we know when they moved up North?' Elliott said.

'They first appeared on the electoral roll in 1962. They were living in Skinningrove by then.'

'I remember Dot telling me she moved to Whitby in the fifties,' Elliott said.

'What's the link between Dot and them?' Jason said.

Elliott pondered. 'Maybe they were just friends from London and got back together when they ended up North.'

'Madge said they had a big fallout,' Brian said. 'We could do with knowing what that was.'

'You can't very well go around there and ask Madge, though,' Elliott said.

'No,' Brian said.

'Have you checked for Geoff's birth certificate?' Elliott said to Jason.

'I can't find one. I looked in Islington, and also around Skinningrove. But nothing.'

Elliott pondered again. 'What do we do now?'

Brian checked his watch. 'I'd better get going. I said I'd meet Geoff back at my place.'

'How are you going to play it?' Elliott said.

Brian shrugged. 'I don't know. He's still our friend. Part of me wants to come straight out and ask him, but another part …'

'Knows what he'll say?' Elliott said.

'Yeah. It's the semi-final of the quiz next week.'

'Let's put this on ice,' Elliott said. 'The question of Geoff and who he is will have to wait.'

Geoff stood outside Brian's cottage with Freddie and knocked. No one answered. Consulting his watch, he knocked again, huffed loudly then took out his mobile.

'Sorry about that,' Brian said, as he hurried along the path. 'I got held up in town.' He pushed his key in the door. 'Come on through.'

Geoff followed him inside. 'How are you, Brian?'

'I'm well. Yourself?'

'Oh, can't complain.'

'Sit yourself down,' Brian said. 'Cuppa or …?' He opened the fridge and pulled out a bottle of beer. 'One of these?'

Geoff grinned. 'I think I'll have a beer. I can get tea anywhere.'

Brian turned away and searched in a drawer for the bottle opener.

'Have you seen much of Elliott?' Geoff said.

Brian picked up the opener and pushed off the top of the beer. 'Not today,' he said, and handed the beer and a glass to Geoff. He pulled a second bottle from the fridge and repeated the process, before sitting at the table with his friend. 'Cheers,' he said as the pair clinked glasses.

'It's the semi-final next week,' Geoff said.

'Yeah, I'm looking forward to it.'

Brian took a swig of beer. 'How did the trip go?'

'Good,' Geoff said.

Brian studied his friend. 'Relatives, wasn't it?'

'Yeah. I haven't seen them in years.'

'Where do they live?'

'Hartlepool,' Geoff said.

'Oh,' Brian said. 'I thought you must have gone to London. Did they move up here?'

'No. They're cousins on my mother's side. I've been promising to visit for years.'

'Isobelle ok?'

'Isobelle?'

'Come on,' Brian said. 'It's the worst kept secret. You two always sneaking about.'

Geoff laughed. 'We were trying to keep it secret from Marion, that's all. Now she knows …'

'And everyone else.'

Geoff smiled. 'You can't keep anything quiet in this town.'

'Is it serious? You and Belle?'

Geoff took a long, thoughtful drink of his beer. 'I think it is.'

'Good for you.' Brian drained his glass. 'I've often wished I had someone to share my golden years with. It can be lonely living on your own. But then, I've got you, Elliott, Jason and Marion, and I'm pretty set in my ways.'

'Have you thought of getting a dog?'

Brian looked over at Freddie, asleep in the corner, and smiled. 'I have. I might just do that.'

Geoff and Freddie were making their way back towards his cottage when his phone rang. 'Hi, Belle.'

'Hi, handsome. I'm back.'

'How did it go with Marion?'

'A bit stilted at first, but ok. She made me walk for miles, though. I'm bloody knackered.'

Geoff paused outside the gate to his property and fished for his key. 'I met up with Brian.'

'Oh,' she said. 'How did that go?'

'Same as you. A bit stilted, until we talked about you.'

'Me?'

'Yeah. Everyone is interested in our thing.'

'A thing. I've never had a thing before.'

Geoff chuckled and placed the key in the door. 'How about you coming round here and we can have a bit more of our thing.'

'I'll be ten minutes.'

Isobelle lay in Geoff's arms. 'Did Brian mention anything while you were round there?'

'No. As I said, it was a bit stilted at first. But then we got back to our usual selves.'

'Marion was much the same. Although …'

'Although?'

'I got the impression she felt a little guilty.'

'Hopefully,' Geoff said, 'they've forgotten all about the Vincent business.'

'Hopefully. They've obviously been talking about it, but I think we may have convinced them.'

'It's the quiz next week.'

'Semi-final,' Isobelle said. 'Are you excited?'

'Yeah. We got to the semi-final four years ago, but The Northallerton Brainbusters beat us.'

'The team we play next?'

'Yeah,' Geoff said.

'A chance for revenge?'

'Definitely.'

Isobelle shifted her position. 'Have you thought any more about a private detective?'

'I'm not sure, Belle. It would involve a stranger knowing about Michael. If he's up to something illegal, the detective would probably feel obliged to go to the police.'

Isobelle sat up. 'If he is breaking the law, wouldn't that be the right thing to do?'

'I could have gone to prison all those years back. I would like to think we can give him a second chance.'

'We don't know what he's doing though. It could be something awful. If it's about the money, I'll pay. I've got loads of the stuff.'

Geoff turned his head away. 'It's not the money, and I know it could be really bad. But …'

'Forget it for the moment,' she said. 'We'll cross that bridge when we reach it. I'll hold off on the private detective for now.'

Geoff squeezed her hand. 'Thanks, Belle.'

'What about talking to Michael? Have you decided what you're going to do?'

'Not yet.'

Isobelle hugged him close. 'I'm thinking of buying a house in Whitby.'

Geoff turned to face her and smiled. 'Are you now?'

'Yeah. I've fallen in love with the place. And also, a certain gentleman. Who knows, he may be interested in moving in with me.'

'Anyone I know?'

Isobelle laughed and kissed him.

Brian sat by the fire, reading. He paused and listened as someone tapped on his door for a second time. He pulled off his glasses, set the book down on the table, and went to answer.

Elliott stood outside. 'Sorry it's late, Brian.'

'Come in and close that door. It's bloody freezing out there.'

Elliott followed Brian into the living room and sat opposite him.

'What brings you around here so late?' Brian said.

Elliott rubbed his hands together and held them out in front of the fire. 'Agnes Grant.'

'What about her?'

'Do you think you would be able to have another chat with her?'

Brian frowned. 'About Geoff Brown?'

'No. Dot and Madge.'

Brian sighed. 'I thought we agreed to put this thing on ice until after the quiz?'

'I can't,' Elliott said. 'It's eating away at me.'

'We're opening up a can of worms, Elliott,' Brian said. 'Geoff and I are just getting back to our usual selves.'

Elliott sat back in his chair. 'I know. I know, but ...'

'But?'

'Don't you think it's funny that Madge knew Dot?'

'I suppose.'

'Jason has looked into Madge and her husband's life.'

Brian stood. 'This sounds heavy. I'll get us a drink.' He moved across and opened the sideboard, pulling out two tumblers and a half-bottle of malt whisky. He poured two liberal measures, handed one to Elliott, and sat back in his chair. 'What about their lives?' Brian said.

Elliott touched glasses with his friend. 'Cheers,' Elliott said. 'They never had any children.'

Brian thoughtfully sipped on his drink. 'Go on.'

'But Dot did. A son. He was registered in London in 1956. She was only seventeen.'

'And the father?'

Elliott gulped his drink. 'Illegitimate.'

Brian rested back into his chair. 'And you think this is why the two women fell out?'

'Madge moved up to Skinningrove with her husband not long after Dot's baby was born. Maybe they adopted Dot's son.'

'Skinningrove Geoff?' Brian said.

'Exactly. Dot came to Whitby a couple of years later. She may have wanted to be closer to her boy.'

'It's a possibility, I suppose,' Brian said.

'Do you think you could talk with Agnes? She may know more.'

'I'd need an excuse to go around to her house.'

'Would that be a problem?' Elliott said.

Brian pondered. 'No. I think I have just the thing.'

Jason logged out of Ancestry world and closed the lid of his laptop. He leant back and stretched before opening the top drawer to his desk. The familiar churning in his stomach started as he looked at the contents and let his fingers gently touch the pile of unopened envelopes inside. Searching the internet for clues to Michael's father had resurrected the yearning and loss he felt for his own family. He allowed his mind to take him back through time to a place of self-loathing.

Guisborough 2000 …

Jason waited in the large front room of the house he shared with his parents. An only child he wanted for nothing. Privately educated and with every evening and holiday filled with activities to keep a young man's mind and body occupied. His father had told him he wanted to talk with him and to wait in this room.

The door opened, and his father marched in clutching a magazine in his hand. He took a deep breath and glowered at Jason. 'Perhaps.' He sneered. 'Perhaps you can explain this?' He shook the magazine at Jason and waited for an answer.

Jason gawped at his father. A mixture of embarrassment and anger washed over him. 'Have you been going through my things?' He lurched forward to grab the copy of *The Advocate* with a picture of naked men adorning the cover. His father, anticipating his movement, snatched it away.

'Jason,' he bellowed. 'I'll ask you again to explain why …' He shook with anger '… you have brought this filth into my house?'

Jason's shoulders slumped as he dropped back onto the seat. He sighed and lowered his head. 'Look,' he began. 'I knew you would find out one day. I know you're going to be a little disappointed in me … The thing is, I've known for a long time that I'm gay. I've tried to fight my feelings, but it's who I am.'

His father's cheeks turned puce as he tossed the magazine to the floor. 'A little disappointed? Good God, Jason. Have your mother and I not raised you correctly?' He turned his back to his son. 'You've had everything a boy could want. How dare you treat us with such disrespect.'

'It's not disrespectful, Dad. This is who I am. I can't go on … I won't go on pretending anymore.' Jason lowered his head. 'Does Mum know?'

His father spun around. His arms folded sternly across his chest. 'That we've got a pervert for a son? Yes, she knows.' He turned away from Jason again and half-filled a glass with brandy. 'I wanted to toss you out like the deviant you are. She begged me to talk some sense into you.'

Jason sat up straight. 'What do you mean—?'

'We thought it would be a good idea for you to go away for a while. There's a place in London that runs courses in curing these …' He sneered at his son, '… feelings you have and make you normal. You'll stay there for four months and then when you come back, we can get you into university and forget all this nonsense happened.'

Jason stood. 'I'm gay, Dad. I'm appalled you think I would want to be cured. It's not a disease. I want to meet someone and fall in love.'

'Jason,' his father roared. 'If you persist with this … degeneracy … I will have no choice but to disinherit you. You'll be left with nothing.'

'I'm not bothered about your money.'

His father drained his glass and banged it down on the table. 'You have twenty-four hours to consider whether being queer is more important than your family and future education.' He strode from the room and slammed the door behind him.

Jason was roused from his memories as Elliott touched him on the shoulder. 'You ok, son? You look miles away.'

Jason jumped to his feet and closed the drawer with the letters inside. 'I was just thinking about my parents.' His eyes glistened. 'With all this family tree stuff, it just got me thinking.'

'Yes,' Elliott said. 'Sometimes, blood is definitely not thicker than water. Family can let you down in a way no one else can.'

Jason lowered his head. 'You … and Babs, have been more of a family to me over the years.'

Elliott smiled. 'Babs thought the world of you. And so do I. You'll have me blubbing in a minute and it's not a pretty sight, I can tell you. I'll fix us a drink.'

Jason forced a smile. 'Yeah, something strong.' He opened the drawer again as Elliott left the room. Taking the letters out, he looked towards the dying embers of the fire in the grate. 'This is where they belong,' he said, and watched as the flames danced higher, curling the paper into black ashes.

CHAPTER EIGHTEEN

Brian parked outside of Agnes' house, climbed out of his car and collected the tray of plants from the boot.

'Hello, Brian,' Agnes said, as the door opened before he reached it. 'I thought it was you.'

'I was passing, and I remembered you love Hostas.' He held out the tray to her.

'Oh, yes. I do.' Agnes accepted the plants and waved him inside. 'I'm just making a cuppa. Sit yourself down, and I'll be with you in a jiffy.'

He entered the living room, sat on an armchair and glanced around the room adorned with photos of children. Some older – her children he suspected – and others much newer, grandchildren, he assumed. On the television, a picture of a younger Agnes next to a man, the pair of them attending some function given their attire.

He turned as Agnes entered carrying a tray with a teapot, mugs and biscuits on it. 'I'm admiring your photos,' he said.

'Children and grandchildren,' she said. 'I do love to show them off.' She sat opposite him and poured the tea. 'Help yourself to a biscuit.'

He poured some milk into his mug, picked up his tea, and selected a bourbon.

'Have you any children or grandchildren?' she said.

'A son, but no grandkids yet. He lives in Australia.'

'One of my kids moved there. I keep threatening to visit, but I'm getting on a bit now. I couldn't face that flight.'

Brian nodded as he sipped his tea. 'I know what you mean. I'd feel the same, and I'd miss the sea air of Whitby.'

'I do enjoy my visits to Whitby,' she said. 'Well, that and my garden. Thanks again for the Hostas.'

'You're welcome. I've been thinning mine out and replanting them elsewhere, but I still had quite a few leftover.'

'Well, I've got just the place for them,' she said.

'Did you have a good time in Whitby the other day?'

'We did.' She lowered her head. 'Sorry about Madge.'

'Madge? Why?'

'She was a little off with you.'

Brian smiled. 'Not at all. She's spritely for her age.'

'She is, but she thinks that allows her to say what she wants.'

Brian chuckled. 'I hope I'm that good on my feet when I reach that age.' He smiled again. 'If I do.'

Agnes laughed. 'Me too. So, you live on your own?'

'Yes.'

'I hope you don't mind me asking. Are you—?'

'Divorced,' Brian said. 'Some years ago now.'

'Ah, I see.'

'When I told you I had a son, that wasn't strictly true.' Agnes nodded for him to continue. 'He's my nephew. I brought him up as my son for a lot of years.'

'You don't have to tell me if you don't want, Brian.'

He cleared his throat. He had never really discussed his past with anyone. 'It was a long time ago. But …' He continued. 'Adam's mother and I had been together for quite a number of years, and then I found out she'd been having a long-standing affair with my brother.'

Agnes put a hand to her mouth. 'And you found out that …?'

'Adam isn't mine. I still consider him my son, though.'

'Of course. Your brother …?'

'We muddle along. He married my ex. I see Adam when I can. He comes over occasionally.'

'No second Mrs …?'

'Shawcross. No. There have been one or two lady friends over the years, but nothing serious. I won a little money, and when I took early retirement from BT, I just got stuck in my single ways.'

'How wonderful. What did you do at BT?'

'I was a jointer,' Brian said. 'I connected the cables together.' He smiled. 'I named my cottage, *Dunsplicing.*' He twisted his fingers together. 'That's what joining two wires together was called. Splicing.'

'Ah, I see.'

'What about you?' Brian said. 'No husband about?'

'My second husband died nearly five years ago.'

'I'm sorry.'

Agnes waved a dismissive hand. 'It happens. He'd been ill quite a while. Still, he left me comfortable. He made sure of that.'

Brian glanced at the photo. 'You look very happy.'

'After Geoff died, all those years ago, I thought I'd never get over it. But then George came along and swept me off my feet.' Agnes reached to her side and plucked a tissue from the box.

'I'm sorry, I didn't mean to upset you.'

She forced a smile. 'You didn't. It's just me being silly.'

'I don't think you're silly. I've lost people, friends, family. You never do get over them.'

'No. I don't suppose you do.'

Brian drained his mug. 'Where's Madge today?'

'She lives at a care home nearby. I try to take her out a couple of times a week.'

'It's good that you two have remained friendly.'

She lifted the pot over Brian's mug and looked at him. Brian nodded, and she refilled it. 'We were always close. Like mother and daughter really.' Agnes put down the pot and rubbed her hands together. 'Can I tell you something in confidence, Brian?'

'Of course.'

'Madge told me this the other day.' She slowly shook her head and smiled. 'You think you know a person intimately, but then they surprise you with some revelation.'

Brian poured milk into his mug. 'Revelation?'

'I think it was meeting you in Whitby that set her off.' She clasped her hands together. 'She told me Geoff, my husband, wasn't really her son.'

Brian sat back in his chair. 'I see.'

'She'd kept it a secret all these years.'

'Did she tell you who his mother was?'

'Yes. A woman called Dot.'

He nodded. 'The one she mentioned the other day?'

'Yes,' Agnes said. 'The one she said she fell out with.'

Isobelle woke early. She decided to go for a walk and took Pip along for company. After walking for over an hour, she stopped at the foot of the steps and telephoned Anton.

'Morning, Belle. Don't tell me you've backed out of the Am-dram?'

'No,' she said. 'A promise is a promise. I need another favour.'

'Go on.'

'Remember I told you about my friend's son?'

'Yeah,' Anton said. 'The one with the dodgy pal?'

Isobelle swapped the phone to her other ear. 'She wants to employ a private detective.'

Anton sucked in air. 'I wouldn't recommend it.'

'Why not?'

'Well,' he said. 'It's expensive for one. Also, they're not like on the television. If they discover a crime, they're likely to report it. Your friend's son could find himself in hot water.'

Isobelle sighed. 'My friend's adamant. Money's not a problem, and she's quite wealthy.'

'There're some crooks out there, Belle. Some of the private detectives leave a lot to be desired.'

'You can't help, then?'

'I'll ask about. If this friend of yours is determined to employ one, we'd better make sure that it's a good one.'

'Thanks, Anton. I owe you a drink.'

'I'm not promising, Belle. Detecting should be left to the professionals really.'

'I understand. I'll have a chat with her again and try to dissuade her.'

'Ok, you do that,' he said. 'In the meantime, I'll make some enquiries.'

Brian sat looking down at his pint as Elliott walked in. Elliott waved at his friend, bought himself a drink, and joined Brian.

'You said you had news?' Elliott said.

'Yeah. I went to Agnes' today. She's a lovely woman. I felt a little guilty for deceiving her.'

Elliott sipped his drink. 'Yeah, I know what you mean. All this creeping about and keeping secrets at our age. But what can we do if we ever want to get to the bottom of this ...?'

'Agnes told me that when she and Madge got home, Madge just broke down and confessed everything.' Elliott nodded for Brian to continue. 'Dot got pregnant at seventeen. You can imagine how bad it was for a woman in those days?'

'Yeah. It must have been hard.'

'Dot's mother persuaded her to give the baby away.'

'To Madge?' Elliott said.

'Yeah. Dot and Madge were good friends. Madge was already married, and Madge and her husband, George, had decided to come north. He was originally from Loftus.'

'I see. And they brought the baby with them?'

Brian took a gulp of his drink. 'Yes. No one suspected. Madge pretended she was pregnant, and Dot kept her pregnancy a secret from friends.'

'You said they fell out?'

Brian nodded. 'When Dot was a little older, she moved to Whitby to be nearer her son. At first, Madge and George didn't mind Dot popping round. They told neighbours that she was Geoff's aunty. But Dot got more and more attached to her son.'

'I see,' Elliott said. 'And she wanted to be involved in Geoff's upbringing, more and more?'

'Exactly. It came to a head. Madge and George threatened to move away and stop Dot from seeing him altogether. They allowed Dot to meet up with Geoff occasionally. Birthdays and Christmas etc. George would travel to Whitby with little Geoff.'

'Why didn't Dot insist on seeing him?' Elliott said. 'He was her son, after all?'

Brian downed a mouthful of beer. 'Because George was the dad. Madge only found out many years later. She forbid Dot from seeing Geoff when he was about twelve, and she and Dot never spoke again.'

Elliott shook his head. 'That's terrible. To think poor Dot kept that to herself. She must have been heartbroken when Geoff was killed.'

'Yeah. Could this have been the big secret she told Babs?'

Elliott shrugged. 'Maybe. We'll never know, though.'

'It still doesn't tell us who our Geoff Brown is.'

'No,' Elliott said. 'This is driving me mad. We need to speak with Geoff.'

'I'm not sure,' Brian said. 'Maybe we should let sleeping dogs lie.'

'I can't, Brian. We've come this far. I need to know.'

'What are you going to do?'

Elliott drained his pint. 'I'm going to see him and have it out.'

Brian gulped. 'Rather you than me, mate.'

Isobelle slipped inside Geoff's house. He looked up from the dining table and smiled. 'Morning,' he said.

Isobelle bent down and planted a kiss on his cheek. 'Where's the breakfast you promised me?'

He stood. 'In the oven.' He glanced at the clock. 'You're late.'

'Sorry about that. I had to put my face on. It seems to take longer and longer as the years pass.'

Geoff laughed. 'You're beautiful with or without make-up. You don't have to get done-up for me.' He cracked two eggs into a pan and tilted it. 'Do me a favour,' he said, 'grab the plates out of the oven. There's a pair of gloves over there. They'll be hot.'

Isobelle pushed on the gloves and pulled out two plates replete with sausage, bacon, tomatoes, beans, fried bread and mushrooms from the oven. She placed them on the table, and Brian popped an egg on both.

'Lovely,' she said.

'There's toast in the toaster,' Geoff said. 'And tea in the pot.'

Geoff joined Isobelle in the lounge. 'That was lovely,' Isobelle said. 'But I couldn't eat it every day.'

'Me too. I have cereal or porridge most days, but I do like to reward myself with a fry-up occasionally.' He smiled. 'Me and Brian usually have one together, once a week. We alternate houses. It's become a little bit of a ritual. Well, it was.'

'You and Brian will get back to the old ways.' She tapped the back of his hand. 'What are we going to do today?' she said.

'How about a walk?'

'Yeah. The weather looks good. Anywhere in particular?'

'Robin Hoods Bay,' he said.

'That's a good walk.'

Geoff patted his stomach. 'We need to walk off those thousands of calories we've just eaten.'

'True enough.' She moved over to sit next to Geoff on the settee. 'Have you thought any more about hiring a private detective?'

He closed his eyes briefly. 'I'm not sure it's a good idea.'

She took hold of his hand. 'It's up to you, Geoff. I don't want to push you into anything you don't want to do.'

'It's just the thought of involving a stranger.'

'I understand. What are you going to do about Michael?'

He rubbed his chin. 'I need to talk to him. Explain about his, and my past.'

'What happens if he tells the police?'

Geoff turned to face her. 'He wouldn't do that, would he?'

She shrugged. 'I don't know?'

'It needs resolving, Belle. I can't just leave it like this.'

'Don't do anything yet. Another week or so won't make any difference.'

'True.'

She stood. 'I'd better go and get my walking stuff on then.'

Geoff pulled her onto his lap. 'Not so fast, gorgeous. You haven't thanked me properly for making your breakfast.'

Isobelle left Geoff's half an hour later. She paused outside and glanced back at the cottage, smiling. Marion, stood nearby with Pip and hidden from view, watched as Isobelle fastened her coat and made her way along the road. Only when Isobelle disappeared from sight, did she emerge. Marion stared at the cottage for a couple of moments, before setting off into town.

Geoff sat on the armchair and pulled on his walking boots. Someone knocked, he smiled and went to answer it.

'You were quick,' he said, as he opened the door. His mouth dropped open. 'Elliott.'

'Hi, Geoff. Have you got a couple of minutes?'

Geoff glanced along the lane. 'Well, I'm going out.'

'Oh, it's ok. We can talk later.'

'I'll be in tonight if you want to come around then. I'll get a couple of beers in.'

'Yes, yes. I'll look forward to that. Have a good day.'

Geoff frowned as he watched Elliott disappear up the lane and out of sight.

'Will I do?' Isobelle said, as she came in to view.

He waved her inside. 'You'll do fine. I'll just grab my coat.'

'I've checked the forecast, and we're set fair.'

He closed his door and locked it. 'You've just missed Elliott.'

'Elliott? What did he want?'

'I don't know. He's coming back later tonight.' Geoff raised his eyebrows. 'I'll let you know.'

'Are we walking back as well?'

Geoff scoffed. 'You're joking. It'll be over six miles along the Cleveland Way. I thought we could have a couple of drinks when we get there, maybe a sandwich. Then we'll grab the bus home.'

Isobelle linked his arm. 'Lead on then.'

CHAPTER NINETEEN

The next day ...
Michael looked up as the pub door opened. Barry strode in and climbed onto a stool at the bar as Michael nodded.

'Bit quiet in here,' Barry said.

Michael shrugged. 'Some days are like that.'

'Any news from our friend Toby?'

Michael sneered. 'He's no friend of mine.'

'Listen,' Barry said. 'If you do what I've asked, there won't be any problem.'

'All I want is a quiet life.'

'Don't we all. Pint of lager.'

Michael placed the glass on the counter and waved away Barry as he held out a note.

The door to the pub opened and Geoff walked in. 'Hi, Michael. Did you remember I wanted a chat with you?'

Michael slapped his forehead. 'Sorry, mate. I forgot about it. Can we do it another time?'

'No worries. Let me know when you're available. No rush.'

Michael nodded. 'I'll give you a ring.' He glanced at Barry.

Geoff followed Michael's gaze then watched as Barry lifted his pint, a tattoo clearly visible on his forearm. He glanced at Barry through the glass behind the bar and narrowed his eyes. 'I'll see you later, Michael.' Geoff hurried from the pub.

Barry glanced over his shoulder at the door Geoff had left by. 'Another Londoner?'

'Yeah. Geoff's lived up here years. I think since the seventies. It's a proper magnet to us Cockneys.'

Barry sipped his pint. 'Where's the best fish and chip shop?' he said. He furrowed his brow and glanced back towards the door as a flicker of recognition arrived.

Michael picked up a menu from behind the bar. 'Here,' he said, and handed Barry the flier. 'It's where I go.'

'Since the seventies?' Barry said.

Michael frowned. 'Seventies?'

'Yeah. The guy that was just in here.'

'Geoff? Yeah, he's lived here for years.'

He took another drink from his glass. 'What part of London was he from?'

'Clapham, I think. Why?'

Barry drained his pint. 'He seems familiar that's all. Probably nothing.'

Michael tapped the empty glass. 'Another?'

Barry placed a note on the bar. 'Here,' he said. 'You'll never stay in business giving away free pints. Get one yourself.'

Geoff raced along the road and stopped. He rubbed his chin and dropped onto a bench. His heart pounded as he sucked in air.

Isobelle came rushing along the path and sat down next to him. 'What's up?'

He covered his face with his hands and leant forward. Isobelle took hold of his hand. 'Geoff,' she whispered. 'What's up?'

'I've just been to see Michael.'

'I thought you were going to—?'

'I know,' Geoff said. 'But I couldn't wait any longer. It's eating me up.'

'What did he say?'

'Nothing. I never got a chance to talk with him.'

She squeezed his hand. 'Why all the panic?'

'Barry was in there.'

Isobelle frowned. 'Barry?' Her eyes widened. 'Barry from the robbery?'

'Yeah.'

She brought a hand to her mouth. 'Oh, my God. Did he recognise you?'

He shook his head. 'I don't think so. He was looking the other way.'

'Are you sure it was him?'

Geoff turned to face her. 'I'm sure. He has the same tattoo on his arm. *Hammers forever.* He's changed a lot. But it was definitely him.'

'Why has he shown up here?'

He shrugged. 'I've no idea, but it can't be a coincidence.'

'What are we going to do?'

'I'll have to keep my head down. If he sees me again, he may recognise me.' He squeezed her hand back. 'Barry has nothing to fear, he's done his time. I haven't though.'

She looked into his eyes. 'We have to keep calm.'

'We?'

'Yes, we.' She nodded at him. 'We'll get through this.'

'Will you do me a favour?' he said.

'Of course.'

He sighed. 'Will you take a letter to Michael from me.'

'Is that wise?'

'He may know why Barry is in Whitby.'

She nodded. 'Yes, he may. We'll go back to your cottage, and you can write it.'

Geoff rubbed his face. 'This is madness.'

She gripped his hand tightly. 'Don't you go to pieces on me, Geoff Brown. I haven't finished with you yet.'

He forced a smile. 'I'll try not to.'

'What about Elliott? Did he show up last night?'

He shook his head. 'No. But I think Elliott is the least of our problems.'

Barry loitered on the corner as Isobelle came out of Geoff's cottage. She hurried along the street and past Barry.

'Excuse me, luv,' Barry said.

She stopped and turned. 'Yes?'

'You couldn't tell me the way to Whitby Brewery, could you?'

She smiled at him. 'You have to go up the 199 steps. Past the Abbey, and it's just on your left. It's well signposted.'

'Thanks.'

She smiled again, then headed off. Isobelle waited until she was out of sight, then pulled out her phone.

'What's up?' Geoff said.

'I think I've just met Barry.'

'Are you sure?' he said.

'He fitted your description, and he had a London accent. He asked me where the brewery was.'

'But you weren't convinced that he actually wanted the brewery?'

Isobelle sighed. 'No.'

'Where was he?'

She stopped and dropped onto a bench. 'Just up the road from your cottage.'

'Christ,' he said.

'Shall I come back?'

'No. Drop the letter off first. See if he's still there when you return.'

'Ok.'

'I'll have a look out of the window. See if he's hanging about.'

Isobelle sucked in air. 'Don't let him spot you.'

'I won't.'

'I'll be as quick as I can.'

Geoff made his way upstairs and across to the window. The curtains were still drawn and, pulling them slightly to one side, he looked down. Barry was there. Geoff watched as he took out a cigarette and lit it. Barry glanced up at the window, and Geoff moved out of sight. His heart pounded inside his chest, but when he dared to look again, Barry was gone. He slumped onto the bed and took in deep breaths.

Michael searched around behind the bar. 'You haven't seen my van keys, have you?' he said to the young barmaid, crouched, restocking the fridge.

'Near the till,' she said.

He moved across to it, snatched up his keys, and pushed them inside his jacket pocket. 'What's this?' he said, holding up an envelope with his name on the front.

'One of the quiz team brought it in.' She pondered a moment. 'Belle?'

'Belle?' he said.

'Yeah. The one who lives on Haggerlythe Street with Marion.'

Michael tore open the envelope and read the letter inside.

'Have we any more tonics?' she said. Michael didn't answer, continuing to stare at the piece of paper. 'Michael,' she said. He looked at her. 'Any more tonics?'

'Yeah, in the cellar.' He folded the paper and put it into his pocket. 'I'll see you later.'

'What time are you back?'

Michael headed out of the door without a word.

'Charming,' she said.

Isobelle handed Geoff a cup of tea. 'You can't keep looking outside all day from your bedroom window. I told you he wasn't there when I came back.'

Geoff sighed. 'What's he going to do, though?'

'I don't know. Maybe we should go to my house in Middlesbrough for a while.'

'I need to speak with Michael,'

'He'll have the letter now,' she said. 'Hopefully, he'll come tonight.'

Geoff sat on the edge of the bed. 'Hopefully.'

'Are we going to go to my house?'

He rubbed his chin. 'If we leave in the early hours, we won't get spotted.'

'That's a good idea. I'll have to grab some clothes from Marion's. I'll come back later tonight, give Michael a chance to call around.'

'What will you tell Marion?'

Isobelle paused at the door. 'Forget about Marion.'

CHAPTER TWENTY

Later that day …
He gasped as he tried to move, the pain in his chest excruciating. He had no idea how long he had been here. Crumpled and broken, lying on the seaweed-slick rocks like a washed-up sea bird. The cold brine slowly lapped at the edges of his body as the copper-tasting, viscous liquid pooled in his mouth. He gagged and coughed, expelling the blood onto a rock to the side of him. He grimaced as a lightning-bolt of pain shot across his head and neck before welcoming blackness crushed him once again.

'You need to come now, he's on the rocks and not moving!' Marion's voice spoke quickly and clearly.

A figure slid back into the shadows, replaced the phone into a pocket and quickly slipped away.

"I can't get to him,' she said. 'The address … Yes, it's Haggerlythe Street. At the very end.'

'Ok, madam,' the voice on her phone said. 'Try to stay calm. An ambulance is on its way.'

A voice boomed through the night. 'Marion! What's happened?' Elliott appeared next to her, breathing heavily.

'It's Geoff. He's down there. An ambulance will be here soon.'

They both turned as footsteps approached through the dim light. Brian hurried towards them, quickly joined by Michael.

'Hey, what are you two doing?' Brian said to them through gasping breaths as a crowd of people gathered at the cliff edge.

'It's Geoff,' Elliott said. 'He's fallen down the cliff. Help is coming.'

'We need to get to him.' Brian zipped up his jacket and placed his boot on the wire of the fence to hold it down.

Marion grasped his shoulder. 'No, Brian. You'll end up in a heap next to Geoff. Help's on its way.'

A blue light lit up their faces as the ambulance turned the corner with Jason jogging along beside it. 'What's going on?' he shouted to the others. 'I heard all the commotion.'

Marion strode over to him. 'Geoff has fallen down the cliff. Brian is trying to get down there, but he'll end up injured too.'

'Geoff's down there?' Jason said. 'Oh my God. How the hell has that happened?' Jason faced Marion. 'Is he ok?'

'I don't know,' she said. 'But it doesn't look good.'

Brian moved closer to the edge. 'How are they going to get to him? We're wasting time.'

Marion took hold of his arm again. 'Stay there and let them do their job, Brian.'

Brian turned to face her, his face ashen, fear and panic etched deeply into his features. 'The water's nearly covering him. He'll drown.'

Marion shook his arm. 'Help's here,' she said. 'Come back from the edge.'

His shoulder's slumped as he allowed Marion to lead him away from the drop. The four friends peered over the cliff into the creeping darkness and watched the still form below as the emergency services neared.

This time he awoke with a feeling of panic. The seawater now splashed at his face and into his nose. He realised he had slipped further down from the rocks and onto the sand. Adrenalin coursed through his veins as he managed to drag his battered body into a half-sitting slump, allowing him to get his face out of the water. 'How the hell did I end up here?' he said to himself. He wasn't sure whether he spoke the words or just thought them.

Screwing his eyes up against the pain, he had a memory of falling. Clawing and grabbing onto anything in a futile attempt to stop his rapid descent. A hand pushing him, a helpless tumble as grass and rock flashed by. 'Yes.' He remembered. 'You were here. Here, with your lies and your accusations.' He could hear the dog barking above. 'Is this it? Is this how I die?' He closed his eyes and waited for the icy sea to sweep over him. His body ceased to shiver, and he lay his head onto the cold rock behind him. 'I'll see you soon, Dot,' he said, as his tears mixed with the salt of the sea. The sound of movement and voices close by fading into nothingness.

Isobelle stood at the window of Marion's house and craned her neck to see further down the road. The noise and sirens alerting her to the commotion outside. It was no good, she would have to go out and see what was going on. She took her coat from the hook, shrugged into it, and hurried out, not even bothering to lock the door. As she walked towards the large group gathered at the cliff edge, she spotted her friends stood there. 'Marion?'

'Oh, Belle. It's Geoff. There's been a terrible accident, and he's fallen down the cliff.'

'Geoff?' Isobelle said. Marion took hold of Isobelle's hands. 'The emergency services are here now.'

'I must get to him,' Isobelle said.

'Belle,' Marion said. 'He's in good hands.'

Isobelle looked at her friend. 'What happened? Is he ...?'

'It was an accident,' Marion said. 'He fell from the cliff.'

'Well, we don't actually know that's what happened yet,' Brian said.

'What do you mean, Brian?' Marion's voice rose. 'It had to be an accident. How else could he have got there?'

'Marion's right,' Elliott said. 'He must have been walking Freddie and lost his footing.'

'It doesn't add up, though.' Jason looked at them all. 'Why would he be so close to the edge? He knows the cliff edge is dangerous, don't you agree, Michael?'

Michael took a drag on his cigarette. 'Looks like he slipped to me.'

Isobelle groaned. 'Sorry to interrupt your amateur sleuthing but does anyone know if Geoff is ok?' Isobelle wrestled her hands free from Marion's grip and walked further towards the edge. She watched as the paramedics eased Geoff onto a stretcher attached to a rope. The others eyed each other.

Another vehicle approached with the words *Mountain Rescue* printed on the side. Four men got out and began assisting the medical team with retrieving Geoff from below.

Twenty-five minutes later, Geoff was placed into the back of the ambulance with a drip attached to his arm, and a silver-coloured blanket draped across him.

'How is he?' Brian asked.

'We'll know more when we get him to hospital,' a paramedic said. 'We can take one of you with him.'

'I'll go.' They all said in unison, apart from Isobelle who had taken a step back away from the ambulance. The sight of Geoff too much to bear. She turned and raced back towards the house with tears streaming down her face.

'Why don't you go, Brian,' Elliott said. 'I'll follow with the rest of us in my car.'

The others watched as the ambulance made its way along the lane. Elliott pulled his car keys from his pocket. 'I'll be two minutes,' he said.

Isobelle felt a panic rising inside her as she reached the cottage. It crept from her stomach and through her chest, cold beads of sweat gathered on her top lip. She had stood like this before. Waiting to hear if a loved one was dead or alive. She touched the gold chain around her neck and let her mind drift back to her first husband, Bill. Standing on a freezing-cold beach, the feeling of helplessness as she watched the paramedic pump his pale, wet torso. Her plans and future lay dead on the sand. Her overriding emotion at the time was annoyance. Why wouldn't he listen to her when she had said he was too old to be subjecting his body to the icy North Sea? Why did he always do as he pleased?

'Why were you so bloody-minded?' Isobelle blurted out.

'What did you say?' Marion said.

Isobelle spun around. 'I couldn't stay there. It was like …' Isobelle rummaged in her pocket for a tissue as Marion thrust a cotton handkerchief towards her. '… like Bill.'

'Belle. Don't upset yourself. Come on. Elliott has gone to fetch his car.' Isobelle followed Marion into the front room.

'I can't go,' Isobelle said, and dropped onto the settee. 'You go.'

Marion placed a hand on her friend's arm. 'Are you sure?'

Isobelle looked away. Her eyes full with unshed tears 'I loathe hospitals.'

'Of course. You get yourself a hot drink. I'll ring as soon as we know anything.' Isobelle said nothing, continuing to look away from her friend until she heard the front door close behind Marion.

Brian frowned at Geoff. His friend lay quiet and still on the stretcher. His breathing barely audible. He reached over and took Geoff's hand as the ambulance bounced along the rough, cobbled road.

Brian closed his eyes, allowing his mind to drift back to the first time he had met Geoff.

Brian moved to Whitby after his wife confessed that she had been having a long-term affair with his brother. And that his son was, more than likely, not his son at all, but his nephew. He clenched his fists. The memory of that day still painful and humiliating. Friends would say to him, *'But, you must have known?'* He genuinely had no idea. So, at forty-four, he moved into a small flat in his home town of Scarborough with no wife, no child and no money. Brian felt that all hope of happiness was behind him. His life consisted of work, pub and bed.

After six months of this existence, he walked into his local newsagent's and bought a lottery ticket. Five numbers and a bonus ball on the Saturday night draw changed the future mapped out for him. The money gave him the freedom to move away but could never take away the pain of losing the child he had brought up as his own for eleven years.

As he parked the hired Luton van outside his small cottage in Whitby, someone knocked on the driver's side window. 'You need a hand, mate?' a man with a London accent said.

Brian opened the door and jumped down.

'I'm Geoff.' He held out his hand for Brian to shake. 'I just live around the corner. We wondered who had bought this place. Needs a good bit of work doing. I'm a builder if you need a quote?' Geoff surveyed the place. 'I nearly bought it myself, but I have my eye on something else.'

Brian shook the offered hand and smiled. 'How about you help me in with this stuff, and I'll stick the kettle on, once we find it. Then you can tell me what you think needs doing.'

'Sounds good to me,' Geoff said.

The noise of the siren jolted Brian back to the present moment, and he looked across at Geoff. 'Lifetime ago, mate. I thought I was doing the right thing. I hope it was an accident.' He rubbed a hand across his chin.

'You ok?' The paramedic looked at Brian. 'What were you saying?'

Brian exhaled the breath he held. 'Nothing important. Just the ramblings of an old fool.'

The ambulance came to an abrupt halt at the doors of the hospital. 'Stay here please and we'll get your friend inside and you can follow on.'

Geoff was wheeled quickly inside with the paramedic striding behind the trolley, relaying figures and statistics to the waiting doctor and her team. A young nurse led Brian to a waiting area. 'You can get a coffee from the machine in the corridor, but it'll be you that needs medical help if you do.' The nurse joked with Brian and opened the door to a brightly painted, yellow room with green and red fabric seats. 'Is there anyone we can contact for your friend? Any family?'

'We're here.' Elliott's massive frame filled the doorway with Jason, Michael and Marion trailing behind.

The nurse moved to let them into the room. 'Are you his family?'

'Friends.' Michael answered for them all. 'He doesn't have any family.'

Brian looked away from Michael and stared at his hands. 'Not that we know of, anyway,' he mumbled.

'Right,' the nurse said. 'I'll come back when we know anything. Don't worry, he's in good hands.'

Jason took a seat next to Brian, and Elliott sat opposite. 'Sit down, Michael. He'll be fine.'

Michael looked at Elliott. 'I should get back to the pub.'

'You can't.' Elliott held up his car keys. 'We're all in my car, and we could be ages.'

Michael rubbed his face. 'I'll get a taxi. It's not like me and Geoff were close. Text me how he is though.' He turned to leave. 'People in the pub will be interested, I expect.'

The door closed behind Michael. Jason whistled through his teeth. 'He's all heart, that one.'

'He's just in shock, it affects people differently,' Brian said.

Jason stood and glanced between Brian, Elliott and Marion. 'I think I will get a coffee. Do you want one?' They both shook their heads in answer.

Marion closed the front door to her property and tiptoed inside.

'How is he?' Isobelle said.

Marion brought a hand up to her chest. 'Bloody hell, Belle, you scared the life out of me. Why are you sitting in the dark?'

'Sorry. I was just thinking.'

Marion pulled off her coat and hung it up. 'He's stable. They've put him in an induced coma.'

'He must have a head injury?'

'I don't know,' Marion said. 'You know hospitals. They never tell you anything.'

'Is Elliott still there?'

Marion shook her head. 'No. He just dropped me off.'

'What if he wakes? Someone should be there.' Isobelle moved towards the hall and grabbed her coat.

'Belle,' Marion said, and took hold of her friend's arm. 'There's nothing you can do. We'll ring in the morning.'

Isobelle stifled a sob and brought her hand to her face. 'Oh, Geoff. What happened, Marion?'

'We don't know. They think he fell.'

Isobelle slowly shook her head. 'Geoff wouldn't fall. He knows the cliffs well.'

'It was dark and raining …'

'Is that what you believe?' Isobelle said.

'I don't know, Belle. Let's sit down. I'll fix us a drink.'

Isobelle scowled at Marion. 'Is that your answer to everything … Get drunk?'

'I was only trying to …'

Isobelle pushed past her and mounted the stairs, closing her bedroom door with a loud thud.

Marion sighed and went to make herself a drink.

Jason handed Elliott a glass. 'Brandy,' Jason said. 'I thought you needed something with a bit of a kick.'

'Thanks, son.'

He sank down opposite Elliott. 'What do you think happened?' Jason said.

Elliott sipped at his drink. 'I don't know. We argued …'

'Argued?' Jason said. 'When?'

'I went to see him tonight.'

'About?'

Elliott sighed. 'About everything. Who he is, why he lied …?'

'What did he say?'

'He was angry. He told me to mind my own business. He said I should leave the past where it belongs. It got quite heated.'

'What time did you leave?'

'I don't know. About an hour before he was found. I just walked about. Thinking over what he'd said. You don't think I had anything to do with his fall, do you? Maybe he was angry? Maybe he came after me?'

Jason patted his arm. 'Of course not. You wouldn't hurt a fly.'

'But what if …?'

'What if?'

Elliott brought his hands to his face then slowly pulled them down. 'What if something I said … Something we said … made him …?'

'Suicide?' Jason said.

Elliott shrugged. 'I don't know.'

'Come on, Elliott. Geoff's not the type.'

'How do you know? He's not who he says he is. Who is he, Jason? Who is Geoff Brown?'

Jason tapped his lips with his fingers. 'The police will probably want to speak to us.'

'What should I say?'

Jason pondered. 'Don't mention his past. Just tell them you went around for a chat. He was fine when you left. That's all you have to say.'

The following day …

Isobelle watched Marion, Elliott and Brian deep in conversation, from the bedroom window. The two men glanced back towards the cottage as the anger in Isobelle rose. She continued to watch as they walked away, and Marion headed back to the cottage.

Isobelle grabbed her case, already packed the night before, and zipped it shut. She pulled it from the bed and lumbered down the stairs. Marion lowered the newspaper and glanced over the top of her glasses, as Isobelle placed the luggage in the hall.

Marion pulled off her glasses and lay them aside. 'Where are you going, Belle?'

Isobelle tugged on her coat and turned to face Marion. 'I'm leaving.'

'Leaving. Why?'

'I need to get away from you all.'

Marion stood. 'Come on, let's talk about this. You shouldn't be on your own.'

'I can't stay here.' Isobelle took hold of her suitcase and turned away.

Marion moved forward and took hold of her arm. 'Belle. You're being silly. Where are you going?'

Isobelle spun around and pulled Marion's arm away. 'It's none of your business where I'm going. This is your fault.' Marion took a step backwards, as Isobelle continued. 'You and the others. Elliott and Brian. Interfering. Digging into the past. Geoff's a good man.' She glowered at her friend. 'A bloody good man.'

'Belle, I'm sure—'

'Sure!' Isobelle snarled. 'Why didn't you three keep your noses out. Poor Geoff. What kind of friends are you?'

Marion lowered her head. 'Go on,' Isobelle continued. 'Crack open another bottle, while poor Geoff …' Isobelle brought a hand to her mouth to stifle a cry as tears pooled in her eyes. 'I can't stay here a moment longer.' She turned and, pulling her case behind her, stormed out. Marion closed her eyes and slumped onto the arm of the chair.

CHAPTER TWENTY-ONE

Elliott hung up and turned to face Jason. 'That was Marion. Isobelle blames us for what happened to Geoff.'

'Us. Is that what she said? Surely it was an accident?'

'Not in so many words. Marion said that they had a row and Belle's moved out.'

'I see. Do you think it's our fault?'

Elliott slumped onto the kitchen chair. 'I don't know. We shouldn't have poked our noses into the past. Whoever Geoff really is … Does it matter? He's always been a good friend to us.'

Jason patted Elliott on the arm. 'What's done is done, Elliott. We'll go to the hospital later today. See how he is.'

Elliott lowered his head and rubbed his eyes. 'Yeah, I'd like that.'

Brian scraped the remains of his half-eaten breakfast into the bin. It had been a bad idea cooking it. He hadn't felt hungry at all. His thoughts drifted to Geoff as he stared outside into the distance. His phone rang and, with a resigned sigh, he picked it up.

'Hello,' he said.

'Brian, It's Agnes.'

'Agnes. Hello.'

'I saw the news on telly last night, about the man who fell. I don't know why … Silly, I suppose, but I thought it was you.'

Brian laughed. 'Why?'

'I don't know. Daft really.'

'I know the man who fell,' Brian said.

Agnes gasped. 'Oh, no. Is he a friend?'

'Yeah.'

'I'm so sorry, Brian. How is he?'

'Comfortable, but still in a coma.'

'I'm in Whitby today.'

'With, Madge?'

'No. On my own. I was thinking of asking if you fancied meeting for a coffee, but …'

'I'd love that.'

'Are you sure? I don't want to intrude.'

'You're not. The truth is.' He coughed. 'I could do with some company.'

'Ok, that's lovely. What time?'

Isobelle pulled on her dressing gown and picked up the ringing mobile.

'Hello?' she said.

'Is that Isobelle Frank?'

'Yes.'

'David Wright, from Wright Investigations. Hello, Mrs Frank. You rang my office yesterday and left a message.'

'Oh, yes,' Isobelle said. 'I got your number from someone I know. Anton Trent.'

'Yes. Anton. He's a good friend and ex-work colleague.'

'I need someone investigating.'

'I see. Not a problem. Maybe it's best if we meet. Shall we say two this afternoon at my office?'

'Two's fine. In Middlesbrough?'

'Yes. 15A Albert Road. Just up from the train station.'

'Ok,' Isobelle said. 'I'll see you then.'

Isobelle wandered downstairs and into the kitchen, filled the kettle and flicked on the switch. She checked her mobile. Marion had left a message for her. Isobelle deleted it without listening and put down her phone.

Michael leant against the counter of the bar, sighed and looked into the mirror. He looked awful. Dark circles surrounded his eyes, a memento for his lack of sleep the previous night.

'Michael,' a female voice said.

He turned and looked at the young woman. 'Yeah?'

'That Toby's here. Out the back.'

'Ok,' he said. He rubbed his face, blew out and walked outside.

'Jesus, Michael. You look like shit,' Toby said.

'I didn't sleep very well.'

'I can get you something for that.'

'No thanks. What is it you want, Toby?'

Toby moved closer. 'The shipments coming soon. I'll have the exact time and location later.'

Michael nodded, wearily. 'Ok.'

'Look,' Toby said. 'It's no good getting all moody over this. Payback time.' He tapped Michael gently on the cheek. 'Just make sure you do what we ask.'

'I hope after this we're even?'

Toby pushed Michael in the chest. 'I'll tell you when we're even. You just be a good boy and do as you're told.'

'Ok,' Michael said. 'But you have to stop coming around here. People are beginning to ask questions.'

'Tell them to mind their own business.' Toby surveyed the pub. 'I don't know why you own this dump. Keep your nose clean, and you could have a decent boozer in Leeds or Newcastle.'

'I'm fine as I am.'

Toby looked him up and down. 'I'll be in touch.' Michael watched as he left, moved across, bolted the door and leant up against it.

Toby Newton climbed into the seat of his car and took out his phone. 'Hi, Wayne,' he said.

'Toby,' Tavistock said.

'I've primed Michael. He knows the shipment is coming in soon.'

'I hope this guy doesn't let us down.'

'I've thought about that,' Newton said. 'Maybe after he's delivered the shipment, we should dispense with his services for good?'

Tavistock laughed. 'You're getting good at this. Do what you feel is the right thing.'

'Your copper friend?' Newton said.

'I've been in touch with him. He's going to keep his ear to the ground. But he doesn't think there are any problems.'

'I'll be in touch.' Newton rang off and smiled.

Newton rang another number. 'It's Toby,' he said. 'The shipment's coming in next week.'

'Great. You know where to deliver it?'

'I do,' Newton said. 'The money ...?'

'As we agreed. It will be in used notes. What about Tavistock? Does he suspect?'

Newton laughed. 'He's clueless. Once I have the shipment and tie up some loose ends ...'

'He won't be best pleased. He'll pull out all the stops to find you.'

'The world's a big place when you have millions of pounds,' Newton said. 'Where I'm heading, he'll never find me.'

Tavistock phoned Barry.

'Yeah, Wayne?'

'I've had Toby on the phone. He's primed the bloke who owns the pub.'

'Do you want me to go round and have a word with him as well?'

'No,' Tavistock said. 'It's probably best if you stay away from the boozer. You just keep your eye on Toby. Once we have the shipment, Toby is going to sort out the landlord.'

'I thought I was doing that?'

'Pointless you doing it when Toby can take care of it for us. Once he's done that, you take care of Toby.'

'Ok. When's it happening?'

'Soon. I'll keep you informed.'

Barry hung up. His phone began to ring again.

'It's Michael.'

'What can I do for you, Michael?'

'Toby's been around. It's happening shortly.'

Barry smiled. 'Good. Keep your nerve. This time next month, it'll all be over.'

Isobelle sat at the bedside of Geoff, holding onto his hand as a young nurse entered.

'How is he?' Isobelle said.

The nurse smiled. 'He's had a comfortable night. No change from yesterday.'

'When will he be out of the coma?'

'I'm not sure. The doctor will decide that. We put him in an induced coma to protect his brain after the injury he sustained.'

'Will his brain ...? Will he be like he was before the accident?'

'It's hard to tell. We'll have to wait until he's out of the coma. But the doctor is reasonably happy at the moment.' The nurse smiled again, did some brief checks of the equipment, and left.

Isobelle gently squeezed Geoff's hand, bent forward, kissed his head, then left herself. She made her way along the corridor, but as she turned a corner, she spotted Brian and Elliott coming from the other direction. Isobelle darted into a toilet and waited until the unaware Brian and Elliott passed.

She paid the taxi driver, climbed out and stared up at the office with *Wright Investigations* emblazoned across the window. She paused, entered, and slowly climbed the stairs to the first floor. David Wright looked up from his desk as Isobelle entered the outer office.

He stood and made his way through. 'Mrs Frank?' he said.

'Isobelle.'

'Isobelle. Do you want to come through?' She followed him and sat in front of his desk as Wright sat opposite her. 'Can I get you a drink?'

'I'm fine, Mr Wright.'

'David. Now, Isobelle, what is it you would like me to do?'

She pulled out a piece of paper. 'I'd like you to investigate a gentleman called Toby Newton. This is his address.' She pushed the paper across to Wright.

'Can I ask why?'

'A friend of mine owns a pub in Whitby. *The Fallen Angel.*'

Wright scribbled on his notepad. 'And his name?'

'Michael Tate,' she said.

Wright smiled. 'I take it these two are connected?'

Isobelle nodded. 'We're worried—'

'We?' Wright said.

'I'm worried. I'm worried that Michael may be getting himself into trouble.'

'And you think this ...?' He glanced down at the paper. 'Toby Newton, may be leading him astray?'

'Yes.'

'Ok,' Wright said. 'I'll run some checks on him.' He appraised Isobelle. 'Is there something else?'

She forced a smile, pulled the letter from her bag and pushed it across the table to him. Wright read it.

'This Michael in the letter, is it—?'

'The same.'

Wright tapped the letter. 'And Geoff?'

'Geoff and I are an item. Geoff is currently in intensive care at James Cook hospital. He fell down a cliff in Whitby on the same night he was to meet Michael.'

'A fall?'

'The police think it was an accident.'

Wright sat back in his chair. 'I take it you don't?'

'No. I found the letter crumpled up on the floor in Geoff's house.'

'What's the connection between Michael and Geoff?'

She sighed. 'Geoff thinks he is Michael's dad.'

'I see. Ok.' Wright rubbed his chin. 'No witnesses to the fall?'

'None that I know of.'

'And Geoff? How is he?'

Isobelle rubbed her hands together. 'He's in an induced coma. They won't know if there's any permanent damage until he's brought out of that.'

Wright nodded. 'Leave it with me. I'll see what I can do.' He opened a drawer and pulled out a sheet of paper. 'This is a list of what I charge. Have a look, and see if it's ok.'

She took the paper from him. 'The cost will be fine.'

Wright offered his hand. 'I'll ring when I have any information. Hopefully, within a day or two.'

'Come on in,' Marion said to Brian and Elliott.

The pair of them followed her inside and into the living room. 'I'll just rustle up some tea.'

'Belle not in?' Brian said. Elliott nudged him.

Marion stopped at the threshold of the door. 'She left.'

'Left?' Brian said.

'Yeah. After our falling out, she ... I think that she's still angry with me, well us, for what happened to Geoff.'

Brian sighed. 'I see.'

'I feel responsible for digging into his past.' Elliott said.

'Yeah.' Marion held up a hand. 'Let me make the tea first.' She moved across to the kettle and flicked it on. Quickly gathering together mugs, biscuits, milk and sugar, she poured the boiling water into the teapot and joined the two men. 'She said we should never have poked our noses in Geoff's business.' Marion stirred the tea and replaced the lid.

'That's a little unfair,' Brian said. 'Geoff has deceived us all these years. We still don't know—'

Marion shrugged. 'I'm only telling you what she said.'

'What do you think?' Brian asked Elliott.

Elliott sighed. 'I spoke with Geoff the other night.'

'When?' Brian said.

Elliott looked upwards. 'The night he fell.'

Brian glanced at Marion and then stared at Elliott. 'Why didn't you tell me about this?'

Elliott rubbed his chin. 'It got quite heated.'

'Heated?' Marion said.

'Yes. He pretty much told me the same as Belle told you. He said I had no right digging into his past. He ordered me out. He was furious. I've never seen him so angry.'

'And you left?' Brian said.

'Of course I left.' Elliott rubbed his face. 'What if I am to blame for what happened to Geoff. What if he fell because …?'

'Because of what?' Marion said.

'What if he fell because he was preoccupied about what we discussed. Geoff knows the cliffs like the back of his hand. Or—'

'Or?' Brian said.

'What if he did something stupid?' Elliott lowered his head.

'No,' Marion said. She shook her head. 'He wouldn't do that.'

'I agree with Marion,' Brian said. 'Geoff's not the type.'

Elliott frowned. 'How do you, how do any of us know for certain? Geoff's not who he says he is. We have to accept that none of us knows him as well as we thought.'

'What do we do?' Marion said.

'Hope he pulls through, and then we beg forgiveness,' Elliott said.

'And his past?' Brian said.

'I think we forget about it,' Elliott said. 'Let sleeping dogs lie.'

Marion poured out the tea. 'I agree. I'm not sure if Belle will ever forgive us.'

'What about the semi-final?' Brian said.

'I've phoned the organizers and explained what happened,' Elliott said. 'They've postponed it for a month.'

'It's not the most important thing,' Marion said.

Elliott nodded. 'No, it isn't.'

CHAPTER TWENTY-TWO

One Week Later …
Isobelle held Geoff's hand as he opened his eyes. He glanced across at her, and then around the brightly lit room.

'Hello,' she said.

Geoff tried to speak. His mouth dry, he struggled with the words. She picked up a beaker from the side table and offered it to him, helping manoeuvre it into his mouth. He sucked at the mouthpiece and drank the lukewarm water.

'Where am I?' he croaked.

'Hospital,' she said softly.

He coughed a little. 'James Cook?'

'Yes. The high dependency unit.'

'How long …?'

'A week,' Isobelle said. 'Can you remember what happened?'

Geoff considered the question. He couldn't. He remembered being at home in his cottage, Elliott was there. Shouting and accusations, but little else. 'No. Not really. I remember Elliott coming to see me but after that … nothing.'

'What did Elliott want?'

Geoff shrugged. 'I can't remember.'

'Don't worry,' she said. 'It will come back.'

'How long will I have to stay here? I hate hospitals.'

Isobelle smiled and squeezed his hand. 'I don't know. But you have to get better first.' She frowned. 'You do know who I am?'

Geoff nodded. 'You're Belle. The love of my life.'

Isobelle hurried along the corridor and into the car park. She pulled the mobile from her bag and searched for the number of a taxi firm.

'Belle,' a voice from behind her said. She turned and looked at Marion. 'I thought it was you,' Marion said.

'Hello, Marion.'

'Have you been to see Geoff?'

'Just now.'

Marion forced an unconvincing smile. 'How is he?'

'He's conscious. He remembers me.' She laughed. 'Which is a good thing.'

'Elliott and Brian are visiting later.'

'Are they?' Isobelle said.

'Where are you off to?'

'I'm about to phone a taxi.' She held up the phone.

'I could drop you off. Where are you staying?'

'At my house.'

'Ah,' Marion said. 'We thought we hadn't seen you.'

Isobelle glanced away. 'I have an appointment in town. I should get going.'

'I'll drop you off.'

'No thanks. You go and see Geoff.'

Marion moved closer. 'Belle … I'm sorry.'

Isobelle turned her face away. 'It's ok. I shouldn't have said such hurtful things.'

'You were right, though. We've discussed it. Elliott and Brian are distraught over what's happened.'

Isobelle turned to face her friend. 'Why don't you pop into Middlesbrough when you've seen Geoff. We could have a coffee and a bite to eat.'

'I'd like that. What time?'

Isobelle glanced at her watch. 'One-thirty?'

Marion nodded. 'One-thirty.' She smiled at Isobelle and disappeared inside.

Isobelle sat in the office of Wright Investigations. David Wright entered and offered her a cup of tea before taking a seat behind his desk. He opened a notebook in front of him. 'I've done some background checks on Toby Newton.' Wright looked directly at Isobelle. 'He's not a nice man. He's got a lengthy criminal history going right back to when he was sixteen.'

'I see,' Isobelle said. 'What sort of crimes?'

'Mainly involving drugs. He's been in prison on two occasions. Both for dealing. He has a history of violence, too.'

'Oh, dear. What about Michael?'

'Michael doesn't have a criminal record. That's not to say he hasn't broken the law. He may have just evaded capture.'

'Michael has always seemed a decent man,' Isobelle said.

'It could be that he's just fallen into the wrong company. Has he mentioned any financial problems?'

'Geoff told me Michael's pub is struggling a bit.'

Wright laced his hands. 'Another problem. Toby Newton is an associate of someone called Wayne Tavistock. Have you heard of him?'

'No.'

'Tavistock is a different animal altogether. He has several clubs in Leeds and on the face of it, he seems quite legit. However, the consensus is that Tavistock deals drugs in a big way. He's been linked to large shipments of a new type of ecstasy arriving from the continent.'

'I can't believe Michael is involved—'

'Isobelle,' Wright said. 'You'd be surprised at who's involved in this type of stuff. Where there are huge amounts of money to be made, people take risks.'

'Why would this …?'

'Tavistock,' Wright said.

'Why would this Tavistock be interested in a small place like Whitby? Surely he would operate in the big cities?'

'Whitby is on the coast,' Wright said. 'The drugs have to come into this country somehow. Where better?'

'What are you going to do?'

'I can't let this go, Isobelle. You realise that?' She nodded, and he continued. 'We're talking about major crime here.'

'Michael could be Geoff's son,' she said.

Wright sipped his tea. 'Yeah, you said. That complicates things.'

'Geoff is still recovering in hospital. What do I tell him?'

Wright steepled his fingers. 'I could speak to Michael.'

'Will that help?'

'He may only be a bit player in this. If he could help the police with information …'

'Wouldn't that be incredibly dangerous?'

'No more dangerous than climbing into bed with this lot.' He tapped at his notepad.

'Yes, I suppose.'

'Did Geoff tell you anything about his fall?'

'No. He couldn't remember. He remembered Elliott coming round to his house, and they had a fallout.'

'Elliott?'

She sighed. 'Elliott is a friend of ours.'

'What did they argue about?'

'I don't know. I haven't spoken with Elliott.'

'You don't think …?'

'No, no. Elliott would never hurt Geoff.'

'If I had a pound for every time I'd heard that,' Wright said, 'I'd be a rich man.'

Isobelle glared at him. 'Elliott is one of the gentlest men I know. He would never—'

Wright held up his hand. 'Ok. Maybe you need to talk to Elliott?'

'Maybe I do.'

Wright leant back in his chair. 'I'll have a chat with Michael. Maybe I can get him to see sense.'

'Ok.'

Wright handed Isobelle an envelope. 'The invoice you asked for.'

'Thanks.' The pair shook hands, and Isosbelle left.

Isobelle entered the coffee shop and scanned the room. Marion sat in a corner staring at her drink. She made her way over to the counter and waved at her friend as Marion looked up and meekly waved back. Once served, Isobelle joined her and slid onto the seat opposite.

'Hello.' Marion said.

'Hi,' Isobelle said. 'How was Geoff when you went to see him?'

'Good. He still has a way to go, but he chatted with me.'

Isobelle laughed. 'I know it's not the most important thing to think about, but a thought popped into my head this morning ...' Marion smiled, and Isobelle continued. '... The quiz.'

Marion smiled again. 'No, you're right. It's not the most important thing at the moment.' Marion sipped at her coffee. 'Elliott phoned the organisers. They've postponed it until next month. Maybe we should cancel it altogether?'

'Leave it for the moment. You never know.'

'Listen, Belle—'

Isobelle took hold of her friend's hand. 'I really am sorry for the hurtful things I said.'

'Stop apologising, you were right. We shouldn't have interfered. Elliott and Brian—'

'It wasn't their fault,' Isobelle said.

'Did Geoff mention anything about the fall when you visited him?'

Isobelle shook her head. 'He said he couldn't remember anything about it. Geoff told me he quarrelled with Elliott on the night he fell.'

Marion's eye's widened. 'I know Elliott went to see him on the night of ...' She coughed. 'But surely ...?'

'He had just woken up,' Isobelle said.

'Do you want me to speak to Elliott?'

Isobelle sipped her drink. 'No. I'm sure he had nothing to do with it. The police say it was an accident. It probably was.'

Marion looked down at her empty cup. 'Have you moved back to Middlesbrough for good?'

'Only while Geoff is in hospital,' Isobelle said. 'I'm selling my house. Being here allowed me to titivate it up again. Having said that, the previous occupants have left it in good order.'

'Yes, you said. Have you thought where you'll live when it sells?'

Isobelle stared directly at her friend. 'With Geoff. I don't know where yet, but we've seen a house that we could renovate together in Whitby. I'll discuss it with him when he's better.'

'Whitby?'

Isobelle shrugged. 'Yes, it's certainly a place that's hard to leave.'

Marion nodded. 'What are you doing for the rest of the day?'

Isobelle drained her cup. 'I thought I'd have a walk around the shops, and revisit Geoff later.'

'Do you want some company? I haven't much on. I could take you to the hospital?'

Isobelle smiled. 'Yeah. I'd like that.'

Michael put the last of the mixers into the fridge and stood.

'Michael?' a voice said.

He turned around. 'Yes.'

'David Wright,' he said, and offered his hand.

'Hello, David.'

'Can I have a private word?'

Michael narrowed his eyes. 'What about?'

Wright surveyed the bar area. 'It would be better in private. It's for your benefit.'

Michael rubbed his chin. 'Ok. We'll talk in the back.' He looked over at the barmaid serving a customer. 'Look after the bar for ten minutes. I've got a bit of business.' She gave a thumbs up.

Michael moved to the opposite end of the bar and lifted the hatch. 'Come through.'

Wright followed Michael through into the back. 'Have a seat,' Michael said, closed the door and sat opposite Wright. 'How can I help you?'

'Toby Newton?' Wright said.

Michael shrugged. 'Never heard of him.'

Wright smiled. 'If we're going to treat each other like idiots, Michael, this isn't going to work. I know Toby Newton, and, I know you know him.'

'Who are you?'

Wright pulled a card from the top pocket of his jacket and pushed it across the table.

Michael studied it, then looked at Wright. 'Yeah, I know Newton. What about him?'

'He's bad news. He has a string of criminal offences to his name. Are you aware of that?'

Michael puffed out his cheeks. 'I wasn't, but I sort of guessed he's no choir boy.'

'How did you get to know him?'

'A friend of mine from Leeds suggested he could help me out.' Michael rubbed at his temple. 'The pub is struggling. Alex, my mate from

Leeds, suggested I give Toby a ring. He said he wanted to invest in a boozer in Whitby.'

'And?'

'He supplied some cheap spirits. No questions asked. It helped a little, but not enough.'

'Then he asked you to supply other pubs?'

Michael put his hands over his face and slowly pulled them down. 'I don't want to get the others in trouble.'

'Others?'

'Friends who run the other pubs. They didn't know. They just thought I was doing them a favour. Most of them are tied to breweries. Let's just say, the profit margin is extremely low. It helped them out a bit.'

'I'm surprised you're telling me all this, Michael.'

Michael glanced at the card. 'Mr Wright, I don't want to get into any bother. I wish I'd never met Toby Newton.'

'So what happened?'

'I said I wanted out, but he threatened me. Said he'd burn down the pub. I checked with my friend, Alex. He dug around a bit and discovered that Toby works for someone called—'

'Wayne Tavistock?'

'Yeah. Apparently, he's a nasty piece of work.' Michael smiled ruefully. 'Alex was all apologetic. Said he didn't mean to drop me in it.'

'Do you believe him?'

Michael shrugged. 'I don't know.' He stared Wright in the eyes. 'All I want, Mr Wright, is a quiet life. One stupid mistake …'

Wright nodded. 'Geoff.'

'Geoff Brown?'

'Yeah.'

'What about him?'

'He's currently in hospital after a tumble down a cliff.'

Michael stood. 'Now listen. I didn't have anything to do with that. The police say—'

'I know what the police say.' Wright indicated for him to sit again. 'He's your dad?'

Michael slumped back onto the seat. 'That's what he told me.'

'So,' Wright said, lacing his fingers. 'What happened on the night of his fall?'

Michael sighed. 'Belle, Geoff's girlfriend, left a letter at the pub asking me to meet him. I went to his house. When he told me …' Michael briefly looked upwards. 'When he confessed, I was dumbstruck. I asked him how he could leave me, and my mum. How …' Michael shrugged. 'It got a bit heated. I stormed out. Geoff came racing after me. He tried to placate me, but I told him to get stuffed. I was so mad. Then I left him. I swear,' Michael said, 'when we parted, he was fine.'

'How far were you from where he fell?'

'A couple of hundred metres.'

'What did you do?'

'I walked so far and stopped.' He half-laughed. 'I'd cooled down a bit. I thought about what Geoff told me. So after a while, maybe twenty minutes, I decided to go back and talk to him again.'

'And?'

'The next thing I know, all hell breaks loose. Ambulances and police everywhere. When I got to the top of the cliff near Geoff's house, some of his friends were there. That's when I heard he'd fallen.'

'Ok, Michael. I believe you.'

'Mr Wright—'

'David,' Wright said. 'Let's keep it personal.'

'David. Are you going to go to the police?'

'Depends,' Wright said.

'On what?'

'What does Newton want you to do?'

Michael briefly covered his eyes again. 'They're bringing drugs over from the continent. He wants me to collect them and deliver the consignment somewhere. I haven't spoken to Tavistock. Toby Newton—'

'We will need to involve the police.'

'I'm going to go to prison for this, aren't I?'

Wright smiled. 'We'll forget about the knock-off spirits, that's small fry. But some of my ex-colleagues, in the force, would be extremely happy to collar Tavistock.' Wright stood. 'Leave it with me. We may be able to keep you this side of the prison walls, Michael. If you assist us.'

Michael nodded. 'I will.'

'Don't tell anyone. Especially our friend, Toby Newton.'

'I won't.'

'I'll be in touch.'

Michael showed Wright back into the bar. Wright thanked him again, then left. Michael rubbed his chin. What about Barry, he thought. Should he go after Wright and tell him? Michael looked upwards and blew out hard. No. It was complicated enough. If the police caught Barry, all the better.

Toby Newton watched Wright leave from his vantage point in the corner and slowly sipped his drink. Michael snatched up a glass from behind the counter and pushed it under an optic.

'Michael,' Newton said.

Michael turned with the drink in his hand. 'Toby? You never said you were coming by.'

'I was just passing and wanted a chat.'

'Yeah, no problem.'

Newton slid his empty glass towards him. 'I'll have one of those. Make it a large one.'

Michael pushed Newton's glass under the optic and handed him the drink.

'Everything all right, Michael?' Newton said. 'You seem a bit on edge.'

'I'm good.'

Newton nodded towards the door. 'Who's that bloke?'

'Bloke?'

'The one you had in the back.'

'Oh, him. A private detective.'

Toby narrowed his eyes. 'A private detective?'

Michael moved a little closer. 'He's investigating Geoff's fall.'

'Geoff?'

'He's a customer who comes in here. He fell from the cliff, and that bloke doesn't believe it was an accident.'

Newton held up his glass. 'Maybe we should have these in the back.'

Michael opened the flap at the end of the bar and beckoned Newton inside. The pair made their way into the rear room, and Michael closed the door.

'Why ask you?' Newton said. 'About this fella falling?'

Michael slumped onto a seat. 'He reckons he's my dad.'

'Who?'

'Geoff. He left a letter at the pub the other day asking me to go around to his house. He said he knows who my dad is.'

'I thought your old man died in prison?'

'Mick wasn't my real dad.'

Newton sipped his drink. 'Go on.'

'I went around to his cottage, and he said he's my dad. I didn't believe him, we argued, and I stormed out. Geoff followed me. We argued some more, and then I left. I swear he was ok when I left him.'

'And this detective thinks you pushed him?'

Michael shrugged. 'Yeah, I suppose.'

'Who's paying him?'

'I don't know. He never said. One of Geoff's mates, probably.'

Newton narrowed his eyes. 'I wouldn't worry, mate. He can't prove anything. If you need an alibi …'

Michael stood. 'He can't prove anything because I didn't do anything.'

Newton moved closer. 'Listen, Michael. I don't care about all this shit. I just want your head in the right place for next Wednesday.'

'Wednesday?'

'Yeah. That's when the shipment's coming in.'

Michael slumped back onto his seat. 'Ok.'

Newton drained his glass. He pushed his hand into his pocket, pulled out a set of keys and an envelope then tossed them onto the table in front of Michael. 'The keys are for a van. Inside the envelope is the address of where you collect it from. You drive it to an address in Leeds and drop it off. Then catch a train back here.'

'What about the shipment?'

'Phone me after you collect the van, and I'll tell you where to go to pick it up.'

'Ok.'

Newton edged closer and lowered his head. 'Make sure you get this right, Michael. The people I'm working for don't take kindly if you mess-up,'

'I won't mess-up,' Michael said.

'Good, because …' Newton glanced around. '… it would be a shame if this place ended up in ashes, especially with you inside.' He grinned at Michael and left.

Michael sucked in air, downed the rest of his drink, and covered his face with his hands.

CHAPTER TWENTY-THREE

Isobelle woke early and made herself a light breakfast before showering and changing. She stared out the window with a cup of tea in her hand as her mobile rang.

'Hi, David,' she said.

'I spoke to Michael yesterday.'

'And?'

'He's being pressurised by our friend Toby Newton to collect and deliver something.'

'What?'

'Well, we didn't discuss that. But I can hazard a guess. Something involving drugs.'

Isobelle sucked in air. 'Will Michael get into trouble over this? I haven't told Geoff anything yet.'

'Michael has agreed to help the police. Newton works for a man called Wayne Tavistock. Tavistock is heavily involved in drugs, but the police have never been able to pin anything on him.'

'Will that help Michael?' Isobelle said.

'I'll lay it on thick with my friend. Hopefully, Michael will avoid prison. I can't promise anything, though.'

'Did Michael say anything about Geoff?'

'He said he went around to see him. Geoff told him he's his dad. Michael and Geoff had heated words, and he stormed off. Geoff came after him, but Michael swears he was fine when he left.'

'So, it could have been an accident?'

'Looks that way. Has Geoff said anything else?'

Isobelle sighed. 'He only remembers Elliott coming to see him.'

'You did say he and Elliott quarrelled?'

'Elliott is a good friend of his,' Isobelle said. 'I'm sure—'

'Things do happen, Isobelle. Believe me. I saw all manner of things in the force.'

'I'm visiting Geoff later today. I'll ask him if he remembers anything else.'

'Is there anyone you can think of that may have harmed Geoff?'

Isobelle thought about Barry. How could she explain him to Wright? That would open up a huge can of worms. 'Er, no,' she said. 'Geoff is well-liked.'

'Good,' Wright said. 'I'll phone later and let you know how I get on with my ex-colleague.'

'Thanks.' Isobelle hung up and pondered. There's no way Elliott would harm Geoff. Not on purpose. Maybe it was *just an accident.* She glanced at the clock, stood, drank the last of her tea, and headed out.

'Isobelle,' Elliott shouted, as she made her way along the hospital corridor.

She stopped and turned to face him. 'How are you?' he said.

'I'm well. Where's Brian?'

'He's just popped to the shop. Geoff wanted something to read.'

'I brought him some magazines last time I visited.'

'I think he's read them,' Elliott said. 'The time drags when you're in the hospital.'

'Can I ask you something?' she said. Elliott nodded. 'The night Geoff fell … you two argued?'

Elliott looked towards the floor. 'It was stupid, really. About his past.'

'What about his past?'

Elliott rubbed his chin. 'This isn't the time or place, Belle.'

'So,' Isobelle said. 'After this argument …?'

'I left. Well, if I'm honest, Geoff asked me to leave.'

'Did you see anyone else as you left?'

'No.'

'What time did you leave?'

Elliott furrowed his brow. 'You don't think I …?'

Isobelle patted his arm. 'Of course not. But Geoff can't remember what happened.'

'About eight o'clock.'

Isobelle nodded. 'Ok.'

'Do you know something?' Elliott said.

'Not really. Listen, I should go. Geoff will be wondering where I am.'

'Are you coming over to Whitby any time soon? We can have a proper chat. Brian and Marion too.'

'Maybe.' She forced a smile, turned, and hurried off.

Elliott rubbed his chin as he watched her disappear.

Michael lifted the glass and studied the contents before tasting it. Satisfied, he clipped the beer name badge onto the front of the pump. His mobile sounded.

'David,' Michael said.

'Can we meet up?' Wright said.

'Yeah.' Michael wandered into the back and closed the door. 'Toby Newton came around here yesterday.'

'Ok. What did he say?'

'He gave me an envelope with keys to a van I have to pick up.'

'Has he told you where you're picking up the consignment?' Wright said.

'No. He said he'd tell me that later.'

'I've got an ex-colleague of mine involved. He'd be delighted if he could nail Tavistock. With your help, we can.'

'I'm worried he'll know I grassed him up.'

'I'll discuss that with you later. If we do this right, he won't suspect.'

'Ok,' Michael said. 'Newton saw you here the other day.'

'What did you tell him?'

'That you're investigating Geoff's fall. I think he believed me.'

'Let me know if he mentions me again,' Wright said. 'We need to meet up. My copper mate needs to see you.'

'I'm going to the cash and carry. It has a little café, we could meet up there.'

'Text me the postcode,' Wright said.

Michael walked into the cash and carry. Spotting Wright, with another man, sat in the café, he headed over to them.

The two men stood. 'Michael,' Wright said. 'This is DI Declan O'Hare.'

Michael shook hands with the officer and sat, as the other two men resumed their seats.

O'Hare glanced at Wright. 'David has filled me in on most of your problems,' he said. 'Now, we just have to get you out of this somehow and spare you a prison sentence.'

'This is all a bit much for me, Declan,' Michael said. 'I never—'

'I know,' O'Hare said. 'But you're involved now. Look ...' He leant in closer. 'If we play this right, Tavistock and your friend, Toby Newton, will end up behind bars. And you'll still have your pub and nobody but us will ever know.'

Michael sighed. 'Ok. What do you want me to do?'

'Collect the van and follow Newton's instructions. Once you know the location of the collection, you relay it to me.'

'I can do that.'

'Then,' O'Hare said. 'We're going to let you travel on to Leeds.'

'Where I drop off the load?'

O'Hare smiled. 'Where you drop off the load.'

Michael groaned. 'But he'll know I grassed if everyone else is arrested except me.'

'This is where David comes in,' O'Hare said. 'I suspect the drugs will be taken on somewhere. I don't suppose Wayne Tavistock will be there himself to meet you. You leave the goods and then come back home. David will be waiting close by. He'll be your alibi.'

Michael looked at Wright. 'Alibi?' Michael said.

Wright nodded. 'Declan and I have discussed it. You'll need an alibi. If Newton tells the police you were driving the van, I'll tell them you were with me. They will just assume you got a mate to vouch for you.'

'I suppose.' Michael shrugged.

'What you have to do ...' O'Hare said. ' ... is make sure you wear gloves and don't leave anything inside the van that can link you to it. We won't investigate too vigourosly. I'll see to that. Just enough to convince Newton and Tavistock that you didn't inform.'

'Ok,' Michael said.

'Do you have a date?' O'Hare said.

'Next Wednesday.'

O'Hare looked at Wright. 'That doesn't give us much time,' O'Hare said. 'I'll get the wheels in motion.'

'What now?' Michael said.

O'Hare looked at him. 'You go home and wait for the call.'

Geoff smiled at Isobelle as she entered the room. 'Did you get me one?' he said.

'One BLT,' she said, and popped the bag on his bed. 'I got you a chocolate bar as well.'

Geoff waved her closer and planted a kiss on her lips. 'You're a smasher, Belle.'

'Has the doctor been?'

'You just missed him.'

'What did he say?'

Geoff opened the packet and pulled out the sandwich. 'He said I may be able to go home next week. He's worried I won't be able to manage on my own. With my broken leg and that.'

'Did you tell him you've got me to look after you?'

Geoff smiled. 'I didn't like to presume. I wasn't sure you wanted a cripple hanging around.'

Isobelle took hold of his hand. 'Don't be stupid.'

'How's Freddie? I'm really missing him.'

'He's fine. Pip and him are getting along great.'

He thoughtfully chewed a piece of sandwich. 'I remembered more.'

Isobelle gently squeezed his hand. 'What?'

'I argued with Michael.' Geoff put down his sandwich and rubbed at his temple. 'He left my cottage, and I followed him outside. He wouldn't listen to me, though.' Geoff gasped and covered his eyes with his hand.

'It's all right, Geoff. Don't upset yourself.'

'I raced after him, but he was so mad. I …'

'Are you saying …?'

Geoff stared tearfully at Isobelle. 'I don't know. I can't remember anymore. Michael wouldn't have … Would he?'

Isobelle squeezed his hand again. 'No. I don't think so.'

'Why hasn't he been, Bellc?'

'I don't know. It must have come as a great shock to him.'

Geoff fixed Isobelle with a stare. 'Don't tell anyone else,' he said. 'I don't want Michael getting into trouble.'

'I won't.'

'Promise me,' he said. 'Promise me you won't tell anyone. Not Brian, not Marion, not Elliott.'

She leant forward and kissed him. 'I won't. I promise.'

Isobelle exited the hospital and took out her mobile. Quickly locating David Wright's number, she phoned him.

'Hi, Isobelle,' he said. 'I was just about to ring you.'

'I've been to see Geoff.'

'How is he?'

'He's doing well. He remembered a bit more about the night he fell. He said he and Michael argued, and Michael stormed off. He followed him outside near the cliffs. After Elliott left.'

'That clears Elliott, then. What Geoff told you coincides with what Michael said. But he maintains Geoff was fine when he left.'

'I got the impression Geoff thought Michael had pushed him. He doesn't want him getting into trouble, though.'

'I understand that,' Wright said. 'We'll keep this between ourselves.'

'Thanks, David. What about Michael and Toby Newton?'

'I met up with Michael and an ex-colleague of mine. He wants Michael to do what Newton tells him. He's hoping to collar Newton and his boss, Tavistock.'

Isobelle sucked in air. 'Isn't that dangerous?'

'It is, but it will get Michael off the hook.'

'When is this happening?'

'Next Wednesday night,' Wright said.

'Will you keep me informed?'

'Of course. I don't need to tell you how delicate this is, Isobelle, so please keep this to yourself.'

'I will.' Isobelle rang off and pondered. The guilt in keeping this from Geoff was awful, and if he discovered she knew? She gave her head a mental shake. 'It's for the best,' she whispered to herself.

CHAPTER TWENTY-FOUR

Isobelle sat back in her seat and looked at the others opposite her.

'This Barry,' Elliott said. 'Have you seen him since?'

She shook her head. 'Not since Geoff's fall.'

'The private detective you've employed,' Brian said. 'You haven't told him about Barry?'

'No,' Isobelle said. 'How could I? He'd want to know why he might try to kill Geoff.'

Marion nodded. 'Belle's right. We don't want him looking into Geoff's past.'

'Geoff's still not certain what happened,' Isobelle said. 'Maybe he did fall.'

Elliott rubbed his beard. 'Barry would have a good reason to push Geoff. If he did try to kill him, he might have panicked and left town.'

'Hopefully, he has,' Brian said. 'He will know that Geoff's alive.'

'But,' Elliott said, 'he'll know that Geoff wouldn't dare tell the police.'

'Let's hope he has gone,' Marion said.

'What about Michael?' Elliott said.

Brian leant forward. 'And this Newton. How's Michael going to …?'

Isobelle sighed. 'Michael is assisting the police. If everything goes well, he'll be off the hook.'

'Does Geoff know about Michael?' Elliott said.

'No,' Isobelle said. 'And I don't want him knowing, not yet. He's still not fully recovered. He has enough on his plate without worrying about Michael.'

Wednesday …

Michael checked the clock for the umpteenth time. The minutes crawled past with snail-pace monotony.

One of the bar staff hurried into the pub, hung up her coat and joined him behind the bar. 'Sorry I'm late.' She looked about. 'You've been busy,' she said.

'I didn't sleep very well.'

'You haven't left me much to do.' She glanced around the pristine bar area. 'You've even stocked up the fridges.'

Michael grunted. 'Yeah.'

'Do you want a cuppa, then?'

He checked the clock. 'No. I think I might go for a walk.' She frowned. 'You ok on your own?' he said.

'Yeah.'

'You're still ok for tonight?'

'God, yeah. A double shift. I'm desperate for the money.'

'Good.' Michael grabbed hold of his coat. 'I won't be too long.'

Marion's car trundled up the lane and drew to a halt outside Geoff's cottage.

Geoff stared outside at the building. 'Where's Freddie?'

'At mine,' Marion said. 'I'll go and fetch him when we get you inside.'

Isobelle took hold of his hand as Geoff continued to stare outside. 'You ok?' she said.

'Yeah. It seems as if it's been months since I was here.'

'Well,' she said, and squeezed his hand. 'Let's get you settled.'

The two women assisted Geoff out of the vehicle. Supporting him, they led him up the path and into the cottage.

Geoff slumped onto his favourite armchair with a groan. 'Stick the kettle on, Marion,' he said. 'I haven't had a decent cup of tea in ages.'

Marion laughed. 'Right you are,' she said over her shoulder as she disappeared into the kitchen.

Geoff surveyed the room. 'It's good to be home.'

Isobelle smiled. 'We'll have this tea, and then I'll fetch Freddie.'

'I've missed the little fella. He probably thinks I've deserted him.'

'According to Marion, he's had a great time with Pip. Like a little doggie holiday.'

'Anything from Michael?'

Isobelle glanced towards the door. 'I'll tell you later.'

Marion came in with a tray. 'Brian and Elliott are coming to see you later,' she said. 'If you feel up to it?'

'Yeah. That'll be good.'

Marion sat. 'Jason sends his love.' She poured the tea into the mugs. 'Do you want me to go for Freddie?'

'Have your tea first. Belle said he's had a whale of a time.'

'He and Pip get on well together, but I still think he's missed you.'

Michael looked into the distance at Geoff's cottage. He steeled himself, then headed towards it. His phone rang, and Michael stopped.

'Toby,' he said.

'All set?' Newton said.

'I'm as ready as I'll ever be.'

'I'm texting you the location of the pick-up. Get there at two in the morning.'

Michael sighed. 'Two?'

'Don't mess this up, Michael.'

'Don't worry, I'll do my part.'

'Good. When you've got the gear phone me, and I'll text you the address I want you to deliver it to.'

Michael hung up and searched his contacts.

'Hi, Michael,' O'Hare said.

'Toby's sending me the location of the pick-up. I have to be there at two in the morning.'

'Good,' O'hare said. 'I'll put the wheels in motion. How are you feeling?'

'Nervous.'

'Just do as Newton says. We'll be close at hand. No mention of the drop off address yet?'

'No. He wants me to text him when I have the gear.'

'Ok. Keep me informed. There's obviously no need to remind you—'

'Not to tell anyone else.'

'Yeah,' O'hare said.

'I won't.'

'Don't forget the tracker. Place it somewhere out of sight.'

Michael sighed. 'I won't forget.' Michael hung up and stared at Geoff's cottage. He pushed the mobile into his pocket, turned around, and headed back to the pub.

Toby Newton slipped the gun into his pocket and started the engine. Putting the car in gear, he sped away as Barry, parked some way from him, followed at a discreet distance.

CHAPTER TWENTY-FIVE

Michael pulled his car up on the industrial estate and stared across at the black van parked a short distance away. He fumbled in his pocket and, removing a crumpled piece of paper, checked the licence plate number written on it. It matched the vehicle. He climbed from his car and made his way across to the van. Pausing at the passenger side, he dropped to his knees and snatched up the keys hidden behind the wheel. He stood and surveyed the area as he made his way around to the driver's side. Satisfied no one was about, he opened the door and jumped in. Michael sighed loudly, took out his phone and texted. *'I've collected the van.'* He waited for the reply. *'Good,'* O'Hare texted back. *'Don't forget the tracker.'* Pushing his phone into his pocket, he pulled out a small, black device. Bending low, so as to see beneath the passenger seat, he placed the device against the frame of the chair. It clanged with a low metallic sound as it magnetically stuck. Pulling his mobile from his pocket, he placed it on the dashboard. He rolled up his trouser leg and felt for the second mobile strapped to his ankle. Taking in a lungful of air, he lowered his trouser leg to cover the phone, sat up straight, started the engine and headed off.

Isobelle locked the front door of Geoff's cottage and joined him in the front room. She picked up a bottle of wine and held it up for Geoff to see. 'Nightcap?' she said.

Geoff grinned and patted his dog. 'I'd love one. Can you get Freddie one of his chews?'

She disappeared into the kitchen, returning moments later with two glasses and a dog chew. 'Here you are, Freddie,' she said, tossing the dog his treat. She slumped onto the seat next to Geoff and handed him the glass. 'Cheers,' she said, and clinked her glass with his.

'You were going to tell me something about Michael?' he said.

Isobelle took a long, thoughtful drink from her glass and turned to face him. 'You won't be mad at me, will you?'

'Mad? Why would I be mad?'

Isobelle put down her drink. 'Michael is assisting the police.'
'Assisting—?'
Isobelle sighed, loudly. 'I'll start at the beginning ...'

Geoff stared towards the floor, and Isobelle took hold of his hand. 'You're not angry with me, are you?'
Geoff shook his head. 'No. I'm just worried.'
'David Wright said he'll be fine. They're determined to catch this drug dealer.'
'When is it happening?'
'Early morning, I think.'
'Do any of the others know?' he said.
Isobelle forced a smile. 'I didn't want to worry you. I've told the others most of it.'
'What did they say?'
'They're fine with it, Geoff. They're your friends. When this is over, you can tell them the full story.'
Geoff nodded. 'I wish I'd spoken with Michael.'
Isobelle shuffled on her seat. 'David Wright is certain Michael had nothing to do with your fall.' She squeezed his hand again. 'Have you remembered anything else?'
Geoff rubbed at his temples. 'Not really. I just have this ... It's hard to explain. A feeling of being pushed.'
'You're sure?'
'Yeah,' he said. 'I couldn't tell you who did it. I just have this ... I can't really describe the feeling.' He furrowed his brow. 'Someone was there with me when I fell. I'm certain.'
Isobelle stared into his eyes. 'If it wasn't Michael ...?'
'Who?' Geoff huffed. 'Barry?'
'Yeah,' Isobelle said. 'It could be?'

Michael parked the van on a rough piece of land overlooking a deserted stretch of beach. He turned off the engine, switched off the lights and waited. He checked his phone for any messages, but there were none. A slow twenty-minutes crawled past as Michael sat nervously waiting. His phoned pinged with a text from O'Hare. *'There's a boat heading your way,'* it said.
Michael stiffened in his seat and strained his eyes across the beach. He spotted it. Bobbing up and down on the choppy water, it edged its way towards the shore. Jumping from his seat, he headed down the slope and across the sand. He glanced around the beach, but nothing stirred. Hardly a breeze upset the stillness of the night. The large rubber dinghy moved closer and, bouncing over the break of the waves, slid to a halt on the sand. Two men quickly jumped from the vessel and

beckoned to Michael. He strode towards them, carefully avoiding the water.

'Michael?' one of the men said. Michael nodded. The three men hauled the boat further up the beach, and free from the water's clutches.

'Quickly,' the man said. 'Help us.'

'The van's at the top.' Michael turned and pointed up the slope.

Michael slammed the back of the van shut, headed around to the front, and climbed in. He watched for a few moments as the men pushed the boat back into the water, and slowly edged their way seawards. He took out his phone and texted Newton. *'I have the cargo.'* His phone pinged back with an address. Michael studied it for a second or two, then texted O'Hare. Slamming the van into reverse, he backed away from the edge, performed a quick turn and trundled off.

Michael glanced across at his phone as it pinged. He studied the message from Toby Newton – a postcode. He programmed the satnav on his phone and set off again, finally coming to a stop in a layby opposite an industrial estate. He peered into the darkness as someone, wearing a parka, walked towards the van and jumped inside. Newton pulled down his hood and stared at Michael.

'Toby?'

'Where is it?' Newton said.

'In the back.'

Newton growled. 'Not the drugs, the tracker.'

'What are you—?'

Newton pulled a gun from his pocket and thrust it into the side of Michael. 'I'll ask you one more time. I know you've been talking to the police. That private detective I saw leaving the pub, he's an ex-copper. Not just any ex-copper. One who worked in the drug squad. So I'll ask you one more time ... Where is it?'

Michael's shoulders slumped. 'Under the seat.'

Newton felt underneath and snatched up the tracker. 'I should put a bullet in you now.' He lowered the window and tossed the little, black box outside. 'Drive.'

'Where?'

'Towards Robin Hood's Bay.'

'I thought we were—?'

Newton nudged him with the muzzle of the gun. 'Change of plan. I'm keeping our little consignment for myself. I've already got a buyer.'

'What about Tavistock?'

'Who gives a shit? He thinks you're taking the van up to Leeds. When it doesn't reach there, he'll come looking for you.'

'Listen, Toby—'

Newton groaned. 'One more word, Michael. One more word, and I'll spill your guts all over this van.' Newton snatched up Michael's mobile and tossed it out of the vehicle.

They travelled on, as Newton gave instructions until they turned off the main road and headed along a narrow track. Michael gripped the steering wheel as the lane opened up into a derelict farmyard. An old, abandoned brick building loomed in front of them. It's roof, and half the walls, missing. Michael pulled up next to another van.

Newton nudged him in the side. 'Get out.' Michael obeyed, and climbed from the driver's seat.

Newton motioned towards the other vehicle with his gun. 'Empty the contents from your van into the other.'

Michael opened the back of both vans and began to load the cargo from one to the other.

Newton took out a cigarette, lit it, and took in a deep draw. 'Hurry up,' he said. 'I don't know who else you've told.'

'It would take less time if you helped,' Michael said.

Newton laughed. 'Just put your back into it.'

He continued his task until he held the last box in his hand. 'What are you going to do with me?' he said, as he paused at the van door.

Newton glanced around and waved his gun. 'Come on, get the box inside. Stop asking questions.'

Michael slid the last box into the van, slammed the door shut, and turned to face Newton.

'Big mistake,' Newton said. 'You should never have involved the coppers.' He stepped closer. 'Big, big mistake.' Newton levelled his gun but turned his head as the sound of a vehicle approaching caught his attention. Michael, grasping his opportunity as Newton was momentarily distracted, fled.

Newton jumped into the van and started the engine. The wheels screeched and skidded on the loose gravel, covering the ground, before he gained traction and roared off after his quarry. Michael turned as the sound of the approaching vehicle neared. Sensing what Newton intended he dived to his left, but the van wing clipped him hard and he was thrown violently into the undergrowth. The vehicle skidded to a stop. Newton got out as Michael pulled his body further into the long grass, trying desperately to evade his pursuer. A second van arrived, and a man jumped out.

'Where the hell have you been?' Newton narrowed his eyes at Barry. 'Where's Jimmy?'

Barry moved closer. 'Car problems. He asked me to do the pick-up.' He nodded at the vehicle Michael had loaded. 'Is it in the back?'

Newton grunted. 'Yeah. The money?'

Barry tossed a set of keys to Newton. 'It's all there.'

Barry watched as Newton opened the back of the van and pulled out a holdall. Unzipping the bag, he viewed it's contents and grinned.

'Is there a problem?' Barry said, as Newton looked away.

Newton nodded towards the grass. 'A loose end to tie up.'

Michael watched from a distance but ducked down as Newton scanned the area Michael had disappeared into.

Newton pulled his gun from his pocket and moved into the grass. 'I have a bit of business to deal with,' he muttered to himself. He wandered further into the long grass as Barry felt inside his jacket for his own weapon.

Newton surveyed the terrain, trying to catch sight of his prey and tiptoed forward. Michael had manoeuvred himself further away from Newton. He now found himself at the edge of a high embankment that sloped steeply down towards the beach before dropping sharply. He glanced back, the form of his pursuer edging ever closer.

'It's pointless trying to hide, Michael. Why drag this out?'

Michael glanced about for a weapon. A piece of wood, a house-brick, anything.

'There's no escape, Michael. You either come back this way or go over the edge.' Newton laughed. 'Maybe that's what should happen. Take a tumble like your friend.'

Michael grimaced, as pain shot down his left leg. He tentatively probed the area. His leg was definitely broken. The bone protruded through his trouser leg, and blood soaked the surrounding area.

'Come on, I haven't got all night, Michael,' Newton said. 'If you show yourself now, I promise I won't kill you.'

Michael groaned as another searing pain traversed his leg.

'Let's not be silly,' Newton said.

Michael rolled further away and felt his body slip from under him as he held on to the edge. He clung to an old tree stump, the only thing preventing him from tumbling downwards. He wanted to scream, the pain unbelievable.

Newton reached him and grinned. 'There you are.' He placed his gun down on a large rock. 'No need for guns. It would only alert someone.'

Barry joined Newton, his gun concealed in his jacket pocket. 'Who's this then?' he said.

'That loose end I spoke about.'

Michael grimaced again and glanced down towards the beach below and then back at Newton. 'What now?'

'You shouldn't have involved the police,' Newton said.

'They'll catch up with you.'

Newton laughed. 'Not where I'm going. I'll leave some incriminating evidence in the van so that they collar Tavistock.'

'Why double-cross him? Wasn't he paying you enough?'

Newton edged closer. ‘He had a friend of mine killed.’ Newton tilted his head and smiled. ‘I was just going to let you take the rap, but—’

‘The police know all about you.’

Newton laughed again. ‘We’ll see.’ He edged closer and stopped a foot away from Michael. ‘You’re struggling to hang on there, mate.’ Newton peered over the edge. ‘Looks like your leg’s in a bit of a mess too. It would be the decent thing to do. Put you out of your misery, like a dog.’

‘Yeah, well. Do your worst, you bastard.’

Newton lifted up his foot and slowly placed it on Michael’s hand. ‘Bye,’ he said, and pressed down.

Barry fired, the gunshot resounding across the area. Newton tumbled forward and barrelled down the steep slope, bouncing as he hit rocks and other objects on his rapid descent, until he came to a stop with a large thud at the bottom. Barry dropped to his knees and reaching for Michael, grabbed hold of his jacket. The pair held in suspension as Barry pulled him up.

Michael lay on the ground and groaned.

Barry reached down and took hold of him. ‘We need to get going. The gunshot might have alerted someone.’

Michael, assisted by Barry, clambered to his feet. The pair slowly made their way across to the vehicle with the drugs inside. 'I didn't mention you to the police, Danny.'

Barry smiled. 'Forget about the police.'

Michael struggled into the passenger seat as Barry retrieved the holdall with the money inside, tossed it in with the drugs, and joined Michael.

Michael groaned. ‘Where are you taking me?’

He started the engine and put a finger to his lips. ‘No questions, Michael. Do as I tell you and you may survive the night.’

CHAPTER TWENTY-SIX

O'hare threw his hands up. 'Jesus,' he said. 'This is a mess.'

A junior officer arrived. 'We found this, sir.' He held out the tracker. 'Newton must have discovered it.'

'If anything happens to Michael …' He sucked in air. 'Comb the area. See if you can find anything.'

'Yes, sir.'

O'hare turned to his sergeant. 'Michael could be dead.'

'Christ, guv.'

'And Newton and Tavistock will get away with it. We should have had him followed.'

Another officer came running up the road. 'We've found this, guv. It's a mobile. It could be his.'

O'Hare rubbed his face. 'Get it checked out. Find out if it is.'

Michael lay on the bed in the caravan. The pain in his leg was incredible. He propped himself up as the door to the bedroom opened and Barry entered.

Michael grimaced 'Where are we?'

'At my humble abode.'

'I need the hospital.' He groaned loudly. 'My leg's killing me.'

'We can't risk the hospital, the police will be looking for whoever killed Newton.'

'But—'

Barry growled. 'But nothing. I saved your life tonight. Don't forget that. If it wasn't for me, it would be you lying at the bottom of that cliff.'

'I'm sorry.' Michael groaned. Tears ran down his cheeks, and he wiped them away with the sleeve of his sweatshirt.

'I've got someone coming here. Someone who will sort your leg out and give you something for the pain.'

Michael slumped back. 'Ok. Have you anything to drink? Anything that will help with the pain?'

'Better not. It's not good to mix painkillers with alcohol.'

Michael closed his eyes and grimaced as another lightning bolt of pain traversed his leg.

'Try to rest,' Barry said. 'He won't be long.'

Barry closed the door behind him and took out his phone.

'What's happening?' Tavistock said. 'I was beginning to worry.'

'Newton's dead and I have the gear. You'll have to send someone across to collect it.'

'Why can't you bring it over?'

Barry sat. 'I've injured my leg. I can't drive. I just about managed to get across to my place.'

'Ok. Have you an address?'

'I'll text it to you,' Barry said. 'The keys are under a rock next to the driver's door.'

'The other guy? The one who runs the pub?'

'That's sorted.'

'Did Newton give you much trouble?' Tavistock said.

'Nothing I couldn't handle. He was definitely going to screw you over. He had a buyer lined up.'

'Who?'

Barry laughed. 'No idea, but he'll have a long wait for Toby.'

Michael slowly regained consciousness. He looked around the room, the pain in his leg still excruciating. He sat up and felt down his uninjured leg. The phone was still there. He pulled it from his sock and pushed it under a pillow as the door to the bedroom opened. Barry, and an older man, carrying a black bag, walked in.

'I've brought someone to look at your leg. This is Dr Smith.' Barry said.

The older man smiled pleasantly at Michael. 'I'll give you something for the pain. He opened his bag and pulled out a syringe and small vial.

'I'll leave you to it,' Barry said.

Barry extinguished his cigarette and entered the caravan as the doctor came out of the bedroom.

Barry raised his eyebrows. 'Everything ok?'

'Yeah. I've done what I can with his leg, but he really could have done with going to a hospital. He may need it pinning.'

Barry shook his head. 'Not an option at the moment, doc. Have you sedated him?'

The doctor nodded. 'It should last a few hours. I've left some morphine and other stuff by the bed. There's an explanation of how to administer it.'

Barry pulled an envelope from his back pocket. 'The other stuff we spoke about?'

The doctor opened his bag and held out a packet. 'Just take the swab and run it around the mouth, then drop it inside the tube. You can send them to this address.' He plucked a card from his pocket and handed it to Barry.

Barry placed the envelope on the table. 'How quick can you get the results?'

The doctor rubbed his chin. '3-4 days, usually.'

Barry smiled. 'I need them sooner than that.' He opened the envelope and poured the contents on the table. Removing a swab, he rubbed it around his mouth then dropped it into one of the large plastic tubes before handing it to the doctor.

Barry walked into the bedroom and over to Michael. 'Open your mouth,' Barry said.

Michael looked at him groggily. 'Why?'

'Just do it, Michael.'

Michael did as he was told, and Barry rubbed the swab around his mouth then dropped it into the plastic container.

He looked at the puzzled Michael. 'With this swab, I'm going to find out who your father really is.'

'Geoff said—'

'I know what Geoff …' Barry sneered, 'or should I say, Vincent, said.'

Michael rubbed at his eyes. 'Who do you think is my dad?'

Barry smiled. 'We'll see. But if it is Vincent, let's just say that wouldn't be good news for either of you.'

Barry marched into the living room, picked up the envelope and handed this and the tube to the doctor. 'There's five grand in there.' He nodded at the envelope. 'As agreed. Get the result of the tests back to me within 24 hours, and there's another two grand in it for you.'

The doctor raised his eyebrows. 'I'll see what I can do. Sounds like you're in a hurry.'

Barry scowled. 'It doesn't do to be too nosy, doc. It could get you in all sorts of trouble.'

The doctor nodded and turned to leave as Barry took hold of his arm. 'I don't need to remind you about discretion, do I? Because I do know where you live.'

The doctor shook his head. 'I was never here,' he said, and left.

The next day …

Isobelle entered Geoff's cottage. 'Everything ok?' Geoff shouted.

Isobelle took off her coat and joined him in the living room. 'He wasn't there.'

Geoff took hold of her hand. 'What is it?'

Isobelle frowned. 'I spoke to one of the staff. They haven't seen him since yesterday.'

'Where the hell is he?'

Isobelle paced the floor. 'I don't know. I'm going to give David Wright a ring.'

He nodded. 'You don't think anything serious has happened, do you?'

She looked directly at Geoff. 'I don't know.'

Geoff stiffened in his seat. 'Ring him now. Something has gone wrong.'

David Wright picked up his mobile and answered. 'You're a hard man to get hold of, Declan.'

O'Hare sighed. 'I've been tied up all morning. Things didn't go to plan.'

'What do you mean, didn't—?'

'Michael's missing,' O'Hare said.

'Missing?'

O'Hare sighed again. 'He picked up the gear from the boat, as agreed. We had a tracker on the van he was travelling in. Somewhere en route to the drop-off, we lost contact. We found the tracker a few miles from the beach.'

'God,' Wright said. 'No answer on his mobile, I suppose?'

'We found that not far from where we discovered the tracker.'

'Do you think Newton has …?'

'You haven't seen the news then?' O'Hare said. 'Newton was found dead at the foot of a cliff yesterday. He'd been shot.'

'Tavistock?'

O'Hare grunted. 'Probably. We've been over to his place, and he claims he knows nothing about it.'

'Well, he would say that. What about the drugs? '

'Gone. Tavistock will have spirited them away by now.'

'Christ, Declan. What a mess.'

O'Hare groaned. 'Tell me about it.'

Wright pulled the mobile from his ear as it beeped. He viewed the name on the screen. 'Isobelle, Michael's friend, is ringing me.'

'Don't answer until we know more.'

'Ok. Keep me in the loop, will you?'

'Definitely.'

The next day …

Michael woke, and drowsily opened his eyes. Briefly confused, he glanced around the room. Realisation dawned on him that he was still in the caravan. His leg didn't feel as painful as previously, and he attempted to sit up. He looked down at his right hand, manacled to the bed. Manoeuvring himself onto his side, he searched underneath the pillow. The phone was still there. He picked it up and flopped onto his back again. His head ached, and a fuzziness still clouded his thoughts. Michael strained to listen. It appeared he was in the caravan on his own. He had to call someone. This could be the only chance he had. Opening the ancient Motorola, he rang the only number he could remember.

'The Fallen Angel.' a male voice said.

'It's Michael.'

'Michael, where the hell have you been?'

'I haven't got time to explain. I want you to find the number for a DI Declan O'Hare at the drug enforcement unit, North Yorkshire Police.'

He laughed. 'Are you pulling my leg, Michael?'

Michael growled. 'Just do as I say. It's in my diary behind the bar.'

'Ok. Sorry.'

'Tell him I'm being held captive at Sunny Horizon's caravan park in Whitby. The caravan is at the far end of the camp near the cliffs. It has a wooden veranda with a few spindles missing.'

'Right. Who—?'

'I can't explain now. Tell O'Hare the man holding me has a gun.'

'Right. I'll do it straight away.'

'Thanks, mate. Please be quick.' Michael hung up and secreted the mobile back under the pillow.

'Anything?' Geoff said to Isobelle.

She shook her head. 'He's not answering.'

He rubbed his face. 'Michael's dead. I just know it.'

Isobelle frowned. 'I'm sure he's not.'

'Where the hell is he then?'

She stood and moved over to the window. 'It's David Wright.' She hurried towards the door and opened it as Wright moved along the path.

'I've been ringing you,' she said.

Wright stopped at the threshold. 'Can I come in?'

She beckoned him inside, and the pair joined Geoff in the living room. 'We haven't heard from Michael,' Wright said.

Geoff glanced at Isobelle. 'Where is he?'

Wright shrugged. 'DI O'Hare is trying to trace him.'

Geoff put his hands over his face and slowly pulled them down. 'What about Toby Newton?'

Wright sighed. 'Toby Newton was found dead at the foot of a cliff near Robin Hood's Bay. He'd been shot.'

Isobelle slumped onto the settee next to Geoff. 'Shot. By who?'

'We don't know that. DI O'Hare ...' Wright took out his phone as it began to ring. 'That's him now. Declan, any news?'

Isobelle and Geoff listened to the one-sided conversation and waited for Wright to finish his call.

'Good,' Wright said into his phone. 'I'm here with Geoff and Isobelle. Ring me back when you have him.' Wright hung up and looked at the other two. 'He's alive. He's been held captive at a caravan in Whitby. The police are heading over there now.'

Isobelle forced a smile and squeezed Geoff's hand tightly. 'Good. Will they …?'

'The DI will ring when they have him.' Wright smiled. 'Maybe we could have a cup of tea while we wait?'

She stood. 'Yes of course.'

Geoff sat on his favourite chair with his broken leg propped on a stool in front of him. 'How did he seem?' Geoff said to Isobelle.

'Very well. He told me the police have questioned him. I'm picking him up with Marion later today when he's seen the doctor.'

Geoff raised his eyebrows. 'And?'

'He told them he escaped but was injured when Newton hit him with the car.'

Marion entered carrying a tray and sat next to Isobelle.

'He was lucky not to be killed.' Geoff said.

Isobelle glanced at Marion. 'Yes, I think he was.'

The three of them sat looking into their teas until Geoff broke the silence. 'I think,' he said. 'It's time for me to come clean. No more lies, no more half-truths.'

'What do you mean?' Marion said.

'I think everyone should be here,' he said. 'Phone Brian, Elliott and Jason, and ask if they can come tomorrow. I'm too tired today.'

Isobelle forced a smile at Geoff. 'It's for the best.'

Barry looked out of his car window and towards the doctor as he made his way over to him. He pushed the passenger door open, and the doctor climbed inside.

'Well?' Barry said.

The doctor pulled out a piece of paper and handed it to Barry. He studied it then looked at the doctor. 'And there's no doubt?'

'No. The test is very accurate.'

Barry opened the glovebox and pulled out an envelope. 'As we agreed.'

'Anything else?' the doctor said.

Barry stared outside. 'No. That concludes all our business.'

The doctor nodded and headed back to his car.

Barry continued to gaze outside for a few moments before starting the engine and roaring off.

Barry pulled the car into the car park of the caravan site as the flashing blue lights up ahead grabbed his attention. He narrowed his eyes and stared briefly towards his caravan then sped back out through the gates. Within minutes he was heading out of Whitby and along the road before turning left, towards Sleights.

CHAPTER TWENTY-SEVEN

O'Hare climbed the steps towards Wright's office, tapped on the door, and entered.

'Have a seat,' Wright said, and pushed a tumbler towards O'Hare. Wright held the bottle over the glass and looked at his friend.

'Just a small one,' O'Hare said.

'Why don't you stay over? Then we can reminisce about old times and sink a few.'

O'Hare smiled. 'I can't with everything that's going on.'

'What did Michael have to say?'

O'Hare sipped his drink. 'He said the guy who held him captive was called Danny. He didn't know his surname. Michael gave a description, but it could be anyone.' O'Hare pulled a piece of paper from his jacket and handed it to Wright.

Wright studied the drawing. 'It's not great, is it?'

'No. Michael said he's sixtyish, with a London accent.'

'What about his car?'

'Michael didn't know.'

'And you've nothing on Tavistock?'

O'Hare sighed. 'No. We're keeping an eye on him, but I'm not optimistic. Michael claims he's never met this guy and doesn't know anyone called Danny.'

'Have you asked Michael's friends? Isobelle and Geoff? They might know him.'

O'Hare groaned. 'I thought you might do me a favour and have a run through to Whitby. I need to get back to Leeds. I gave Michael a copy of the sketch. He said he would ask around his pub.'

Wright folded the paper and placed it in his pocket. 'Yeah, ok.'

Michael sat in the wheelchair as Isobelle pushed the last of his clothes into his bag.

'Is that everything?' she said.

'I think so. Thanks for doing this, Belle. Where's Marion?'

'Outside in the car.' Isobelle laughed. 'Parked illegally, no doubt.'

'She's such a rebel.'

She forced a smile. 'Geoff would like to see you. If you're up to it?'

He nodded. 'Ok. I think it's about time we had a chat. There's something I need to ask him.'

'Is it about the police?'

Michael shook his head. 'No. Take me across to Geoff's, and I'll tell you then.'

'What did the police say about your part in the drugs?'

'I'm off the hook. They're keeping me out of it.'

'It's me,' Isobelle shouted as the two friends helped Michael into Geoff's cottage. 'I brought someone with me.'

Geoff sat with his broken leg on a stool in front of him, as Isobelle, Marion and Michael entered.

'Michael,' he said. 'It's great to see you.'

Michael struggled into a chair. 'It's great to see you too.' He rubbed his chin. 'I have a few questions.'

Isobelle raised her eyebrows at Marion. Marion smiled. 'I'll give you some privacy. I'll see you later.'

The others waited for her to leave.

Geoff glanced at Isobelle. 'Fire away,' he said, as Isobelle sat next to him.

Michael pulled a piece of paper from his pocket and handed it to Geoff. 'Who's this?' he said. 'I got it from the police.'

Geoff studied the drawing then passed it to Isobelle. He sighed. 'Barry Hunt.'

'And he is?' Michael said. 'He told me he's called Danny.'

'I knew him way back. He was a friend of Mick's.'

'My dad?'

'Well, the one you thought was your dad. Barry was the other man who robbed the van with Mick. He's the one who shot the security guard.'

'I see. Mum never mentioned him by name.'

Geoff glanced at Isobelle. 'He and your mum had a thing.'

'An affair, you mean?'

'Yeah,' Geoff said.

'He could be my dad, then?'

Geoff shook his head. 'He told your mum that he couldn't have kids.'

Michael smiled. 'He lied.'

'How …?' Geoff said.

Michael frowned. 'While he held me captive, he made me take a mouth swab.'

'A what?' Geoff said.

'He ran a swab around my mouth,' Michael said, 'and then he put it in one of those plastic tubes. He told me it was to determine who my dad is.'

'Do the police know this?' Geoff said.

'I didn't tell them. I wanted to ask you first.'

Isobelle glanced at Geoff. 'You had better tell Michael the whole story about the robbery and your fall.'

Michael listened as Geoff told him how he had driven the getaway car and escaped north with the money.

Michael sat back in his chair. 'And you think Barry pushed you?'

'I'm certain of it. I couldn't tell the police, though. If they found out about the robbery ...'

'Yeah,' Michael said. 'I understand.'

'I had no idea he would involve you,' Geoff said.

'What if he is my dad?'

Geoff shrugged. 'I don't know.'

'He may come back,' Isobelle said.

'We can't tell the police who he is,' Michael said. 'That would implicate you.'

'He's dangerous, though,' Geoff said.

'We'll have to hope …' Michael said. '… that we've seen the last of Barry.'

'What about us?' Geoff said. 'I could still be your dad.'

Michael smiled. 'We'll do a test of our own if you're willing?'

'Of course,' Geoff said.

The next day …

Isobelle entered Geoff's cottage with Freddie. 'That's a good walk he's had.'

'Did you post it?' he said.

'Yeah. A week to ten days to get the result.'

Geoff rubbed his chin. 'I hope Michael is mine. I'm just getting used to the idea of having a son.'

She sat next to him. 'Let's hope for the best. I'm not sure how Michael will take it if you're not.'

'No,' Geoff said. 'He won't be keen on Barry being his dad either. Let's hope he isn't.'

'It might not be either of you. You did say that Yvonne was a bit flighty.'

'She was,' Geoff said. 'Did you manage to sort out when Elliott and the others are coming around?'

'Yes. They'll be here at four.'

Geoff sucked in air. 'Let's hope they take it well. I feel guilty that I've kept it secret from them all these years.'

Geoff beckoned Brian, Elliott, Marion, and Jason into the front room. 'Have a seat you lot,' he said, and slowly lowered himself into his seat. 'Belle is rustling up some drinks for us.' The four of them sat. 'How have you all been since I got out of hospital?'

Elliott glanced at Brian. 'Very well,' he said. 'We've missed you at the pub, though.'

'I'll be back there soon. I'm dying for a pint.'

Isobelle entered carrying a tray. She sat next to Geoff and took hold of his hand. 'Help yourselves,' she said.

'So,' Brian said, picking up his mug. 'This is all very intriguing.'

Geoff glanced at Isobelle. 'I haven't been completely honest with you all. You're my dearest friends and …' He took a deep breath. '… I feel that now is the right time to tell you everything.'

'Geoff,' Elliott said. 'Whatever it is, we won't judge.'

Geoff smiled thinly. 'I'll begin in the seventies …'

Silence descended on the room, and Brian leant forward. 'This will stay between us all.' He glanced at his companions, who nodded their approval.

'Did you ever meet the real Geoff Brown?' Elliott said.

'No. Dot told me about him, though. She moved up to be closer to him. She was devastated by his death. It was Dot who suggested using his name. I wasn't keen on that, but she insisted.'

'And Michael?' Brian said. 'Is he your son?'

'I'm not sure. We've talked, and his mother insisted I, or rather Vincent, was Michael's dad. However, there's another possibility … Barry.'

'The one who held Michael captive?' Brian said.

'Yeah.'

Elliott rubbed his chin. 'Have you told the police you know who he is?'

'I can't,' Geoff said. 'He could tell them about my involvement in the robbery.'

Brian scoffed. 'They'd never prove it after all these years.'

'I daren't take that chance.'

'How are you and Michael going to …?' Elliott said.

'We've sent our DNA samples away for testing. It'll prove once and for all if I'm his father or not.'

'What about your fall?' Jason said.

'I was pushed by Barry.'

'How do …?' Brian said.

'Bits of it keep coming back. I'm certain it was him.'

'What happens if he returns?' Marion said.

'We'll just have to hope he doesn't.'

Elliott furrowed his brow. 'He's tried once. He may try again.'

Geoff glanced at Isobelle. 'We're hoping with the police looking for him, that he's headed back to London.'

'At least that Newton character isn't a problem for Michael anymore,' Brian said.

'I heard on the news he was killed,' Elliott said. 'He got what he deserved if you ask me.'

Brian chuckled. 'It's certainly been an eventful few days.'

'Listen,' Geoff said, smiling broadly, 'why don't we all go to the pub? I'll get the drinks in.'

'Yeah,' Elliott said. 'That sounds like a great idea.'

CHAPTER TWENTY-EIGHT

One week later …

Barry pulled out his mobile and called his cousin Danny.

'Barry,' Danny said. 'How are things going?'

'Not as smoothly as I'd hoped.'

'Why?'

Barry grunted. 'Long story. Has anyone been asking after me?'

'No, why?'

'I had a bit of trouble up here. I'll tell you when I get back. Made a few quid though.'

'When are you coming home?'

'Soon. I have a couple of things I need to do first.'

'Yeah?' Danny said. 'Sounds ominous.'

'We'll see.'

Geoff stood at the bar as Michael limped across to him. 'What can I get you?' Michael said.

'Can we have the same again?'

'I thought the others would be getting the drinks for you? With your leg and that.'

'I insisted. I'm not an invalid. How's your leg by the way?'

'Still a bit painful, but I'm like you. Stubborn. Have the others mentioned the quiz?'

'No. I completely forgot about it. When is it?'

'Monday. Elliott was on about organising a minibus.'

Geoff looked back at his friends. 'Not a bad idea.' He smiled at Michael. 'I'll see you shortly.'

Geoff made his way back, slumped onto a chair, and leant his crutches against the wall. 'The drinks are on their way.'

'You're a stubborn bugger, Geoff Brown,' Marion said. 'We'd have got the drinks.'

'I'm not being treated like I'm useless.' He took hold of Isobelle's hand. 'Michael mentioned the quiz. Why didn't you remind me?'

Elliott glanced at Brian. 'We thought you had enough on your plate'.
'Michael said you're thinking of organising a minibus?'
'Yeah. I've booked it. We'll all meet at six-thirty on Monday.'
Geoff picked up his pint. 'Here's to The Whitby Wailers.'
'The Whitby Wailers,' the others joined in.

Michael turned off the lights to the pub and made his way upstairs slowly. His broken leg and crutches, making the journey an arduous one. He sat on the edge of the bed, undressed, and slid underneath the duvet. He yawned, turned off the light and lay his head on the pillow. Within minutes, he was asleep.

Barry, dressed in black and wearing a beanie hat, carried the large holdall up the slope to The Fallen Angel. He stopped outside and checked in all directions before climbing the gate to the back of the pub. Throwing the holdall to the floor, he eased himself down into the back yard, took out his torch and searched around for a means of entry. He ran his fingers along the length of the window, dropped to his knees and pulled a gemmy from his holdall. The window quickly yielded under the assault of the tool. He pushed it open and glancing inside, stared into the kitchen.

Shoving the holdall through the opening, he gently lowered it to the floor. He pulled a small torch from his jacket pocket and shone the beam inside, paying particular attention to the ceiling corners where a sensor might be. There were none. Barry eased himself up and adroitly dropped to the floor. Opening the bag again, he pulled out a plastic bottle and a small candle then moved towards the door. The door opened silently into a hallway with stairs to the upper floor about half-way down. Barry crept on his stomach, and slowly, almost noiselessly made his way along the carpet. Stopping at the foot of the stairs, he poured the contents onto the floor, allowing the liquid to cover as large an area as possible. Then, placing the candle in the middle of the now sodden carpet, he lit it. He crept back the way he had come and gently closed the door to the kitchen behind him. Barry opened the bag again and removed a second bottle, dousing the contents around the kitchen.

He opened the gate and glanced outside into the darkness. The deserted street greeted him, and satisfied, he closed the gate behind him, slung the holdall over his shoulder, and hurried off.

Isobelle sat up in bed and rubbed her eyes. Geoff stood at the window, supported by one of his crutches, staring outside. 'What is it?' she said.
'Something is happening up the road. There are flashing lights.'
Isobelle climbed out of bed and joined him. 'What?'

Geoff grunted. 'Can you get me my binoculars from the coat hook in the hall? I can't see from here.'

Isobelle padded out of the room and down the stairs, returning moments later with the binoculars.

He put them to his eyes and zoomed in. 'Christ,' he said.

Isobelle took hold of his arm. 'What is it?'

'The Fallen Angel's on fire.' He handed them to her. 'There are police and fire engines.'

'Oh, God,' she said. 'Michael.'

Geoff stared at Isobelle. 'Can you get dressed and head up there? I need to know what's happening.'

She nodded. 'Of course.'

Geoff stood at the threshold of his cottage as Isobelle turned and kissed him. 'I'll come back as soon as I know anything,' she said.

'Belle,' Marion shouted, hurrying to join her. 'I heard the commotion,' she said. 'It's The Fallen Angel.'

'Quickly,' Geoff said. He watched as the two women disappeared up the street and out of sight.

Geoff's phone rang. 'Elliott,' he said.

'The Fallen Angel's on fire,' Elliott said breathlessly.

'I know. Belle and Marion are on their way there now.'

'I'll phone Brian. Jason and I are almost there. Don't worry, I'm sure he's all right.'

'Phone me, Elliott. Let me know as soon as you know anything.' Geoff paused to catch his breath and put away his phone before hobbling his way into the lounge. He stopped in his tracks as someone knocked on the front door.

Isobelle and Marion rounded the corner and paused for breath. Elliott, Brian and Jason stood across the road staring at the burning building. Isobelle and Marion joined the three men.

'What's the hell's happening?' Isobelle said. Her eyes wide. 'Is Michael ...?'

'Michael's alive,' Brian said. 'He's in the ambulance.'

'Ambulance? Is he injured?' Isobelle said.

Elliott forced a smile. 'I think it's just a precautionary measure. They think that ...' Elliott glanced back towards the building.

'What, Elliott? What is it?' Isobelle said.

'They think it's arson.'

Isobelle slumped back against the wall. 'Arson?'

'It's just rumours at the moment,' he said.

'I need to tell Geoff.' She struggled to her feet again. 'I need to phone him.' She took out her mobile. Isobelle groaned. 'He's not answering.'

She turned to face Marion. 'I'll go back. Ring me if there's any more news.'

Marion held up her mobile. 'He'll be fine, I'm sure. Go and tell Geoff. He'll be beside himself.'

CHAPTER TWENTY-NINE

Geoff sat on the settee and stared across at Barry who held a gun loosely in his hand.

'What are you going to do, Barry, kill me?'

Barry sneered. 'I knew setting fire to the pub would have your lady friend running up there.'

'You started the fire?'

He glared at Geoff. 'He's your son. He knows too much.'

'This is between us.'

'Not anymore. Twenty years I did. You and Mick screwed me over good and proper. Where's my money?'

Geoff laughed and waved a hand around the room. 'You're looking at it. I bought this cottage for my aunt.'

'I did think for a moment that Michael was my son. I gave Yvonne a cock and bull story all those years ago. I didn't want to be tied down with a nipper. But the test came back negative. It appears you have a son.' He grinned. 'Well, had one. I would imagine Michael is burnt to a crisp by now.'

'You bastard,' Geoff said.

Barry stood and levelled his gun. 'I'd walk you over to the cliff and do it properly, but I don't think you'll make the journey. You were lucky the night I pushed you. You can imagine the satisfaction I got from watching you tumble down the hill.'

'What now?'

Barry grinned. 'We're going on a short ride. It'll only be a matter of time before everyone realises it was arson and puts two and two together.'

'I'm going nowhere,' Geoff said.

'If you don't,' Barry said. 'I'll wait here for … Belle … isn't it?'

Geoff ground his teeth and glanced around the room.

Barry laughed. 'Don't waste your time looking for a weapon. You're an old man, and a cripple.'

Geoff stood unsteadily. 'Ok. It appears I have no choice.'

Geoff hobbled towards the door as Barry kept his gun trained on him. He opened the door and glanced outside. 'Ok,' Barry said. 'Just a short drive.'

The two men stepped into the chill night air. Barry nodded towards a car parked a little way up the street. 'Off you go,' he said.

Geoff limped to the end of his path, closely followed by Barry. 'Faster,' Barry said, as he pushed Geoff in the back with the gun. 'I haven't got all night, Vincent.'

Barry groaned as the piece of wood came crashing down across his shoulders. He stumbled forward onto the ground as his gun fell from his grasp. Isobelle stooped and picked up the weapon, levelling it at the prostrate Barry.

Barry clambered to his feet and turned to see Isobelle, now stood with Geoff, pointing the gun at him.

He roared. 'I'll kill you, bitch.'

'Move an inch,' she said. 'And I'll fire.'

Barry sneered. 'You won't fire.'

Geoff took the weapon from her and aimed it at Barry. 'I will, though.'

'You've never had the balls, Vinny.'

Geoff narrowed his eyes. 'Let's see, shall we.'

'I've phoned the police,' Isobelle said. 'They'll be here any minute.'

Barry glanced along the road. 'This isn't over.' He turned and moved for his car, but stopped several yards from it as flashing lights headed towards him. Barry glanced about for a means of escape and headed for the beach.

Geoff turned to Isobelle. 'Michael?' he said.

'He's fine.'

Two police vehicles screeched to a halt, and several officers jumped from them. Geoff, realising he still had the gun in his hand, allowed it to fall to the ground.

'He's headed that way,' Isobelle said, pointing towards the cliff. 'He threatened to kill us.'

Geoff pointed to the ground at the weapon, as an armed officer neared. 'His gun's here.'

The officer turned to one of his colleagues. 'Secure that weapon and follow me.'

Barry glanced over his shoulder at the figures pursuing him. He paused for breath and to gather his thoughts. He was lost, the darkness of the night both helping and hindering his escape. The voices grew louder as he started off again. He reached a fence and clambered over the top and along the fence line. Barry searched desperately for a means of getting down the steep incline as the officers closed in.

'Over here,' shouted one of the men.

Barry blinked as a torch shone in his direction. He reached into his pocket for his mobile phone. The evidence stored within it, damming.

'He's got a gun,' an officer shouted. 'Put down your weapon.'

Barry dropped the phone. His right foot slipped, as the loose soil beneath it gave way. He grasped helplessly at a shrub growing from the cliff. The plant, unable to support his weight as he leant back, easily came away from the rock and, along with Barry, tumbled downwards. He crashed and bounced as his body barrelled its way down the steep incline, finally coming to a crumpled heap at the bottom.

O'Hare put down his coffee and pulled out his phone. 'Morning,' he said. 'You're up bright and early.'

'Someone torched Michael's pub in the early hours,' Wright said.

O'Hare swapped the phone to his other ear. 'You're kidding? How is he?'

'Isobelle rang me. He's ok. It was the bloke who held him captive.'

'I'll make some calls. I'm just off into work now. I'll ring you when I know more.' O'Hare downed his coffee in one, pushed his phone back inside his pocket, and hurried off.

Isobelle opened the door of Geoff's cottage and viewed O'Hare and Wright stood on the step.

'You had better come in,' she said.

The two men followed her inside and into the living room. Geoff sat on a chair with his leg propped up. 'Have a seat, gentlemen,' he said.

The pair sat, and O'Hare leant forward. 'What the hell happened?'

Geoff glanced at Isobelle as she sat next to him. 'The guy who held Michael captive is called Barry Hunt.'

'And your connection with him?'

'I knew Barry years back, in London. He was a mate of a friend of mine.'

'Did you know it was Barry Hunt who abducted Michael?'

Geoff sighed as Isobelle gently squeezed his hand. 'Not until last night.'

O'Hare sat back in his chair. 'I've spoken to some of my colleagues. They've interviewed Michael, and he says that Hunt tried to kill him because he knows too much about Tavistock and the drugs.'

'That's probably true,' Geoff said.

'What I don't understand,' O'Hare said, 'is why he should try and kill you?'

'Barry thought Michael was his son. He came up here looking for him. I don't know how he knew the guy smuggling the drugs—'

'Tavistock,' Wright said.

'Yeah, Tavistock. But Michael isn't his son.'

'He's yours?' O'Hare said.

'I don't know that. Michael and I have sent a test off which we're hoping to have the result of soon. Barry thinks I'm Michael's dad.'

'It seems a bit of an over-reaction,' O'Hare said. 'Killing someone because they're the father of someone you believed was your son.'

'Barry Hunt was always a mental case.'

O'Hare glanced at Wright. 'Sorry, Geoff. I'm not buying that,' O'Hare said.

Isobelle squeezed his hand again. Geoff sighed. 'Barry went down for a robbery years ago. The police were waiting for them. He thought I grassed him up.'

'And did you?' O'Hare said.

Geoff shook his head. 'No.'

'Who did?' Wright said.

'Yvonne.'

'Yvonne?' O'Hare said.

'Michael's mother.'

'Why would she do that?' Wright said.

Geoff shrugged. 'She had this idea that me and her had a future. She thought if Mick, her husband, and Barry were sent down, we could move away and start afresh.'

'And you weren't keen?' O'Hare said.

Geoff shook his head. 'There was never anything serious between us. It was a one-night stand. Mick was my best mate. When she told me what she had done, I went ballistic.'

'When did you move up here?' O'Hare said.

'In the seventies. My aunt had lived up here for years, and I used to visit when my dad was alive. After Mick went to prison, I moved up and stayed.'

O'Hare glanced at Wright, who shrugged. 'Ok. We'll leave it there.' The two men stood and Isobelle showed them out.

'Do you think they believed you?' she said to Geoff.

'I hope so.'

Wright climbed into the car next to O'Hare. 'Do you believe him?' Wright said.

O'Hare stared back towards the cottage. 'Not fully. I think something happened between the pair back in London. The only two people who know what are Geoff and Barry Hunt. The dead can't talk, and I'm pretty sure Geoff won't either.'

'To be honest, Declan,' Wright said. 'Do you want to get involved in a case from the seventies?'

O'Hare smiled. 'With my workload ...? No way. In any case, Barry Hunt's phone has thrown up some interesting details.'

'Regarding Tavistock?'

O'Hare nodded. 'Yeah. We might just have enough to pin the smuggling on him.'

'Good.'

The pair glanced back at Geoff's cottage then set off along the cobbled street.

CHAPTER THIRTY

The next day …
Isobelle placed a mug of tea in front of Geoff. 'That'll sort you out,' she said.

Geoff laughed. 'Thanks, Belle.'

She slumped into the chair opposite him. 'I had a walk to the pub with Marion while you were sleeping.'

'And?'

'It's in a terrible state.'

'How's Michael?' he said.

'Michael's fine physically, but he's cut up about his pub.'

'The insurance will fix it. They'll—'

'He didn't have insurance.'

Geoff shook his head. 'Why?'

'He said he didn't have the money. When it comes out that there wasn't any insurance, he may lose his license.'

Geoff closed his eyes briefly. 'I need to see him.'

'All in good time.'

'But I need to see him. He could be my son …'

She leant forward. 'I know. We'll see what we can do.'

'Where is he?'

'Marion's putting him up. He can't stay at the pub. I'll have a walk up shortly and ask him to come here.'

Geoff shook his head. 'Poor Michael. What are we going to do?'

'Drink your tea. We'll think of something.'

Three Months Later …
Geoff, stood with Isobelle, smiled. 'It looks fabulous,' he said, as he stared across at the newly refurbished pub.

'It does,' she said.

Elliott and Jason joined them as a small group of people gathered 'Where's Michael?' Elliott said.

'He's gone to get a pair of scissors,' Geoff said.

Brian, panting, reached the group. 'I thought I'd missed it.'

Michael came out of the pub. 'Geoff,' he said. 'Will you do the honours.' He held out a pair of scissors as Geoff made his way across the road.

'Still using the stick, I see,' Michael said.

'I'm not as young as you.' He took the scissors from Michael. 'What do you want me to do?'

'Cut the ribbon,' Michael said.

'Do you want me to say something?'

Michael laughed. 'If you like.'

Geoff turned to face the small crowd. 'I'd just like to say ...' He glanced at Michael, '... that it's a wonderful day today. It's also a great honour to be cutting the ribbon on Michael's newly refurbished pub. So, without further ado ...' He grinned and cut the ribbon.

Michael moved along the bar and stopped opposite Geoff. 'Thanks for all this,' Michael said. 'I would never have been able to reopen without the money you and Belle gave me.'

Geoff glanced across to a table where Isobelle, Brian, Jason and Elliott sat. Isobelle smiled and waved at the pair.

'It was Belle, really,' he said. 'She put the most in.'

'Well, I'm determined to make a real go of it. The new chef starts today.'

'What's he like?' Geoff said.

'She,' Michael said, and grinned. 'She's very nice.'

'Ah,' Geoff said. 'It's like that, is it?'

Michael reached under the counter. 'I nearly forgot.' He pulled out a carrier and opened it. 'The trophy.' Michael placed it onto a shelf behind the bar. 'Pride of place.'

'North Yorkshire pub quiz champions 2019,' Geoff said. 'The Whitby Wailers.'

Michael studied the trophy. 'Wait a minute,' he said. 'They've spelt your team name wrong.'

'No, they haven't,' Geoff said.

'But I thought—?'

Geoff laughed. 'We call ourselves the Whitby Wailers because we all have a sob story to tell. We used to laugh about it when you misspelt our name.'

'Ah,' Michael said. 'All these years you've had the quiz here, and I never knew.'

The door opened, and Agnes entered. She glanced around and spotting Brian, moved across to his table.

Brian stood. 'I don't think you've met my ... friend Agnes,' he said.

They all smiled at her. 'Have a seat, Agnes,' Isobelle said.

'I'll get you a drink,' Brian said.

Elliott held out his hand to her. 'Are you any good at quizzes, Agnes?'

Three Months Later ...

Michael popped the glasses onto the bar and turned as the door opened. O'Hare and Wright came in. The pair made their way over to him.

'Can we have a word?' O'Hare said.

'Yeah, sure. Come through.'

The pair followed Michael into the back. 'Have a seat,' Michael said.

'We got the result we wanted,' O'Hare said.

Michael slumped onto a seat opposite. 'I'd forgotten that's today.'

'Tavistock will be going away for a very long time,' O'Hare said.

Michael lowered his head. 'Good.'

'I'm sorry we didn't bring Toby Newton or Barry Hunt to justice, though,' O'Hare said. 'Maybe it's for the best that they're dead. It keeps you out of it.'

'Do you think my involvement—?'

'Don't worry, Michael,' O'Hare said. 'No one will find out. It's not in their interests to mention it either.'

'The pub looks good,' Wright said.

'Yeah. Geoff ...' He smiled. '... My dad, and Isobelle helped out with the money. It's doing really well.'

'And the license?' O'Hare said.

'It was touch and go,' Michael said. 'But the word you put in helped.'

'Glad it worked out,' O'Hare said.

Wright tapped the table. 'How about a drink to celebrate?'

Michael stood. 'Of course,' he said. 'On me.' He looked at Wright and then at O'Hare. 'Thanks, again.'

O'Hare shrugged. 'No problem. Just keep on the right side of the law, will you?'

Michael smiled. 'You can be certain of that.'

Isobelle carried the glasses outside and onto the patio. She sat next to Geoff and handed him his drink.

Geoff smiled at her. 'What do you think, Belle?'

She gazed out across the garden, and beyond to the sea. 'It's gorgeous. The house is fabulous.'

'Brian's promised me some plants for the far corner. This time next year it'll look fantastic.'

'It looks fantastic now.' She took a sip from her glass. 'We've got about half an hour until they all descend on us.'

'What about the caterers?' Geoff said. 'Have they finished setting up?'

‘Yes. I know it’s a bit extravagant, but nobody wants my cooking inflicted on them.’

Geoff took hold of her hand and kissed the back of it. He lowered his head. 'Without you, Belle, without you …'

Isobelle put a finger to his lips, then kissed him.

NOTES ABOUT THE AUTHOR

John Regan was born in Middlesbrough on March 20th, 1965. He currently lives with his partner in Stainton Village near Middlesbrough.

This is the author's seventh book.

At present his full-time job is as an underground telephone Engineer at Openreach and he has worked for both BT and Openreach for the past twenty-one years.

He is about to embark on his eighth novel and hopes to have it completed next year.

December 2020.

The author would be happy to hear feedback about this book and will be pleased to answer emails from any readers.

Email: johnregan1965@yahoo.co.uk.

OTHER BOOKS BY THIS AUTHOR

THE HANGING TREE

Sandra Stewart and her daughter are brutally murdered in 2006. Her husband disappeared on the night of Sandra's murder and is wanted in connection with their deaths.
Why has he returned eight years later? And why is he systematically slaughtering apparently unconnected people? Could it be that the original investigation was flawed?
Detective Inspector Peter Graveney is catapulted headlong into an almost unfathomable case. Thwarted at every turn by faceless individuals, intent on keeping the truth buried.
Are there people close to the investigation, possibly within the force, determined to prevent him from finding out what really happened?
As he becomes ever more embroiled, he battles with his past as skeletons in his own closet rattle loudly. Tempted into an increasingly dangerous affair with his new Detective Sergeant, Stephanie Marne, Graveney finds that people he can trust are rapidly diminishing.
But who's manipulating who? As he moves ever closer to the truth, he finds the person that he holds most dear threatened.
Graphically covering adult themes, 'The Hanging Tree' is a relentless edge of the seat ride.
Exploring the darkest of secrets, and the depths people will plunge to keep those secrets hidden. Culminating in a horrific and visceral finale, as Graveney relentlessly pursues it to the final conclusion.

'Even the darkest of secrets deserve an audience.'

PERSISTENCE OF VISION

Amorphous: Lindsey and Beth, separated by thirty years. Or so it seems. Their lives about to collide, changing them both forever. Will a higher power intervene and re-write their past and future?

Legerdemain (Sleight of hand): Ten winners of a competition held by the handsome and charismatic billionaire, Christian Gainford, are invited to his remote house in the Scottish Highlands. But is he all he seems, and what does he have in store for them? There really is no such thing as a free lunch, as the ten are about to discover.

Broken: Sandi and Steve are thrown together. By accident or design? Steve is forced to fight not only for Sandi but for his own sanity. Can he trust his senses when everything he ever relied on appears suspect?

Insidious: Killers are copying the crimes of the dead psychopath, Devon Wicken. Will Jack be able to save his wife, Charlotte, from them? Or are they always one step ahead of Jack?

A series of short stories cleverly linked together in an original narrative with one common theme — Reality. But what's real and what isn't?

Exciting action mixed with humour and mystery will keep you guessing throughout. It will alter your perceptions forever.

Reality just got a little weirder! Fact or fiction...You decide!
Seeing is most definitely not believing!

THE ROMANOV RELIC – The Erimus Mysteries

Hilarious comedy thriller!

Private Detective, Bill Hockney, is murdered while searching for the fabled *Romanov Eagle*, cast for The Tsar. His three nephews inherit his business and find themselves not only attempting to discover its whereabouts but also who killed their uncle.

A side-splitting story, full of northern humour, nefarious baddies, madcap characters, plot twists, real ale, multiple showers, out of control libido, bone-shaped chews and a dog called Baggage.

Can Sam, Phillip and Albert, assisted by Sam's best friend Tommo, outwit the long list of people intent on owning the statue, while simultaneously trying to keep a grip on their love lives?
Or will they be thwarted by the menagerie of increasingly desperate villains?

Solving crime has never been this funny!

THE SPACE BETWEEN OUR TEARS

If tears are the manifestation of our grief, what lies within the space between them?

After experiencing massive upheavals in her personal life, Emily Kirkby decides to write a novel. But as she continues her writing, the border between her real life and fiction begin to blur.

Sometimes even the smallest of actions can have far-reaching and profound consequences. When a pebble is cast into the pool of life, there is no telling just how far the ripples will travel.

A rich and compelling story about love in all its many guises. A story about loss and bereavement. A story about guilt and redemption, regret and remorse. But mainly, chiefly, it's about love.

THE FALLING LEAVES

One of the most perplexing cases Inspector Peter Graveney has worked on. A car is dredged from the bottom of a deep pond after twenty years. The grisly remains of two bodies locked inside. Why is Graveney certain that this discovery is linked to a dubious businessman and the murders of the men working for him? And why does a young woman's name keep surfacing within the investigation after her release from prison for murder?

As Graveney digs deeper, he finds more missing pieces to the puzzle and is faced with his biggest struggle yet – his own mind. As the body count escalates, Graveney battles with his own demons and in his desperation to solve the case, he allows himself to be guided by an unlikely source from his past.

A gruesome and provocative sequel to the author's first novel, 'The Hanging Tree'. The Fallen Leaves takes the reader on a breath-taking journey, from the graphic opening chapter to the emotionally charged denouement.

If you bury the past, bury it deep.

THE LINDISFARNE LITURGY – The Erimus Mysteries

The boys from The Erimus Detective Agency are back in the funniest adventure to date. The search for an ancient Celtic Cross – The Lindisfarne Liturgy – saved from the marauding Vikings and missing for centuries. Could this cross have somehow ended up on Teesside? Sam, Phillip and Albert assisted by their friends, attempt to discover its whereabouts, while simultaneously trying to wrestle with the vicissitudes of everyday life.

A hilarious romp containing canine offspring and Pilates. Spikey auras and misaligned chakras. Orange shirts and cravats. Monogrammed flip flops, waders and fishing flies. Irate coppers, monocles and puppy pads.

A side-splitting adventure from beginning to end. Will the boys find the cross, or will they be thwarted by a collection of individuals intent on owning it?

Mystery and intrigue have never been more enjoyable!

Printed in Great Britain
by Amazon

54036129R00132